"I CAN'

Hannah's voice rose, and she wrapped her arms around herself to keep what composure she had fenced behind her rib cage. "I just can't."

"A couple of hours. Keep it together for a couple of hours, and that's it."

Her eyes were wide and dry; she slumped against the foot post on her bed. "He's evil. And I keep thinking . . . I almost—" She stopped and put a hand over her mouth.

Yates stepped in front of her, took her hand from her face, then grasped her shoulders. "This is what you need."

He took her face in his hands, touched his mouth to hers. Hannah's breath stalled and her senses narrowed, focused on the rough velvet of Yates's mouth.

PERFECT EVIL

E.C. Sheedy

ZEBRA BOOKS
KENSINGTON PUBLISHING CORP.
http://www.kensingtonbooks.com

Always Tim, because without his love and support there would be no "wind beneath my wings."

And to my talented Red Door friends, Gail Crease, Vanessa Oltmann, and Bonnie Spidle, a very special trio of sharp, talented, and insightful pen warriors who know exactly when to give a good push! You're the best.

Chapter 1

It was past four in the morning when Hannah heard him, his voice a cracked whisper, his words labored, urgent. Heart pounding, she abandoned her book, threw back the covers, and reached for her robe in one reflexive motion.

The bedside lamp cast a garish pool of light over a chrome hospital bed sitting stage center in the luxurious room. The man in the bed lay sprawled over its bunched linens as if the effort to reach the intercom had been his last. His hand still rested on the call button. Pungent antiseptic clashed with the lingering fragrance of the sandalwood he'd burned every evening for as long as she'd lived with him. A task that in the past six months had become hers.

Hannah hurried toward him, her bare feet stepping from hardwood to carpet without registering the difference.

"Milo, what is it?" She lifted his hand, rested it on his chest and caressed his sunken cheek. *Not cold. Not yet.* "It's Hannah, Milo. Can you hear me?"

His eyelids slid open, and his eyes slowly focused on her. Relief flooded through her, but ebbed quickly when she saw the depth of his suffering.

"Hannah," he mumbled. "I'm going."

"No." She shook her head, held his dull gaze, willed him to hang on. *No, you can't go. I won't let you. Not now. Not ever.* "No," she said again, with more conviction than she felt. She would hold him here. She had to. He was her life—her linchpin.

"You're in pain," she said. "I'll get you something." She righted his bedding, smoothing the linens with trembling hands before reaching for his pills.

He grasped her arm with surprising strength, dug his nails into her flesh. "No. No pills," he said, his lips compressing against the pain. "The drawer. Open the drawer." He made a weak gesture with his head toward the opposite wall, where a George III bureau sat beside a window draped in blue velvet. His grip slackened.

She knew the drawer he wanted open. Years ago she'd sold him the bureau when—

Not now. Don't think of that now.

"Please," he urged. "There's no more time. I should have done this sooner, but I was . . . weak." The words rattled in his throat. The last coins in the bank, few and precious.

"I'll do it, Milo. Rest now." She stroked the hair back from his forehead, then crossed the room to the bureau.

The eighteenth-century piece had a base comprised of three drawers, a drop-front desk area with a series of cubbyholes, and a glass-fronted bookcase on top. She pressed her index finger on a rose carved into the molding at the base of the book-case, then tugged to open a narrow drawer. Inside were three sealed and numbered envelopes, one thicker than the others. She'd never seen them before. She carried them back to his bedside. Closer to the light, she saw that two of the envelopes had her name on them. The other was unmarked; Milo gave her no time to wonder about any of them.

On sight of the envelopes, he drew in a ragged breath and fixed his gaze on them. The pain in his eyes deepened to beyond the physical, gave way to fear when he took the letters from her hand to crush them against his chest.

"Water, please," he murmured.

A water glass with a bent straw sat by his bedside. She put the straw to his lips and held his head as he sipped. "I'm calling the doctor."

"Too late." He inhaled as deeply as his ruined lungs allowed and stroked the envelopes, as though to ensure himself they were still there. "You know I . . . love you, Hannah," he whispered.

She didn't answer, didn't know what to say. Was love their bond? Or was it merely an accommodation—two isolated souls sharing the same shadowy, secluded place giving small comfort to one another. But when she thought of his leaving, her brittle spirit quivered with hurt. Yes. She did love him as much as her shriveled heart allowed. He was her protector, her guardian angel, and she'd entrusted him with what was left of her life. She wouldn't know how to live without him.

"Shush," she finally said. "I'm with you. I'm always with you." *I'd die for you if I could. Isn't that a kind of love? Or is it only the terror of being left behind?*

He wheezed, the air making a scraping sound across his palate as he labored to pull in another breath.

How many did he have left?

How many breaths made an hour, a day, a life? *Oh, Milo, don't go. Please, please, don't leave me.*

"I love you, too," she said, fighting a growing desperation. She would say the words. If she couldn't hold him, perhaps the words would.

A tear caught lamplight at the edge of his eye and glowed a golden course into his thinning brown hair. "When you read these, you'll hate me."

"Never! I could never hate you."

"You don't know..." He shook his head and lifted his hand from the letters resting on his chest. "Back in the drawer. Until... after. When you're strong again. I didn't mean for it to be you, didn't want that. But I trust you. You won't hurt her. It was so long ago. So long. I tried to make it right... can't ever. God, Hannah, I'm sorry, so sorry." He swallowed hard, shuddered convulsively.

She didn't know what he was talking about. But it didn't matter. Nothing mattered except his leaving. "Oh, Milo—" She wanted to console, but the words knotted in her throat. Useless. There was no solace to be given, no promises to make. Even on the edge of death, Milo would see the missing truth. She owed him better.

"Please," he murmured, touching the letters. "The drawer."

She scarcely glanced at them as she did what he asked, returned quickly to his side. This time she sat on the bed and took his hand in both of her own. Cool. *Too cool.* Not the hand of the warm-hearted man who'd come for her five years ago. Only bones under skin now. Kindling.

His fingers curled around hers, so tight they hurt. "Read yours first. Alone." He raised his death-glazed eyes to hers. "I wanted you to be safe, I never thought I'd go before—"

"Be still, Milo. It's all right. Everything will be all right." Impotent words, useless against the dread webbing tighter in her belly, the vile disease in his lungs.

"Try to forgive me . . . to understand?"

"I'll forgive you anything. You know that. You're more to me than life and—" Her voice broke. "Nothing you could say, or write, will ever change that."

He rolled his head, the subtle negative thick with resignation and disbelief. "I've left you everything—" He stiffened, grimaced, and clenched his eyelids closed.

Hannah knew the enemy in his body had renewed its merciless assault. She gripped his hand and held tight, leaning to kiss his knuckles. So little comfort for the life he'd given her. It seemed forever before he exhaled and the tension in his body eased.

How many breaths?

"You'll take care of Mother? Tell her I love her and that I left . . . peacefully." He managed a faint smile.

"I will."

"And yourself. Take care of yourself. Promise me that."

She nodded, swallowed against the building pressure to weep.

"Good." He moved his thumb over the back of her hand. "If I could," he murmured, "I'd say hello to Will and . . . little Christopher. Tell them how you miss them. How much you love them."

His soft words were a warm hand on her heart; the moan was hers. It was too cruel, this life. First love, then mistakes and unthinkable losses, leaving nothing but broken souls adrift in a bleak and empty wake. Alone. Always alone. And now Milo. She buried her head near his shoulder and wept.

He reached for her, used his waning strength to nudge her head onto his shoulder. "Lie with me, Hannah," he whispered.

She stretched out beside him, pressed her cheek to his, her tears heating their skin. He caressed her hair, soothed her, the almost dead consoling the not alive.

"Warm. So warm." He continued to stroke her hair, his fingers stopping at her nape. "A woman in my arms." He kissed her forehead softly. "My first woman."

With that he ran out of breaths, his last wafting over her cheek on an endless sigh.

Yates woke to a headache—and a tongue like a bloated carcass. He rolled to the side of the bed, planted both feet on the floor, and finger-combed his too-long hair. He rested his head in his hands, then became dimly aware of movement on the bed. He shifted his head, using only one eye to peer at the bed behind him.

He cursed, rummaged his scotch-fogged brain for her name. No luck—as usual. Also, as usual, he didn't care. He wasn't much into post-fuck discourse anyway—or pre-fuck, for that matter. He rubbed his tongue along his teeth, swallowed in distaste, and headed for the bathroom.

When he hit the switch, the light retaliated, zapping his brain with a thousand-volt charge. "Shit."

He vised his head between his hands and applied pressure to his temples, waited until the thumping stopped. He hoped his headache wouldn't bloom into the one he damn well deserved. He straightened and cautiously rolled his head. Okay.

Toothbrush. Where in hell was his damn toothbrush?

Ten minutes and one shower later, he vaguely resembled human. Five minutes after that, while he was shaving, the reflection of his morning-after brunette joined his in the mirror, her expression sultry, expectant. Her hair was almost as dark as his, he noticed. He wondered idly why he never brought home a redhead, maybe a blonde.

"Mornin' . . . sweetheart," he managed.

"Tracy," she said calmly. "My name's Tracy."

Yates took a final swipe along his lower jaw with the razor, rinsed it, and turned to lean against the sink, blotting his jaw with a hand towel. He looked at her. "Tracy who?" he asked, not entirely sure if he cared to know.

She shook her head and smiled indulgently. "Bastard."

He wiped the remaining foam from his face and tossed the towel aside. "Bathroom's all yours. How about you move that perfect little ass of yours. I've got an appointment." He didn't bother to tell her it was for late afternoon.

"That's it?" She looked confident, unperturbed by his casual dismissal.

"That's it."

"I don't think so." She moved closer, ran a hand palm flat through his chest hair and down. "You're everything they say you are, Yates Lang." She fondled him boldly through his briefs. "And more—a lot more."

He took her hand in his, held it in his fist. "If you know so much about me, sweetheart, you'd know I'm the one who makes the moves." He let go of her hand, strode past her and out of the bathroom.

"Bastard," she said again, this time with a vengeance.

In the morning hours after Milo's death, Hannah Stuart pulled herself together and saw to his remaining requests.

Do this, now do that, take care of this, she instructed herself, forcing her pain aside, putting her grief on hold until everything needing doing was done.

Methodically, she'd moved from task to task, plodding through the closing of Milo Biehle's life in the same way she'd plodded through her own years before.

Milo, following a lifelong habit of note-taking and list-making, had made it easy. His directions were clear right up to his dispassionate instructions on the "disposition of the cremains." Hannah went through his list item by item, made the necessary calls to the funeral home, his two remaining business associates in Seattle, and his attorney, whom she'd reached at his home shortly after six.

Now it was time to tell his mother, Miranda. Milo

had asked Hannah not to telephone, but to wait until she was "composed," and tell her in person. "Be there for her, Hannah, that's all I ask."

Hannah would have been there already if Milo's lawyer, Gerry Vonecker, hadn't insisted on driving up from Seattle immediately. He'd arrived within two hours of being called and had just left. A coolly efficient man, he'd expressed the proper condolences, then asked Hannah if she'd mind his taking Milo's remaining papers and files back to his office. He wanted one final, thorough review, he said.

Most of the estate work was already done, he'd advised her, reminding her Milo's passing was "while certainly regrettable, not unexpected." He'd been preparing for it for months now. Hannah had the dim impression Gerry Vonecker would like all his clients to die on schedule, leaving as few loose ends as possible.

Milo's instructions to Vonecker were also precise: complete the liquidation of the specified assets begun immediately upon Milo's diagnosis and turn all proceeds of those sales, along with his other holdings, over to Hannah. The sizable fortune consisted of real estate and blue chip stocks. Milo had never been a speculator. The hundred-year-old, forty-room mansion, which he'd named Kenninghall after an English village he'd visited on a buying trip, was not to be sold, nor was the antique collection. Those had been transferred into her name before Milo's death with the instruction she do with them as she wished—no conditions attached.

Hannah Marie Stuart, at age thirty-two, was a wealthy woman.

Although the early October day was warmed by a rich autumn sun, she drew a black coat over her brown sweater before opening the door and stepping onto the wide porch that swept halfway around the large house. That the coat had worn cuffs, and the sweater sagged from too many washings, she ignored. It didn't matter how she looked, hadn't for years.

She walked down the six front steps and took the path to the garage. There were five cars there, an ancient Rolls Royce, an even older Ford, a 1937 Cord sedan, a 1946 Chrysler with wooden trim, and a two-year-old Saab. She got in the Saab and placed the box she carried on the seat beside her. Gripping the wheel firmly, she drew in a calming breath.

It had been a long time since she'd been behind the wheel of a car. Since coming to the La Conner area of Washington State, she'd walked the three miles to and from town only if she had to, preferring solitary rambles across the flat, untilled fields in winter, the quiet country roads in summer.

When there was driving to be done, Milo did it. When there was *anything* to be done, Milo did it, and Hannah let him, slipping without protest or complaint into an undemanding dependency. Content to let him manage things, she resisted all his efforts, stronger since his cancer diagnosis, to force her into a more active interest in the business—and in life. And while he'd grown increasingly insistent, she'd demurred in silence, refusing to accept a future without him.

She took her hands from the wheel long enough to get the keys from her pocket. Her vision blurred when she looked at them.

Now Milo was gone and everything was hers,

even this car she'd never driven. Milo had given her his life, and she didn't know what to do with it.

"Relearn how to live, Hannah," he'd said last week. "Become the strong, resourceful woman you once were." She hadn't listened then, didn't want to now. She put the key in the ignition, but didn't start the car. Instead she gripped the steering wheel and rested her head on her knuckles. That woman was gone. This woman didn't want to re-learn anything. She wanted to hide—to sleep, then wake up and have someone tell her she'd been locked in an extended nightmare. That it was over now and everything would be all right.

That's not going to happen.

She looked at the dash, then the key embedded in the ignition. She would do this. For Milo she would start this car and drive to the funeral home; there she'd drop off the nineteenth-century Chinese ginger jar he'd requested his ashes be held in. But first she'd stop at Miranda's house and tell her that her son had died early this morning.

Hannah stared across the flat, now dormant, tulip fields of La Conner to where Miranda's house, easily seen from Kenninghall, sat sprawled beneath two overwhelming chestnut trees and prayed she'd find the right words.

She breathed deeply, steadied herself.

One. Two. Three. That was how things got done. One simple step at a time.

One. She turned the key and the car responded instantly.

Two. She slipped the car into drive and eased out of the garage. She had a promise to keep. Milo had been dead since early morning. It was past time to tell Miranda.

* * *

"There's nothing here. Nothing. That son of a bitch!" The client shoved the mass of documents off the desk with one angry sweep of his arm, swung back to face Gerry Vonecker, hands on hips. "You're certain this"—he gestured roughly with his chin toward the papers scattered over the desk and floor—"is everything?"

Vonecker had never seen him like this, but he wasn't unduly concerned. He was accustomed to placating upset clients, although it hadn't yet been necessary with this one. Shrewd, and possessed of an icy control, until now he'd been a pleasure—a very lucrative pleasure—to work with.

"Everything I could find given the situation," he said, careful to keep his tone authoritative, confident.

"What the hell is that supposed to mean?"

Gerry looked up into a pair of cold, uncompromising black eyes. "It *means* Biehle's house has over forty rooms. What you see here"—he nodded at the papers still in his hands—"is everything from his private office, den, safe, and bedroom. And bear in mind, Biehle was only hours dead, and his assistant was, of course, distraught. Given the circumstances, I couldn't very well ask to inspect the attic," he said, injecting a hint of disapproval. This interrogation was getting tiresome. And the task was impossible. How could he be expected to find a record of a safety deposit box in that mausoleum Biehle called home? And the key itself? Forget it. It irritated him to be used as if he were a third-rate private eye. Not to mention, should he find the key, there was nothing extra in it for him.

"With what I'm paying you, you should have looked up his *assistant's* skirts."

Gerry thought of Hannah, her sad but luminous blue eyes—her recent inheritance. "Now there's a thought," he said, and risked a smile.

He shouldn't have.

The man lunged across the desk, grabbed his throat, and yanked him halfway across the desk. "You think this is funny, Vonecker? You see humor in this?"

Vonecker's breath bunched under the man's viselike grip. His throat closed. In every line of the face mere inches from his own lay threat—a barely leashed menace. Panic gathered under his rib cage.

The man's fingers were steel talons, and his glare was ice over fire. "You know what you are, Vonecker? Expendable, that's what. You'd be smart to remember that." He growled the words, his face so close Vonecker could smell his minty breath.

As suddenly as he'd attacked, he let go, shoving Vonecker backward to the seat he'd pulled him from.

Vonecker's knees buckled as he tangled with his chair. His cheek slammed into the edge of his desk before he crumpled to the floor. He came up gasping, struggling to fill his empty lungs. Unable to speak, he rubbed at his throat and blinked while his heart hammered in his chest, wild and erratic.

"Get back out there and try again." The man reached for his coat and slipped it on, casually aligning its collar, then rolling his head to ease his tension. He strode to the door and turned back.

"And this time, Vonecker, don't fuck up."

Chapter 2

At Miranda's roomy cedar-shaked house, Hannah was met at the door by Claire Bergen. Claire had moved in shortly after Miranda's second heart attack over a year ago.

Miranda knew, at eighty-eight, after two attacks, it was either get help at home or go into one, the latter a prospect loathed by both her and Milo. Milo had argued for her to come to Kenninghall. "God knows, there's room to spare, Mother!" he'd said, but she'd refused. "You've got your life, Milo, and—such as it is—I've got mine. That's the way it's going to stay." After a war of words, they'd settled on Milo expanding and renovating Miranda's home, so all the living could be done on the main floor, eliminating Miranda's need to use the stairs, and providing enough room for a live-in caregiver. And they'd agreed on Claire Bergen as Miranda's nurse and companion. Since then the two women had become friends; the only hint of conflict com-

ing when Miranda accused Claire of "constantly
fussing." As a plan, it worked: Miranda was well
cared for and had her independence. And Milo
could look out his second-floor bedroom window
and see the lights of her house.

Claire took Hannah's coat, asked quietly, "Is he
gone?"

"Early this morning."

Claire's eyes watered, then she nodded. "I'll
make tea," she said. "Miranda's in the sunroom."

"Thanks."

Miranda was sitting in her wheelchair staring
out the window into the autumn sun. Shasta, her
small Border terrier, was asleep at her feet. Upon
Hannah's arrival, he opened one eye, saw it was
someone he knew, and closed it again.

"Miranda?" Hannah took a hesitant step forward.

The old woman lifted her head and turned. Her
eyes, once blue, now grayed with age, were also
grayed by tears. When she saw Hannah, her eyelids
fluttered to a close, and she nodded solemnly, her
face creased in grief.

"It's not natural," she said, "for a mother to out-
live her son."

"You know?" Filled with remorse, Hannah quickly
crossed the room and knelt beside Miranda's chair.
She should have come sooner. Milo wanted Miranda
to hear of his death from her.

"Yes." She nodded, again closing her eyes. "Milo
came to me. Shortly after four this morning."

The time he died.

Hannah didn't try to dissuade Miranda from
her vision and didn't discount it. If souls did come

back, and if Milo could say good-bye to anyone from the other side, it would be Miranda. He'd loved her unreservedly.

Hannah felt a stab of envy.

No one came back to her. No matter her cries in the night; her truth was darkness, a cold pillow, and an empty crib.

Miranda unfurled a balled-up hanky, dried both eyes, and straightened to look directly at Hannah. "Well, at least there's one good thing about being eighty-eight; I'll see him soon. There's consolation in that. Tell me, Hannah. Did he suffer?"

Hannah took her hand. "He went quietly. There was very little pain at the end." And no hurt in a small lie, she told herself.

"Less than in his life, I hope." Miranda gazed at the sky through the glass ceiling of the sunroom as though there were a secret there, a journal on the past.

"He was happy, truly he was," Hannah said, not sure if it were true.

"Because of you, dear. And I'm grateful for that— and so was Milo."

"I owed him so much." Hannah worked to not cry, to stay strong for Miranda. "He saved my life."

Miranda touched Hannah's hair, smoothed loose strands behind an ear. "Only you can save your life. Only you. Remember that."

"That's what Milo always said."

"He was right. The tragedy is he didn't apply it to his own life."

"I don't know what you mean."

"I'm not sure *I* do. But somewhere along the way my son changed, withdrew somehow. He'd always been such a happy boy, then—" She stopped. "When

I tried to find out about it, he said I was imagining things." She looked at the sky again and smiled. "Maybe given an eternity, I'll make him talk."

"I'm sure he'll be up there"—Hannah swallowed, dammed up the tears—"waiting for you."

"Yes. I'm sure of it. Because if Milo doesn't make it, there's little hope for the rest of us." She started to cry. "He was a good man, my son." She opened her arms and Hannah went into them. Their embrace was desperate, each drawing from the other's life force, Hannah acutely aware that Miranda's body, although terribly frail, was immeasurably stronger than the one she'd held in the hours before dawn.

An hour later Hannah pulled into the parking lot of the funeral home where they'd taken Milo that morning. She glanced at the blue and white ginger jar resting in the bubble packing in the open box beside her. It had been Milo's choice. Rare and perfect—like the man himself.

She lifted the jar from its packing and looked at the imposing oak doors of the funeral home. Was he still there, she wondered? Or was he gone, already the ashes he'd longed to become. She would never know.

"No service, no coffin, no tears," he'd told her firmly.

"Two out of three, Milo, my dear friend," she whispered, wiping dampness from her cheeks. "That's the best I can do."

Wilson Bone pried a paper napkin from its metal cell, folded it precisely in half, and wiped the sweat and grime from his forehead. He set the napkin, stain up, beside his cup.

He watched the dark-haired woman sitting across from him shift back, saw her nose twitch. The bitch wanted space. Looked real pissed when she didn't get it. The tiny booth didn't yield an inch.

"Ever hear of soap and water?" she asked, using her chin to indicate the soiled napkin, her lips to show distaste.

When he didn't bother to answer, she shook her head.

"Fifteen grand," she said. "Five now to cover expenses. The rest later."

"You got a time frame?"

"Before the end of October."

Bone let on he was considering this, as if his dance card was full. Using both hands, he lifted his mug to his lips and slurped at his coffee. The flesh on both hands was puckered and dry. Discolored. Three fingers ended in stumps, and two more were fused to his palm. The bitch looked away.

"My way," he stated, giving her his no-shit stare. "Nobody tells Wilson Bone how to do his business."

"I don't give a damn how you do it." She clicked open the slim briefcase sitting beside her, took out an envelope, and slid it halfway across the table. The envelope linked them, his wrecked hands on one end, her long, scarlet-tipped nails on the other. Her gaze was hard. "Just make it tidy. Understood?"

He pulled the envelope from her grasp and slipped it into the inside pocket of his windbreaker. "Just call me Mr. Clean."

"Yeah, right." She snapped the briefcase closed and stood. "I'll be in touch." She dug a five-dollar bill from her bag, tossed it on the table, and looked down on him. "You bet-

*ter be as good as your reputation, Bone, or the next guy I
hire does you."*

Through the dirt-streaked window, Bone watched her
fold her long legs into a red Lexus SC 430 convertible,
settle her sunglasses on her nose, and drive off.

Hot car. Cold bitch. The rich prick's reward.

You wouldn't catch Wilson Bone wasting his money
like that. No fuckin' way. Well . . . maybe on the car.

He rifled his jeans' pocket, exchanged her fiver for the
exact change, and slid out of the booth.

Outside, he lit a cigarette, drew the smoke deep, and
pulled his collar close to his chin. Damned chilly for a San
Diego September. Probably freezin' up there in Washington
State. Damn near Canada up that way.

He thought about the woman, the fifteen grand. If the
bitch was goferin' for some rich prick, he was one dumb,
overpaying sucker. Hell, for that kind of green he'd do his
own grandmother and throw in a six-pack of relatives to
boot. Too bad, though. He'd hoped it would be a torch job.

He took another deep drag on his smoke. Hell, it was
his rules. He could do whatever he wanted. And he couldn't
think of a better way to cover his tracks than with a heap
of hot ash.

"What's with Vonecker? He looks as if he woke
up on the wrong side of the law." Yates arced his
apple core into the center of Anne Chapman's red
lacquered trash can and lifted his chin in the direction of the door.

She followed the toss, gave him a skinny look from
over the top of her chained reading glasses, then
looked to where he'd indicated. Gerry Vonecker
stood outside her glass-walled office. One of their

paralegals talked at him, her expression as earnest as Vonecker's was distracted.

Anne stopped her paper shuffling long enough to frown thoughtfully in the direction of her partner. When she again started to dig through the tower of files centered on her otherwise clean desk, it was with more vigor.

"He's busy," she said. "We all are. The law firm of Simpson, Chapman, and Vonecker is on a roll. It's amazing what a little hard work and commitment can accomplish. You ought to try it sometime."

"Now, Annie, honey, you're not going to launch into that 'dust off the degree and join the firm bit,' are you?"

"Humph. Not in this lifetime. You're not exactly my idea of a team player. And take your size twelves off my damn desk." She whacked his scuffed boots. He grinned, dropped his feet to the floor, and picked up a photograph from her desk.

"Who's this," he asked, giving the photo mock-serious perusal. "Your Great Aunt Bertha? A sister maybe?"

She grabbed it from his hand. "Funny, Yates. Very funny." She put the picture of her golden retriever carefully back in place before waving a file at him. "This is it. Strome and McMann." She opened it, adjusting her glasses and reading posture at the same time. "They're partners in a company called Lotsa Beans, Inc. They import coffee and related paraphernalia from around the world. Been partners for"—she ran her index finger down the page—"eight years. Strome's convinced McMann's cheating the partnership." She closed the file and thrust it at him. "It's all yours, wise guy. You've got a month."

Yates groaned. "Haven't you got something with

more blood and guts, Chapman? I'm not a bean counter."

"We specialize in corporate law here, Yates, not *corpus delicti*. If you want blood, go shoot yourself. Besides, that piece of paper saying you're a CPA says bean counter to me."

"Another life." He rifled through the file, distinctly unenthusiastic.

"And the aborted criminology degree? What life was that?"

"I always wanted to be a policeman when I grew up. Something about those blue suits."

"And the law degree?"

"A poorly marked turn in the highway of life."

"Well, that turn and the initials CPA add up to the juicy task of nailing a coffee tycoon. That's all I've got. Take it or leave it." She walked around to the front of her desk and leaned against it, arms braced under her breasts.

He tossed the file on her desk and stood. "I'll leave it." He shrugged into his beat-up leather jacket. "Thanks anyway."

A worry line creased her forehead. "You need the money, Yates. Take the job."

He looked at her. At fifty-eight, she was a plump but striking woman with a voice rasping enough to strip the veneer off courtroom walls. He liked her, and he didn't like many people. She was also a damn fine lawyer.

He kissed her cheek and smiled into her sharp eyes. "Try me next month. I should be desperate enough by then."

"You're certifiable. You know that. An over-educated, unmotivated—" She was working up a full head of steam.

Just then Vonecker stepped through Anne's open office door. A red welt stained his cheek and a bruise shadowed the left side of his neck. "Sorry, Anne. I didn't know you were busy." His gaze darted between them.

"Just doing some missionary work," she said, giving Yates a deadly glare. She went back to the chair behind her desk. "Might as well save my breath," she mumbled.

Vonecker offered Yates his hand and a smooth smile. "Yates."

The two men shook hands. "What happened to you?" Yates asked, gesturing at his face. "A close encounter of the physical kind?"

Vonecker touched the welt carefully, as though it were still tender. "Would you believe my car door attacked me?"

No, Vonecker, I wouldn't. "Must have been one mean door." Yates didn't miss that his neck's left-side bruise had a twin on the right. Turning back to Anne, he said, "Call me when the blood starts to flow, Chapman."

The remark earned him another irritated glare.

"Right now the only thing flowing is coffee—poured by Strome and McMann." Her look was stern. "Think about it, Yates."

"Yeah." He nodded at Vonecker. "Better get some ice on that."

"I will. Thanks." Again Vonecker touched his cheek.

Yates walked out, wondering where his next month's rent was coming from, and who'd gotten pissed enough to try and throttle Vonecker.

* * *

"Hannah?"

Hannah forced her eyes open. Her mouth was woolly, her lids heavy from drug-induced sleep. She blinked in slow motion, dimly aware of a voice. *Milo? She must go to Milo. He was calling her.*

"Milo . . ."

She felt a hand on her shoulder, a firm grip then a shake. The voice was louder now.

"Hannah, the phone. It's Mr. Vonecker." The lamp went on beside her bed. *Was it nighttime? Who was talking to her?*

"Wake up." The voice again, louder now. Exasperated.

It was Meara, the housekeeper. *Fool. Milo's gone. Dead. Has been for days.* The truth shot into her and a pain made of acid and fog settled in her forehead.

"The telephone," Meara said, raising her voice. "Please take the phone."

Hannah reached for the phone, knocked over an empty glass, and watched blearily as Meara picked it up. *Who was on the phone?* Her head threatened to explode.

She held the receiver to her chest, clutching it in both hands. She looked dumbly at Meara, who stood by her bedside.

"Mr. Vonecker," Meara repeated. "Mr. Biehle's lawyer?"

"Oh. Yes. Of course," she muttered, the words sand in her mouth. She sat up, shoved her hair back from her face, and tried to ground herself. This was her room, pale green walls, deep rose carpet, high windows with stained glass at the top. Familiar. Everything the same. She let out a breath. Still shaky, she put the receiver to her ear, closed her eyes, and concentrated.

"Mr. Vonecker. This is Hannah. Is everything all right?" she managed to ask, her voice only slightly ragged. She watched Meara mouth the word *coffee* before quietly closing the bedroom door behind her. Her eyes stayed fixed on the door. When her eyelids drifted closed again, she shook her head to jar them open. Pain arced to the back of her head.

"Yes. Everything's fine," Vonecker said briskly. "A small matter. A former business associate of Milo's called. He's looking for a deed on a property once jointly owned by him and Milo. I looked through the documents I have here, but can't find it. I was wondering if I'm missing a couple of Milo's files."

"I don't think so, but I can check if you like." Hannah struggled to register the conversation, to make sense of it. Her mind moved slowly from dead stop to sluggish awareness. With that came the tightness in her chest, the dull ache that had been her companion since Milo's death. She was alone again—and afraid.

"I hate to trouble you at a time like this, but . . ."

Hannah scarcely listened as she scanned the marble top of her bedside table, then opened its single drawer. She took out an amber vial, its contents hidden by a wraparound prescription sticker. She shook it. It didn't rattle. She rested her head back against the pillow and let the bottle roll from her hand. Vonecker was still talking.

". . . be better if I came out there. Had a look myself. Easier all round, I think. Say, this afternoon, about two or two-thirty? It might take a while."

"Fine. Good. See you then." Hannah couldn't wait to get off the phone. She clicked off the re-

ceiver, retrieved the amber vial, and read the label.
"For refill contact your physician." She considered
her chances of refilling a prescription for a dead
man. Not good.

She should go to her own doctor, get her own
pills. *And maybe she should pull herself together!* She
pushed the second thought aside. She had nothing to get together for.

Her bedroom door opened, and Meara came in
with a tray laden with coffee, orange juice, and toast.
She set it across Hannah's knees and went to open
the drapes. Pale light seeped into the room, doing
little to brighten it. Hannah stared at the glass of
orange juice but made no move to pick it up.

Meara stood beside the bed and pointed at the
tray. "Eat something, girl. You need your strength."

Dutifully, Hannah picked up a piece of toast
and nibbled at its edge. It tasted like straw.

Meara, oozing disapproval, bunched her fists on
her hips. "You always do what you're told?" she
asked.

Hannah frowned. Meara had said something,
but the words wouldn't take shape in her dulled
consciousness. "I'm sorry. What did you say?"

Meara tilted her head and gave her a curious
look. "Put the toast down and drink some of that
orange juice."

Hannah did as she was told; the summer scent
of orange filled her nostrils.

Meara spoke to the ceiling and drew in a noisy
breath. "That's it. You're coming with me."

Hannah only had time to blink before she was
hoisted out of bed and tugged toward her bathroom. Without ceremony, Meara stripped off her

nightgown and shoved her into the shower. It wasn't difficult. Meara probably outweighed her by sixty pounds.

A sluice of frigid water hit Hannah's face and breasts with the virulence of an arctic wind. She shuddered violently, twisted to free herself from Meara's grasp. Useless. She was dismally weak, wasted from more than a week of pills, mindless sleep, and scant food. Meara gripped her chin, lifted her face into the stream of cold. Cutting water now punished her naked body with the fierceness of a rawhide. When her knees started to give out, Hannah lifted her hands, locked them over the shower head, and hung on. Suddenly, she didn't want the water to ever stop.

Minutes later Meara was rubbing her back and shoulders energetically with a bath sheet. "There. Isn't that better now? It's about time you joined the land o' the livin', girl." She rubbed harder. "Like my mother used to say, 'no grievin' for the leavin', it's the livin' who bring in the wood,' " she said, going heavy on the Irish.

Hannah wrapped herself in a dry towel and turned. "Did she really say that, or did you make it up?" she asked, noticing her headache had lessened and rearranged itself into dull throb.

Meara McCoy smiled noncommittally.

Hannah smiled back. The mouth shape so alien, she was sure it sat on her face like a pumpkin's grin.

Meara nudged her toward the bedroom. "Now. You get dressed and come down to the kitchen. That coffee and toast I brought you will be cold by now. I'll make you a real breakfast." She headed for the door, issuing one last instruction. "Don't be long. Hear?"

Hannah nodded.

Twenty minutes later she followed the aroma of frying bacon into Milo's kitchen and perched on a stool at one end of what she always called Meara's island, a slab of ancient oak, designed for the cook and staff of a fifteenth-century castle kitchen. Slightly higher than a normal table, its top was scored by thousands of ancient knives, poultry saws, and pounding mallets. It had taken ten men and a hoist to install it in Kenninghall's kitchen not long after Milo bought the estate twenty-five years ago. He'd joked how the shipping costs were as much as he'd paid for the table, but that it was worth every cent. Walking into the Kenninghall kitchen was stepping back in time, and it wasn't only the scarred, ancient table. Not a modern appliance was in sight, every one of them artfully hidden behind period oak cabinetry. Milo bought the best, and the latest, but he never wanted to see anything newer than the nineteenth century.

Hannah glanced at her watch; barely noon, but the rain-darkened sky made it seem like early evening.

This time when a mug of coffee was placed in front of her, she didn't need to be told to drink it.

Meara filled her own cup and sat opposite her. "Mr. Biehle's gone, you know, and he won't be coming back."

Hannah looked at her through the steam rising from her coffee. "I know that," she said quietly. "I know."

Meara's expression softened. "Yes, I suppose

you do." When Hannah didn't answer, she paused before going on. "Will you be wantin' me to leave, then?"

Hannah swallowed so quickly she burned her throat. "Leave? Of course not. Why would you think that?" Meara couldn't leave. She belonged here, as much a part of Kenninghall as the antiques and curios that filled every square inch of Milo's odd old mansion. It had been Meara who opened the front door when Hannah first came here five years before.

"I didn't know. What with Mr. Biehle gone and all. You haven't said, and I—"

"My God. I'm so sorry. Your check! I haven't paid you." How could she be so irresponsible? Milo always left the household accounts strictly in her hands. She'd let him down.

"It's not the money. Mr. Biehle took good care of that. Bless his good soul. Like I said, what with him gone, I—"

"You have to stay, Meara." Hannah reached across the island and took her hand, held it—too tight. "This was your home before it was mine. It wouldn't be the same without you. You're comfortable in the cottage aren't you?" She knew there was a trace of desperation in her voice but couldn't contain it.

"You know I am. But . . ."

"But what?"

The woman, a hale sixty years old, straightened her shoulders, leveled her gaze to meet Hannah's. "I won't sit by and watch the place go to wrack and ruin, Hannah Stuart. I won't. Mr. Biehle wouldn't like it." She sealed her mouth into a stubborn line.

"I—" Hannah didn't know what to say. She let go of Meara's hand. She was right, of course. It was her role now, to keep Kenninghall running, to maintain the collection, do the work as Milo would have wanted it done. In life he'd trusted her to take care of things. Now it was a legacy. Why hadn't she seen that? She would keep things as they'd always been. Milo would be proud of her.

Meara went on. "That nice Mr. Vonecker has called almost every day since Mr. Biehle died, and you wouldn't take his calls. And Mr. Biehle's mother. She's phoned three or four times to see if you're all right. And—"

"Miranda called? When?"

"When you were sleepin', that's when."

Meara's words were baldly accusatory—and justified. The kitchen calendar told Hannah she'd slept away more than a week. She winced as Meara went on.

"And there's the roof to be looked after—the man from town called about it yesterday—the broken window that needs replacing, a new cleaning service to be hired, now Peggy and her daughter have gone, and the garden to be seen to. By this time last year, you'd already ordered the spring bulbs. And that woman . . . Mrs. King? She's called, too. Twice. Wants to know about"—she dug into her apron pocket and pulled out a folded note—"the Worcester sugar bowl. And an Erin Calder, inquiring about some candlesticks." Meara put the paper on the table, rested her clasped hands over it, and waited for Hannah to reply.

Hannah listened to her list of sins in silence. Ignoring one or all of the things on it wouldn't lead them to immediate "wrack and ruin" as Meara so direly predicted, but even knowing her comments were a play on her sense of duty, Hannah admitted there was work to be done. Work Milo entrusted to her. And Meara couldn't go. It would change things, and Hannah had grappled with enough change to last her a lifetime.

She gripped her coffee mug tighter and nodded at Meara. "You're right. I have been letting things go. But don't worry. I'll make out your check this afternoon. In the meantime, I'd appreciate it if you'd write everything down, Meara. Make me a list. I'll get started on it as soon as I've finished eating. I'll take care of things. I promise. There's no need for you to leave." She pushed the coffee aside and picked up a fork. She would eat now. Get some strength back.

Meara opened her mouth as if to say something, then shook her head. "A list, is it? Fine, then, I'll make you a list."

"Yates?"

"Hey, Chapman." Yates tucked the phone between shoulder and ear, cupped the back of his head in his hands, and propped his bare feet on the coffee table. "Found some of that blood and guts I'm looking for?"

"No." She hesitated. "But I do have an, uh, internal problem—quite delicate—I'd like to talk to you about. Can we meet? Somewhere away from the office?"

"Sounds promising. Can't think of a thing I'd rather do than explore the wicked underbelly of the law firm of Simpson, Chapman, and Vonecker."

Anne Chapman didn't come back at him with her usual snappy rejoinder. "This is serious, Yates, or could be. On the other hand it could be completely unfounded. Still, when it involves a senior member of the firm—"

"Vonecker?" Yates straightened, gripped the phone in one hand, and reached for a pen with the other.

"How'd you figure that?"

"Unless you're the guilty party—"

"No one's guilty—at least not yet."

"Yeah? Well, unless you're the *alleged* guilty party, Chapman—whereby I assume you'd hire a much less competent person than myself—I figure I had a fifty percent chance of being right. Because try as I might, I can't see old Simpson involved in anything sleazier than cheating at solitaire. That leaves Vonecker."

"Yes."

He pulled the newspaper forward and spotted available white space around a car ad. "When and where?"

Anne named a restaurant several blocks from her Union Square office and he wrote it down.

"Tomorrow, noon. Got it." He hung up and again leaned back in the sofa.

I guess if I can't find any blood and guts, Vonecker's welt and two bruises will have to do.

Chapter 3

Wilson Bone decided to use gasoline, make it look like some amateur firebug was the starter. Amateurs liked gasoline. So did Bone. He even liked the smell of the stuff. Gas was uncomplicated, reliable—and untraceable. Now all he had to worry about was timing.

He lit a cigarette, dragged deep, and parked it in the corner of his mouth. One eye squinted against the smoke but didn't water as he bent once more over the map.

Interstate 5. That looked good all the way. He ran a nicotine-stained finger up the map and stopped it on Seattle. The town he wanted was pretty much straight north of there. Maybe a couple of hours' drive. Hell, the whole trip wouldn't take any time at all. He'd take care of some leftover business here and be on his way. Maybe make a bit of a holiday out of it. Yeah, that's what he'd do, take it slow and easy.

Pick up what he needed along the way.

* * *

Hannah was leafing through seed and bulb catalogues when Gerry Vonecker walked into the kitchen. He looked harried and nervous.

"Find what you were looking for?" Hannah asked, setting the catalogue and her notes aside. She hoped he had. Meara's list was only the beginning. She'd made one of her own—consoled to see a plan emerge, a steady, predictable series of jobs. A path to follow. She had lots to do.

He shook his head. "No. Are you sure that's everything? Perhaps Milo had another safety deposit box somewhere?"

She shook her head. "You say it's an old deed you're looking for?" She wanted to help. And not for altogether unselfish reasons. The sooner he found what he was looking for, the sooner he'd be gone, and the quiet of Kenninghall would be hers again.

"Yes." His eyes leveled with hers. "Is there anything—anywhere—that I might have missed?"

Maybe her brain was still fogged by the sleeping pills, but Hannah couldn't think of anything that might help him. She shook her head. "Sorry. As far as I know Milo gave you everything, and he was very organized." She forced a smile. "I'm sure you'll find it."

"There's always the chance he mislaid it, put it with other documents or more personal papers?" He peered at her over his reading glasses.

The letters! Maybe what he wanted was in the letters. Her throat muscles tightened and her thoughts stumbled. She should have read them by now. If she had, she'd know the right thing to do. Milo obviously trusted Gerry Vonecker; he *was* his lawyer.

He'd handled Milo's affairs for years. Perhaps she should trust him, too—tell him about the letters.

She clasped her hands together, worried an index finger, gripping it with the other hand and rubbing the knuckle. If she gave Vonecker the letters, she could forget about them. As much as she tried to hold it back, fear gnawed her bones at the thought of them.

She started to speak, glanced up to see Vonecker watching her closely, too closely, and she closed up.

"You've seen everything," she lied, then stood to take her cup to the sink. There was an odd quivering in her stomach; she hoped it hadn't manifested in her voice. "And really, other than the antique collection, and the buying and selling associated with that, I know next to nothing about Milo's other affairs, business or personal. So if there are more personal papers . . ." She shrugged to indicate her impotence in such things. It helped that what she said was true. Her relationship with Milo thrived in privacy and seclusion. Neither of them talked about the past. They lived in the day they were in. Hannah knew her reasons for this, but not Milo's. She simply accepted them.

"I see," Vonecker said as though he didn't see at all. He stood to go. "I did wonder, though. About the room on the third floor? The locked one."

"Linen storage," she lied again, this time without knowing why. "Irish mostly, old and very fragile. The room is moth proofed and temperature controlled."

"Hmm." He nodded. "Then I suppose I'll have to tell my client the deed is lost. But you will let me know if you think of anywhere else I might look. Anywhere at all."

"Of course."

She walked Vonecker to the door. When she closed it after him, she leaned back against it and looked up the broad staircase. Bracketed by two elegant Regency rosewood tables, each bearing a lily lamp from the twenties, and carpeted in rich Persian red, it was the showpiece of Kenninghall's entrance. It led to the second floor. Milo's bedroom.

She'd been there only once since the night he'd died. She'd tried, but hadn't found the courage to read the letters. She told herself it was too soon; she was too tired, too mired in grief, which didn't come close to the truth.

She wished her reluctance was so easily explained.

But, that night, when she'd opened the hidden drawer and taken out the first letter addressed to her, it had crouched in her hand like a cursed crystal. Milo told her the letters would change things, knowledge that drained her of curiosity. She wanted predictability, uniformity, one day indistinguishable from the next. This house was her refuge, a place to nurture her guilt and chain her demons. More than she deserved, but she was desperate to preserve it.

Alone in the dim and cavernous room, filled with dread, yet trapped by her promise to her dying friend, she'd slipped the letter back in its hiding place—and opened a bottle of his sleeping pills instead. Over a week ago.

Milo said to open the letters when she was ready. She didn't know when that would be and didn't care.

The restaurant buzzed with hurried lunch-hour conversations, a social white noise ensuring no one heard anything coherent from more than a foot away. Anne Chapman looked nervous as hell. After she and Yates took their seats, her gaze shifted constantly to points beyond his shoulder. So far all she'd said was how confidential everything was.

"Would you relax, Chapman," he said, when she'd cast yet another furtive glance at the table behind them. "There's not a chance in hell of anyone over-hearing you in here. The damn place is probably full of lawyers, and everyone knows they don't listen to anyone but themselves."

"This place is about as far away from a legal eatery as I could find," she snapped. "And quit with the lawyer jokes, would you. Right now they're the last thing I need."

"Just trying to fill the dead air." He signaled for the overworked waiter before looking at her again. "C'mon, Anne. What'd Vonecker do, run off with the company's gold-plated gavel? Fornicate with a competitor? What?"

She picked up a spoon, made circles with it on the tablecloth. "The gavel analogy's close."

"Let me guess. A few unauthorized trust fund withdrawals?" Yates figured Vonecker wouldn't be the first lawyer to "borrow" from the company trust accounts, nor would he be the last. And hadn't he nabbed himself a trophy wife sometime last year? They were expensive, particularly when you were supporting the original Mrs. Vonecker in the style to which you'd made her accustomed.

"It's more the company he's been keeping lately."

"You mean there's a subspecies lower than the legal beagle and Vonecker's found it?"

She glared at him. "I come to you with a serious

problem—and cash for services—and you make jokes. There's more than one P.I. out there, Yates."

"There's thousands of them. I'm not one of them."

"Oh yes, I forgot. You're a crime consultant—whatever the hell that is," she grumbled.

"It's whatever I want it to be."

"How convenient for you."

"Exactly." He glanced up to see the waiter heading their way. "How about we order lunch, then discuss Vonecker. Dishonest lawyers go down easier on a full stomach."

"You are—" she started.

"Ready to order?" The waiter arrived, stood over their table, and brandished his order pad with enough officiousness to deflect Anne's quelling look from Yates to himself.

They both ordered the pasta lunch special, and both stuck to shop talk until the food arrived. Anne, it seemed, was again reluctant to broach the subject that was the reason for their lunch. Maybe he'd been too hard on her. The woman looked worried, real worried.

"Okay." Yates pushed his plate back. "Let's get down to it. Who is Vonecker seeing that's got you looking as if you're fully invested in a bear market?"

"His name's Donald Hallam, and the company is called Zanez Shipping. Owns five freighters. Carries goods between Seattle and various Asian ports on a regular basis. Vonecker brought them on board about three years ago—"

"And you're only starting to worry now? I don't get it."

She lifted her coffee cup from the saucer and held it in front of her mouth, not drinking. "Oh, I worried then, all right. When I heard the company's business was importing wood products from Southeast Asia, particularly Thailand—otherwise known as narcotics central—I told Vonecker to be extra cautious, to check them out thoroughly. I left him to it, of course, having no reason not to.

"Actually we never had many dealings with them. Kept their company registry up to date, a couple of letters of opinion. That sort of thing. Then, a couple of weeks ago"—she took a drink of her coffee—"I received a phone call, anonymous, of course, telling me Zanez is up to its corporate armpits in a trade as nasty as it gets."

"Drugs."

She shook her head, pulled in a long breath. "They import kids, Yates. Mostly young girls, but some boys, too. As young as twelve, maybe up to sixteen. They bring them in by the container-load— using Zanez' ships. Gerry, apparently, looks after the legalities while this Hallam character makes the deals. Once here, God knows where they end up. But no doubt there are enough creeps around to provide a lucrative and ongoing market. Most of the kids are probably presold before they hit Seattle." Anne looked at him, her expression a combination of revulsion and weary cynicism. "Did you know, according to UNICEF, over a million kids a year are sold as sex slaves?"

Yates had a knack for numbers. But he sure as hell didn't like this one. He'd read about the Seattle Port Authority discovering illegal immigrants in shipping containers, but they'd always been adults or families. Many of them simply desperate people looking for a better life and placing themselves into bondage to the criminals who'd promised it. Ugly enough. But kids . . . Think about *that* long enough, and you'd heave, public restaurant or not.

"The caller? Man or woman?" He focused on getting back to business.

"A woman. Or to be more accurate, a girl."

"Anything familiar about the voice?"

"No. But it was Asian. Young. Terrible English. But what I got from her was she'd been brought in by ship three years ago from Thailand. Thirteen then. Sixteen now. She sounded scared—terrified, really. I tried to get her to meet with me, but there was no way. And when I tried to ask more questions, she panicked, couldn't get off the phone fast enough. Kept saying, 'They kill me, they kill me.' "

"And you believe her."

She rubbed her forehead. "I don't want to. Hell, who needs this kind of trouble. But she was so damn . . . real. I can't ignore it. But if you come up with nothing, no one will be happier than me."

"And she specifically named Vonecker?"

"Specifically and *very clearly*—considering her English. His was the only name she gave. His and the name of the ship she'd come in on—the *Naarmu*. The *Naarmu* is registered as belonging to Zanez."

"How in hell would a thirteen-year-old girl being herded out of a container know that?"

"She said she 'put name in head' and she 'not forget.' "

"That's it?"

"It's enough, isn't it? Vonecker plus *Naarmu* equals Zanez Shipping. And Zanez equals Donald Hallam."

"You've checked Vonecker's files, his office?"

She pulled at her unadorned earlobe, as if frustrated. "Yes."

"And?"

"Other than confirming Zanez operates the *Naarmu*? *Nada*. A big fat zero. Which is exactly what I expected. Gerry's too smart to leave a convenient trail of bread crumbs."

"You checked everything?"

"Every file, memo, and sticky note. Nothing. Spent more than a few late nights going through his trash can. And all I can tell you is he eats a lot of apples."

"And you've never met this Hallam character?"

"Once. Briefly. About a year ago. A chance meeting at lunch." She stopped a moment. "Gerry couldn't get away from me fast enough. But Hallam? He was a charmer. Handsome. Mid-forties, I'd say. Six feet or close to it. Dark hair. Expensively dressed. Kind of . . . sleek, if you know what I mean."

"Not exactly."

"Tanned. Fit." She paused. "The kind of man you'd expect to wear monogrammed silk underwear."

"Chapman, I'm shocked." But he got the picture. "And that's it? That's all you know about this guy?"

She nodded. "But given the business Zanez is in, I'd be surprised if his name is really Hallam. I checked out his address on the company records. It's an abandoned apartment over a delicatessen in downtown San Francisco. Hasn't had a tenant in years. Basically it's used for storage by the deli below." She let out a frustrated breath, sipped her water, then met Yates's gaze. "So, where are we on this? Do I get your help?"

"Harry knows you're talking to me?" Harry Simpson was not a Yates Lang fan.

"He knows. He's not happy, but he agrees this is something we can't handle on our own. I hate to say it, Yates, but you're the only one we can trust with this. And we're prepared to be generous."

He ignored her reference to money. "So the plan is if old Ger is guilty as charged, you want to change the firm's name to Simpson and Chapman as quickly as possible. Right?"

"That's a given. But what I really want is to hang Gerry by his balls from the Space Needle." Her expression set to flint. "Those girls they bring in? They're kids, Yates. Kids! It doesn't get sicker than that." She rubbed her chin with her index finger. "But if the city objects to that particular use of the Needle, I'll settle for a nice long prison term."

"You could call the cops." He knew she wouldn't, and knew he didn't want her to.

"I could—" She lifted her gaze to the ceiling. "It truly pains me to admit this, but I'd rather work with the best. If there is a case, I want it solid. No screwups, no advantageous technicalities. You give me that—then I'll call in the police. Give them everything you find."

"This isn't going to look good for you and Harry. You know that."

"I know." She stood and looked down at him. "Hate to disappoint you, but even lawyers have standards. Dig deep enough, we even have a few ethics." She dug into a large tote she'd stashed by her chair, pulled out a fat manila envelope, and tossed it on the table. "That's all I have on Zanez. The rest is up to you."

He didn't touch the envelope. "I didn't say I'd take the case."

"Yes, you did," she said, smug as hell. "You asked me at least three questions, Yates. And now you have to answer them."

Anne was right. Yates hated unanswered questions—He also hated sick bastards who preyed on innocence and despair. Bastards who'd do anything to line their own pockets—anything at all.

He remembered one in particular.

He picked up the envelope.

Chapter 4

Hannah looked out her bedroom window to watch Meara's Honda pull out of the driveway. She was going to spend the weekend with her sister in Blaine, the U.S./Canadian border town an hour or so north of La Conner.

It was barely after four o'clock, and day was already replaced by an early rain-swept evening, shadowy and gray. Tonight, for the first time since she'd come to Milo's home, she'd be completely alone.

She let the sheer white curtain she'd been holding fall back into place over the window and turned to face the emptiness of her room. Shivering suddenly, she rubbed her upper arms.

If Milo were here, they'd be in the library, the fire on the old grate crackling and snapping at the encroaching coolness of the damp West Coast night.

If Milo were here . . .

They would read for awhile, then Milo would

say something like, "What do you think of the Lalique I bought today?" He would peer at her over his newspaper, his glasses resting precariously on the tip of his nose. "Worth twelve thousand, don't you think? Fetch at least sixteen, I'd guess. Maybe more. But should I sell or hold? That's the question." That was *always* the question.

Milo was a passionate collector and a reluctant seller, second-guessing the sale until the last possible moment. His clientele, wealthy and discerning, trusted him to deal only with the finest and rarest of antiques. His collection filled Kenninghall and a secured storage facility in Seattle. For five years, Hannah had helped him accumulate and manage it.

Five eternal years. Ever since—

Pain, sharp and predictable, invaded her chest. She stepped briskly away from the window and walked toward the door, stopping as abruptly as she'd begun. Standing in the center of the room, she realized she had no place to go, nothing to do. No chores, no lists, no responsibilities, no distractions.

No direction.

She cocked her head, listened.

No sound, save her own uneven breathing.

The dark house enveloped her, its oppressive quiet compressing her lungs with the weight of lead.

She fidgeted with her sweater sleeve, pulled at the threads, disturbed to discover the fullness of the silence put her on edge, the emptiness made her uneasy.

Get real, Hannah, this is your life, get used to it.

Her bedside phone rang, a sound so shrill and

unexpected she started like a frightened hare. She picked up on the second ring.

"Hannah, how are you, dear? When I called a couple of days ago, Meara said you weren't feeling well."

"Just the flu, Miranda, I'm fine." Her voice was fluttery but clear. She was pleased. She was always pleased when her inner turmoil stayed deep, hidden and muffled.

"Milo wouldn't want you to get sick. You know that."

"Yes . . . I know."

Silence.

Miranda broke it. "I had a visit from Mr. Vonecker yesterday."

"Is there a problem? What did he want?"

"I'm not sure," Miranda said. "He said he was sorry about Milo—brought me some lovely flowers. But I don't believe it was his only purpose in coming to see me."

Neither did Hannah. "What else could it be?" she asked, telling herself she was suspicious over nothing.

"He wanted to know if Milo had left any personal papers with me. He's missing a share certificate, he says. I referred him to you, of course, told him I knew nothing at all about my son's business affairs. Did he call?"

"He was here a few days ago. I wasn't much help, I'm afraid—but I think it's a *deed* he's looking for."

She was silent for a moment. "I was sure he said share . . . but it really doesn't matter, does it?"

"No, I suppose not." But Hannah wasn't sure. Miranda might be eighty-eight, but her hearing was thirty-eight, and there was a big difference between a share certificate and a deed.

She switched on her bedside lamp, her gaze following its swath of light to her open door. Beyond it was Milo's room. The letters.

"Hannah? Are you there?" Miranda asked. "And are you really all right in that big drafty place by yourself?"

"Yes, I'm here. And I'm fine."

"Why don't you come by tonight? I know it's late, but I'm expecting a visitor, and I'd appreciate your being here." She paused. "I'm not overly fond of him, and you'd be a welcome buffer."

"I don't know . . ." She could drive over. Ten minutes and she'd be there—away from here. Odd, but she didn't feel as anxious about driving as she had two weeks ago.

"He's coming shortly after eight. If you came now, we could have dinner together before he gets here. I'd like that. And Claire's made that marvelous chicken thing she does—as usual enough for an entire seniors' home instead of just us two old bats. Do come, dear."

Hannah thought of the long night ahead of her. "All right. That would be nice."

"Wonderful! I'll see you in a bit, then."

Hannah replaced the receiver, glad for a sense of purpose. Dinner with Miranda was infinitely preferable to her other choice, the first of what would be years of nights alone at Kenninghall.

She'd walk, she decided. Rain or not. Fifteen minutes of evening air would be good for her. And if you didn't walk in the rain in the Pacific Northwest, you didn't walk at all.

Her mind skipped back to Gerry Vonecker.

She looked toward her open door, tapped a fingernail on her front tooth, then telling herself she was ridiculous, stood and followed the path of light into the hall.

She stopped outside Milo's bedroom. Before she'd touched the latch, her throat was dry and tight, her heart a dull drum. She took strength from the unyielding brass knob in her hand before turning it and opening the door.

She took a step into the room. The hospital bed and medical cabinetry were gone. Meara had seen to that. In their place stood Milo's intricately carved seventeenth-century tester bed, velvet drapes flowing lushly from its oak canopy. Hannah had teased Milo about this bed, telling him all he needed was a nightcap and candle and Scrooge would live again. When she stepped farther into the room, her nerves spiked to expectant life, wary and unpredictable. Another step and the lingering scent of disinfectant scurried up her nose. Death's deodorant. She looked at the George III bureau bookcase that held the letters and moved toward it. One step. Two. She shivered and stopped.

The room was cold. Too cold. Another step.

Fear leached into her chest, squirmed and pulled until her breath broke into painful uneven bursts. The void itself assaulted her, froze her in place with icy, invisible hands. The shadows moved toward her now, shapeless and dire. Pushing her away.

She stepped backward into the hall and pulled the door closed behind her. She leaned against it, took deep breaths, and pressed both hands on her thrumming heart.

She couldn't do it.

She locked her hands into fists and straightened. "Not yet, Milo, not yet."

Her answer was the silence of the dead.

Three days into it and Yates was nowhere on the Zanez thing. When it came to records, this Hallam guy was invisible, not a trace of him anywhere. He was a man who intended not to be found. Yates's sniffing around Zanez Shipping today, a cramped, second-rate office on the pier, netted zero. If the employees did know Hallam, they didn't let on, or were happy enough to keep their mouths shut as long as the paychecks kept coming.

So he was back to Vonecker. At least Yates knew what the hell *he* looked like.

He picked up the phone and punched a memory sequence.

"John? It's Yates." If anybody could get a line on Vonecker, it would be John Crayne, friend, computer hacker, and—conveniently—a licensed Washington State private investigator.

"It's been awhile. How the hell are ya?"

"Good. Need a hand, though."

"For hard cash you can have both of them and a damned good nose." Crayne laughed, then coughed for an easy half minute. Crayne was also a dedicated smoker, a dying breed, he called himself. Yates agreed. "So what's up?" he added when he got his gravelly voice back.

Yates heard him suck hard on a cigarette, then blow a hurricane of smoke. He visualized the usual heaping ashtray beside Crayne's computer keyboard. "When are you going to quit those damn things?"

"When I get a date with a real woman."

"Be awhile then, I guess."

"Probably." Crayne laughed again, but this time the coughing fit was shorter. "So, what can I help you on?"

"I need a tail. On a guy named Gerry Vonecker. You can pick up on him at his home or the offices of Simpson, Chapman, and Vonecker, downtown. Two Union Square." He gave Crayne Vonecker's home address, told him the make and model of his car. A Jag. And the plate number.

"An attorney?"

"You got it."

"Love it!" He took another drag on his smoke. "You want pictures?"

"Of who he meets, yes. But what I really want is to know where he goes and when. I'm looking for a place to start."

"You want an ear?"

Yates considered the tap, but decided against it. There was still the remote chance Vonecker was more sucker than sinner, and wiretapping the guy's phone under such circumstances wouldn't be a bright move. If you were going to bend the law, best to do it with someone who couldn't bend it back—around your neck.

"No," he finally said. "A few mug shots and a list of addresses will be enough. I'll handle the rest." He relaxed into his high-backed leather chair. It and his king-sized bed were his only luxuries in the loft/office space his sister, Stella, called a minimalist's heaven. Yates didn't like a lot of things around. "When can you start?" he asked.

"I'll pick up on him tomorrow at his house. Good enough?"

"Good enough. Thanks."

"We'll be talkin' then. See ya."

Yates matched Crayne's sign-off with his own and turned back to the two files Anne had given him, Zanez's incorporation papers and its list of shareholders, of which there were only two. Don M. Hallam held ninety percent and L. Ray Tenassi the other ten. Vonecker was listed as the company's attorney, and the accountant of record was Baynes and Croft. Other than Vonecker, they all had San Francisco addresses—except for Hallam, who, according to Anne, had no address at all. Anne had scribbled the Baynes and Croft telephone number in the margin.

He tapped a pen on the sheaf of papers. Stopped. Tapped again, then reached for the phone. He was slipping. First rule: validate the information you have—or invalidate it. The latter was the most likely.

He'd already come up empty on Hallam, and Baynes and Croft—they'd closed the firm months ago.

He looked at the other name on the shareholder's list. Probably a waste of time. He dialed. This time he connected to San Francisco information.

"A number for Tenassi? L.R. Tenassi." He read the address from the file on his desk. "And would you check your new listings. He may have moved."

"One moment please."

Yates doodled—circles, trees, a picket fence— already thinking about his next move. You had to check the basics, but he'd bet Tenassi would be as deep underground as Hallam and the accounting firm. Crooks and sleazebags were seldom obliging.

"Sorry, sir, that number is classified as unlisted."

Bingo! He surged forward in his chair.

"Okay, thanks."

He hit Crayne's number. "Yates again. I need an unlisted telephone number."

He heard John chuckle, suck up some tar. "In these modern times, my man, 'unlisted number' is an oxymoron."

Claire let Hannah in, took her coat, hugged her, and sent her along to the living room. Miranda sat by the fire doing a crossword puzzle, Shasta in a curl by her side.

When she started to push herself to her feet, Hannah quickly closed the space between them. Miranda's time out of her wheelchair was short and precious, but she insisted on getting up and taking a few steps every day. They embraced and Hannah was immediately glad she'd come, relieved to be away from the lonely house—and Milo's deathless letters.

The room was so cheery, Miranda asked Claire to bring her "chicken thing" dinner to the living room so they could eat by the fire.

Miranda watched every bite Hannah took, but didn't say anything until after Claire picked up their dishes and left for the kitchen.

"You should eat more. You're too thin." She tilted her head to eye Hannah speculatively. "And you should get your hair cut—not short, that wouldn't suit you, but shaped softer around your face."

Hannah touched the misshapen knot of hair at her nape. Miranda *would* notice her lack of style. All her working life was spent in the beauty business. Milo talked proudly of her supporting them as a hairdresser in a second-rate salon before eventually owning five of her own.

"If my hands weren't so unpredictable—damned arthritis—I'd do it myself," Miranda went on. "You have wonderful hair. Wickedly black. It's a shame to hide it like you do. I'll bet that's an elastic band you're using to tie it back." She shook her head in dismay. "Tears the hair shaft to shreds, you know."

"It's easy this way. No trouble." Hannah smoothed some stray hairs behind her ear.

"And that's the way you like it, isn't it? No trouble."

"I guess so. Yes."

Miranda pursed her lips thoughtfully. "Were you sleeping with Milo, Hannah?"

Hannah, in the midst of raising her water glass to her lips, froze. Miranda's gaze was riveted to her face. She looked oddly hopeful.

"Miranda!" She set her glass on the table between them. "That's a bit personal."

"About as personal as it gets. Old age grants me the privilege of putting my nose where younger noses should never go. Well, did you?"

Hannah shook her head both in disbelief and to indicate a negative, adding a "no" for good measure.

Miranda looked disappointed. "Why not?"

"I can't believe—" She shook her head again, tried to adjust to the turn in this conversation. "That wasn't what Milo and I were about. Neither of us wanted . . . that." Her words tumbled into an uncomfortable void. There'd been a time when, had Milo asked it of her, she'd have given it. But he never had. In the end, they'd settled for more.

"Then what did you want?"

Hannah stood, paced a few steps to the window,

and turned to look back at the petite older woman, her white hair bronzed by the firelight, her eyes, so much like her son's, fixed on her own. In the years she'd been with Milo, she'd seldom been with Miranda without Milo being present. Those visits, although frequent, had been between mother and son with Hannah an uninvolved third party. She had no idea what, if anything, Milo had said about their relationship—or about her.

"A friend," she said. "A safe place. Our work. That's what both of us wanted."

"I see." If Miranda did see, she didn't look happy about it, only confused.

"Why do you ask? Why do you care?"

"Because, I'd always wondered if . . . oh, forget it. It doesn't matter anyway."

Hannah studied her a moment, added softly, "Milo wasn't gay, Miranda. If that's what you're asking." Hannah didn't know why she was sure of this. Certainly she'd never seen Milo bring a woman to Kenninghall or heard him speak of one. But sure she was.

"No. That wasn't it. Had he been, he'd have told me. He would have known it wouldn't affect my feelings for him." She lifted a pale hand, fluttered it, let it fall back to her lap. "I was hoping he'd found something . . . something more than you described."

"But he did! He loved his life, his work. We were happy. Truly." Hannah reached over and took her hands. "And I *so* loved him. Milo was the kindest, most generous man I've ever known."

"You must be referring to my late cousin." A deep male voice came from the doorway.

Hannah looked up to see a tall, well-dressed

man walk to where she and Miranda sat. "If Milo was anything, it was good—to the bone," he said to her. He turned to Miranda, his voice soft when he added, "I've missed him over the years."

Miranda's fingers tightened briefly around Hannah's palm before releasing it, and Shasta growled, stopping immediately when Miranda rested her hand on her head. "Shush, you silly thing."

Hannah stared—dumbly, she was certain—at the man towering over them, a *very* handsome man, carrying a showy bouquet of flowers. He must be the visitor Miranda was expecting.

"Miranda." He leaned to kiss her on the cheek. "I hope you don't mind. Your housekeeper let me in."

"You're early, Morgan," she said, taking the flowers he offered her, but offering no thanks, no warm smile of appreciation. How odd, Hannah thought, and settled herself in the background.

"Traffic was light." His gaze again fell on Hannah. Miranda's followed it.

"Hannah, this is my nephew, Morgan Greff."

"Ah, yes. Milo's second-in-command," he said. She shook his cool hand. Milo had a cousin? Hannah tried to remember, sure she'd never heard the name Greff before. And if this was a family meeting, why had Miranda asked her to be here? A buffer, she'd said.

Greff glanced at the chair left by Claire. "May I?"

Miranda nodded.

Morgan seated himself between them and turned to Miranda; his brown eyes softened when he said, "It's been a long time, Miranda, but I was truly sorry to hear about Milo. I know how close you were."

He touched a leaf of the bouquet, now abandoned on the table. "If there's anything I can do, anything at all, I hope you won't hesitate to ask."

"There's nothing I can think of, thank you." Her response, verging on the dismissive, made Hannah uncomfortable.

Morgan went on as though she hadn't spoken, his tone solicitous, his smile engaging. "Anything. Unfinished business matters, selling off of assets. I'm sure Milo's estate is quite complicated—"

Looking impatient, Miranda lifted a hand to cut him off. "Morgan, why not get to the point? Tell me why you're here—and what it is you want."

Chapter 5

Morgan Greff sat back in his chair, confident and relaxed, seeming unfazed by Miranda's sharp, direct question. "What makes you think I want something?"

Miranda continued, "I haven't seen you in more than fifteen years. And as far as I know, you and Milo haven't talked since you were teenagers. Why this show of familial concern now?"

Morgan shifted in his seat. He looked unaffected, but Hannah thought not; she was embarrassed for him. He got up, looked down on Miranda, his expression sober. "The truth?"

She nodded, not taking her eyes from his face.

"I'm fifty-eight years old. Don't you think it's past time for familial concern?" He lowered his voice and went on. "I have no hidden agenda, Miranda. You and I? We're all that's left. I thought I could help. That's all."

Hannah was surprised. The man didn't look a day over forty-five—a fit, attractive forty-five.

Miranda's gaze didn't waver. "Milo didn't like you. You know that."

"Yes, I do, and he had cause. That's one reason I'm here."

"A little late, don't you think?"

"For Milo? Yes. For us? Only if you say so."

"What happened between you and Milo?" Miranda's expression was curious, but distrustful. Hannah had never seen her like this.

"Damn kids' stuff." Morgan tugged his earlobe, looked frustrated. "I took his girl. No, that's not the whole truth. I took *both* his girls. Back then I took every girl I could get my hands on. The first time he forgave me, the second time he didn't. He said if he couldn't trust me, he'd just as soon I stayed the hell out of his life." He smiled thinly. "He was right, of course. He couldn't trust me. Not then. But people change. Even me. I tried to call him—countless times over the years—to set things straight, but he wouldn't take my calls."

Miranda continued to stare at him. "That's it?"

He lifted his hands, palms up and open. "That's it."

"I don't think I believe you," she said, her old eyes sad but unwavering.

Greff looked disappointed but resigned.

"I'm sorry then. Because I think Mother would have wanted us to at least keep in touch."

Miranda's gaze hardened. "I think my sister would have liked you to keep in touch with *her* more than with me, Morgan. As I recall, you weren't the most attentive of sons."

He nodded. "Guilty."

"I suppose you're sorry about that, too?"

"It was no secret Mother and I didn't get along, but yes, I'm sorry for that. I did what I could."

"Her funeral was magnificent, I'll say that much for you." Miranda's tone was caustic.

Hannah saw Morgan tense, the bright flare of anger in his eyes before his angular, handsome face set to impenetrable. To hide the hurt, she thought. She couldn't believe Miranda was so unforgiving.

"I was wrong to come." Morgan straightened his shoulders and headed toward the door. "It seems neither of the Biehles is of the forgive-and-forget school. I regret that. For all our sakes."

He glanced down to where Hannah sat silently in the chair across from Miranda, nodded. "Nice to have met you. I hope we'll meet again—under better circumstances."

He turned his back on them and strode to the door.

Miranda didn't mention his name for the rest of the evening.

It was nearly ten when Hannah left Miranda's. The rain had stopped, leaving a moonless, cloud-filled sky offering scant light, but Hannah didn't mind. The country road was safe and well-known to her, although she'd never walked it quite this late before.

She was maybe a quarter of a mile from Miranda's when—

"Hannah?"

Startled, she spun around. A man leaned against a low-slung car she hadn't noticed under the tree shadows.

It was Morgan Greff.

She let out a breath and pressed her right hand against her chest. "Oh, it's you."

"I'm sorry. I didn't mean to frighten you."

"You didn't. I—"

He was close enough now, she could see he was smiling at her. She took another, deeper breath and calmed herself, although her heart still thumped triple time.

"Can I buy you a cup of coffee?" he asked.

"Me?" She knew her reply was stupid, but like her reaction to his voice in the darkness it was knee-jerk.

"There's a coffee shop about fifteen minutes down the road."

She knew of it. But she didn't know this man, and didn't want to be disloyal in any way to Miranda—or Milo, who'd never once mentioned his cousin's name.

When she didn't answer, he added, "If you're thinking about what happened in there"—he gestured toward the house—"I'd like you to hear my side."

"Why?"

"Believe it or not, Milo and I were like brothers once. I'd like to hear something about his later years. I know you lived with him, that you were his friend."

Hannah glanced back as the last of the lights in Miranda's house flickered off, then looked at Morgan. She wasn't sure she could talk about Milo. Her grief was too fresh—too raw. And she certainly wasn't sure about this man. But she was curious. For the first time in years, she was curious.

"Please," he urged. "I'm really not the ogre Miranda believes I am and I don't eat small children for breakfast." He cocked a brow, waited.

"All right."

She got into his black Ferrari and traveled with him in silence along the rain-slicked road. He was comfortable in silence, much like his cousin had been.

The Rose Berry Coffee Shop was crowded with mismatched tables and odd chairs. The lighting bounced off white walls, chrome, and canary yellow Formica tabletops. Three booths lined the window, and Morgan guided her to one of them, his hand on her elbow. He helped her off with her coat, then sat opposite her.

Hannah thought him completely out of place sliding into the fifties-style booth. This sophisticated man belonged in an elegant restaurant where the owner knew him by name. One with no prices on the menu. She estimated that for the price of his suit and topcoat, he could have bought the entire diner. Again, she thought how extraordinarily good-looking he was, strong chin, skin taut and tanned. Nothing at all like Milo, who in the past few years had softened without protest into middle age. Even in a fluorescent glare, Morgan Greff looked years younger than his age.

The waitress came, filled her coffee mug, and brought Morgan a bottled water. She left menus on the table.

"Would you like something to eat?" he asked.

She shook her head.

"You don't say much do you?"

"Enough." Hannah couldn't remember when she'd last needed small talk to break the ice with a stranger. That particular brain function rusted out years ago. She didn't miss it.

"And you're adept at one-word replies."

"Why use two when one will serve?" She stirred cream into her coffee.

He poured water into his glass. "How long were you and Milo together?"

"Five years."

"Strange."

She gave him a questioning look.

"You're not at all what I'd expected," he said.

"How could you be expecting anything? You haven't been in touch with Milo for years." She looked across the table at him, puzzled.

His jaw tightened, then he smiled to show perfect white teeth. "I guess I was thinking of how he was when we were kids. Back then he went for the flashier type."

Milo with a flashy woman? She couldn't see it. But she hadn't really known him as a young man— and she'd never seen him with a woman. Any woman. "If what you told Miranda was true, so did you—*if* they were with Milo."

"Why would I lie?"

She lifted a shoulder, dropped it. She didn't know why she'd said that.

"Testosterone overload," he said.

"Excuse me?"

"I was a wild kid. The town bad boy. I liked fast cars—and fast girls. So did Milo. But I was three years older and that gave me an edge. And, though I hate to admit it, I took it. Every chance I got." He paused, gave her a slow grin. "It was a game to me. I guess I thought it was with Milo, too." His expression turned somber, regretful. "Turns out it wasn't. Damn! I'd like to have made things right between us before he died." He lapsed into a moody silence.

"I'm sorry," she said finally, surprised she meant it.

"What do you have to be sorry about?"

"That you didn't get to see Milo before he . . . died. He was a forgiving man, a spiritual man. I'm sure you could have at least talked to him."

"Maybe. More likely he'd have told me to take a hike."

Uncertain how to respond, Hannah said nothing.

"Did he suffer?" he asked abruptly.

Hannah fidgeted with her paper napkin. "His wasn't an easy death. But he bore it well. He spent the last few months putting his affairs in order."

He smiled as though in memory. "Now *that* sounds like Milo. Even as a kid he was a detail man."

"Yes, he was that."

"And you helped?"

She nodded. "That was my job."

He tapped a finger rhythmically against the rim of his cup. She was beginning to think he'd forgotten she was there until he set his gaze on her—and locked it there. "I heard you tell Miranda your relationship to Milo wasn't a sexual one. Is that true?"

She stared at him, couldn't speak. Why in hell was everyone so interested in whether or not she slept with Milo? First Miranda, now this strange relative. Anger lent heat to her face, a tightness to her throat. The emotion was alien, long unused.

She shoved her coffee aside and reached for her coat. "I can't see how that's your business."

When his fingers circled her wrist to stay her

movement, his grip was warm and vital. It was also loose. She could easily have pulled back her hand if she chose to. She didn't.

"It isn't my business." He stroked her wrist idly with his thumb, exerted a gentle pressure on her pulse. "I just don't like to think of Milo rolling over in his grave when I take you out to dinner."

Chapter 6

Yates stepped out of the shower in time to hear his door buzzer. He wrapped himself in a bath towel and dripped his way to the door.

"Yates Lang?" Without waiting for a reply, a refugee from grunge city, wearing the ubiquitous reversed baseball cap, held out a large manila envelope.

Yates nodded and took the envelope and a clipboard from the kid's hand.

The kid looked over his shoulder, surveyed the open space behind Yates. "Hey, cool place," he said. "You could drive a Harley around in there."

Yates grunted, scanned the form for a signature line, and scribbled his initials. He turned the envelope over in his hand. Crayne had come through in record time—four days.

"Pretty shitty security though," he added, jerking his head in a backward movement to indicate the wide hall with its peeling wallpaper. "Old guy was sleeping downstairs when I came in." He retrieved the clipboard and gave Yates a hotshot grin. "A guy could rip you off easy, man. Real easy."

Yates, water dripping off his nose, stared at him. "A guy could try," he said, and slammed the door.

He wasn't about to explain the guy downstairs was a tenant. Norm "The Fist" Fisher. A boxer in his day, now he was an old guy fighting a daily war against the ever-widening black hole in his mind. Most days he was okay, and when he was, he sat in the foyer of the run-down apartment building, a self-appointed security guard in a part of Seattle that needed a lot more firepower than a fearless old man with a baseball bat. But Yates had to admit that, when roused, old Norm was still a presence to be reckoned with. More than one smart-ass kid in the neighborhood could attest to that.

Yates had his own ideas about security. If you didn't have stuff, nobody tried to steal it, so he didn't accumulate anything he couldn't lose—or leave—in a heartbeat. Life was simpler that way.

He strode across his large, empty loft toward the storage wall on the other side of his bed, tossing the envelope on the coffee table on the way. In seconds, clad in jeans and a Mariner's sweatshirt, he was back tearing open the envelope, hoping like hell Crayne had done better than he had.

Yates had tried the Tenassi number and discovered two things: Tenassi was a woman, and she was traveling in Europe. A dead end. For now.

Yates pulled out a dozen or so five-by-eight photos and leafed through them.

Vonecker and Chapman coming out of their building.

Vonecker and his ex, Mona. Neither of whom looked happy.

Vonecker and a woman.

Vonecker and another woman.

The next two were of men. Yates didn't recognize anyone; he'd check them out with Anne.

The last one . . .

Yates's heart rammed his rib cage, knocked the air out of him.

"Shit!"

He tossed the pictures on the coffee table, slumped back into the sofa, and forked his fingers through his wet hair.

This can't be happening. This fucking can't be happening!

A weird coincidence, he told himself. He shifted forward on the sofa and set the picture squarely on top of the others. He studied it again. Hard. He cursed again. Coincidence? Maybe. But there wasn't any doubt in his mind who the man with Vonecker was.

His damn hand was shaking! Irritated, he fisted it, flexed it, then reached for the phone. He dialed Anne's private line. When he heard the line open, he didn't wait for a hello.

"Does the name Morgan Greff mean anything to you?"

"I have someone with me, Yates. I'll call you back." She sounded pissed.

"*The name,* Chapman. It's important. Greff. Morgan Greff." He rubbed his chest, but his pounding heart ignored his less than gentle massage.

"Never heard it before."

"He's not one of Vonecker's clients?"

Pause. He sensed her turning away from the people in her office.

"No. I know his files. That name isn't in them."

Silence.

"Have you found something?" she asked, lowering her voice.

Yates hoped to hell not. "Maybe. I'm coming over. I've got some pictures I want you to see."

"Not now, you're not. After this meeting—which ends in two minutes—I'm heading straight to the courthouse."

"When, then?"

"One."

"Good enough." It wasn't, but it would have to do. He looked at his watch. Ten-forty-five. Two hours and fifteen minutes to kill. "See you then," he said, and hung up the phone.

His gaze fell to the coffee table, and Morgan Greff stared up at him, filling his vision. Yates forced himself to pick up the photo. It had been sixteen years since he'd seen him, and the guy hadn't aged a day. Yates wasn't surprised. He knew Greff's discipline: his daily regimen of muscle-wrenching exercise, his obsession with proper diet, his endless cache of vitamins.

For a long time Yates stared at the face of the last man on earth he wanted to see. The tight coil in his gut twisted to pain, then bloodied to rage. He turned the photos over, slapped them on the table, and stood, letting out a long breath to clear the heaviness in his lungs.

He'd go to the gym. He needed to beat on something.

Hannah backed the Saab out of the garage and headed for the road, not thinking twice about the fact that she was driving—again. It had quickly become a necessary task, a part of her day, and today she had business in Seattle. Milo wouldn't want her to let his customers down. *My customers now,* she reminded herself.

She turned onto the road and mentally reviewed her schedule, a list of activities neatly, and uselessly, transcribed in the green leather diary in her tote bag. Hannah wouldn't need to look at it again. Everything was organized in her mind. First, she'd deliver the Worcester piece to Mrs. King, then she'd go to Dan Monk's shop on Linnet Street and have a look at the early twentieth-century Daum vase he wanted to sell. If she could get it for under ten thousand, it would be a genuine bargain.

After that she'd stop in at Gerry Vonecker's office, drop off the papers she'd found. Yesterday, while looking for the original purchase price on the Worcester, she'd found an old lease, misfiled five years ago. It probably wasn't what he was looking for, but it had calmed her to find something and eased her suspicions about his interest in the letters. And the lease might at least point him in the right direction. Judging from the date, the misfile was her mistake.

She'd made more than her share during those first months with Milo. Her black cloud period, Milo called it. Gradually the requirements of the business and the quiet life they'd led became a workable pattern and Hannah's inborn work ethic and penchant for detail reemerged, comforting and mind-occupying. Routine and pattern. One foot after the other, carefully, repetitively until the rut was deep enough to hide in, to disappear in.

But today there was something new on her list. Item 4: *Buy a dinner dress.*

On Saturday night she was going out to dinner with Morgan Greff. Her acceptance of his offer wrought dueling emotions, fear and temptation. Her mind remained wary, but she couldn't ignore the whispers of her spirit, a spirit quivering to new life. And there was something . . . fascinating about Morgan.

She glanced at the clock on the Saab's dash and speeded up. If she were to keep on schedule, she'd better hurry. She intended to be in Vonecker's office before one o'clock.

"Lena, when are you coming back?"

"Maybe never, darling. Spain is such an improvement over the Pacific Northwest in October. All that rain drives me crazy. Besides," she said, a husky touch of humor in her voice, "I just got here. I've barely put on my first bikini."

"You've been gone a week." Shit! He sounded like a whining adolescent. He downed the single malt scotch in his hand and blocked the image of Lena in a bikini, all curves and silky skin. It didn't work. Even the sound of her voice gave him a hard-on.

She laughed. "It's only been four days, Morgan. I take it you miss me?"

He wasn't taking that hook, or she'd start with the marriage crap again. One of those was enough. "We have a business here, sweetheart. And in case you've forgotten, there's a lot of money riding on the next shipment." He'd be damned if he'd admit to missing her.

"You worry too much." Her voice lowered to a seductive murmur. "And as for business, I've met worthwhile people here. Big money. The right appetites. It seems Americans aren't the only customers for our product."

"We don't need more customers. It's over. This shipment is *it*. I'll be out of the business clean, with all the time in the world to spend fucking you."

"Sounds like heaven to me, lover."

"And the sooner we get there the better." The plain truth was he was tired, fresh out of ambition, and . . . spooked. There were times his damn heart nearly palpitated itself out of his chest. Scared the hell out of him.

So far he'd beat the odds. But nobody beat them forever. Hell, if it weren't for the blindfold Old Lady Justice wore, he'd have been behind bars years ago.

He didn't intend for that to happen. Ever.

He intended to be one of the smart ones. Quit while he was ahead. All he needed to do was take care of his family problem. The Stuart bitch would help him do that. And she'd do one other thing. Once he got her on her back with her clothes off, she'd go a long way to relieving his itch for Lena.

"But aren't you the teensiest bit interested in the international market?" Lena asked. "I made a couple of excellent contacts last night."

"I hope you made those 'excellent' contacts with your legs crossed."

"You're jealous." She laughed again, and it irritated the hell out of him.

"No. Cautious. I don't intend to spend my last years taking AZT. We made a deal, remember. The only one to stroke that soft little pussy of yours is me."

"How about I stroke 'little pussy' right now and

tell you all about it?" Her smoky voice, low and dark, crawled through the phone line and clutched his crotch. "Hmm, you're right, lover, it is soft . . . and wet. So wet."

"Lena . . ." he groaned, touched himself.

"Hmm?"

"Forget the vacation—and the damn customers. Haul that sweet ass of yours home. You got that?"

"Soon, baby. Soon."

Chapter 7

Hannah arrived at Vonecker's office at 12:30, and stepped up to the reception desk.

She waited while the man in front of her asked the receptionist to call a person named Chapman. She heard the receptionist tell him the person he wanted to see was still in a meeting with a client, and she'd be at least another half hour or so. Unfazed, the man lowered his voice and leaned over the desk. Hannah, standing behind him, couldn't see his face, or hear what he said. She did see the receptionist smile and reach for the phone.

"Hannah. This is a surprise. What brings you here?" Gerry Vonecker stepped out of an office near the reception area, wearing a raincoat and carrying an umbrella. He smiled broadly. She hadn't expected to see him, hadn't wanted to. She'd hoped to simply to drop off the lease and head home.

"I found this." She lifted the ten-by-twelve envelope she was carrying.

"What is it?" He quickly reached for the envelope.

"A lease on a property near Pike's Market. It expired years ago, but I thought it might be what you're looking for," she said. "Although I'm not sure what that is exactly. Miranda said something about share certificates, but I thought you'd said deed."

"Share certificates?" He looked momentarily confused. "No, you have it right. Miranda must have heard wrong. But then it was an inopportune time to ask—much too soon after Milo's death. I get overzealous at times." He turned the envelope over in his hand without enthusiasm.

Hannah became aware that the man she'd been standing behind was now beside her.

Gerry noticed him at the same time. "Yates," he said, looking up.

The man was well over the six-foot mark. Lean, with broad shoulders and a sharp . . . ascetic face, all definite lines and angles. When Hannah realized she was staring, she glanced away for a moment, fussed with a coat button.

The man called Yates nodded his acknowledgement to Vonecker, and immediately shifted his gaze to Hannah; its studious intensity made her squirm. His eyes were a deep green, but even under the fringe of dark lashes, they were cold. Cynical eyes, she thought. Intelligent eyes.

Gerry was about to introduce them when a woman, about fifty or so, strode into the reception area as though she were a general and her troops were at illegal ease. She glanced at, but didn't speak to, Gerry Vonecker, glaring instead at the tall man beside Hannah. "You're early, Yates," she said. "This better be good."

"Chapman, have I ever disappointed you?" He lifted a brow either in sarcasm or to imply a double entendre. Hannah wasn't sure.

"Every chance you get," the woman replied without hesitation, centering her glasses with a sharp jab of her index finger and looking at her watch. "I've got to go back into my meeting, so you've got five minutes. If I were you I wouldn't waste it trying to charm a barracuda who hasn't had time for lunch." She looked at Vonecker. "Could we use your office for a couple of minutes?"

"Be my guest," Vonecker said. Hannah noticed he'd followed the exchange between the two people with interest. "You on the payroll again, Yates?" he asked.

"Very hush-hush, Gerry," Yates replied. "Chapman's closing in on the great American coffee caper."

Vonecker chuckled. "Ah, the infamous McMann. Getting anywhere with that, Anne?"

"I might if I could get the hell out of this reception area." She jerked her head to the office Vonecker had stepped out of and started toward it. "Let's go, Yates."

"Right behind you," he said, again focusing on Hannah, his expression softening. Something close to a smile played over his mouth. "And you are?" he said, offering his hand. The words, the gesture were polite, utterly conventional, although Hannah was sure this man was anything but.

"Hannah Stuart." When she took his outstretched hand, he held hers in a strong grip, but didn't shake it. His dark-lashed eyes met hers squarely, curiously.

"Hannah." He repeated her name carefully, never

taking his steady gaze from her face. "Nice to meet you, Hannah Stuart."

He'd done nothing extraordinary, yet Hannah sensed a subtext; her face grew warm. She pulled her hand back, acutely conscious of her fingertips sliding over his when he loosened his grip on her hand, let it go.

"Yates." Anne Chapman tapped her watch. "Give me a break—I've got three people in my office. Can we get on with whatever it is that 'absolutely won't wait'?" She shot an irritated look at the receptionist who started paper shuffling in quick time.

Yates smiled down at Hannah. The smile was cool, but the wink he gave her held a conspiratorial warmth. "Duty calls. If I'm lucky we'll meet again."

He gave her another quick grin and trailed Anne Chapman into Vonecker's office.

Hannah's gaze tracked him until he disappeared behind a firmly closed door. "Who was that?" she asked Vonecker.

"Lang?" Vonecker reorganized his umbrella and case. "He does contract work for the firm. Forensic accounting, research. Things like that. Good friend of Anne's."

An accountant. He didn't look like any accountant Hannah had ever seen. She wanted to ask what forensic accounting was, but Vonecker didn't give her the chance. He took her arm, started them both toward the door.

"Do you have time for a cup of coffee?" he asked. "I have a few minutes and there's a coffee shop downstairs."

"No, I don't, really. I have shopping to do." She pulled her eyes from the door Yates was behind and looked at Vonecker. "But thanks anyway."

Gerry Vonecker got in the elevator with her. And while he chattered, her thoughts focused on Yates Lang.

There was no blur in the focus. The man in her vision was etched in coal—the color of his hair. He was all edges and shadows. His hand had been warm, but she sensed his spirit was not. Something about him made her feel anxious, but intrigued, too: the cool, penetrating eyes, yielding nothing, the smile no deeper than a curve of the lips, and the wink, so charmingly flirtatious, so utterly mechanical. Facile gestures for society's sake, but underneath it all a remote soul.

Takes one to know one, Hannah.

She pushed further thoughts of him aside. Her silly analysis didn't matter, because chances were she'd never see him again. After one morning in the city, her thinking process was skewed. She needed to get back to the quiet of Kenninghall.

". . . good of you to stop by," Vonecker said.

The elevator doors opened and they stepped out.

"Excuse me? What did you say?"

"I was saying thank you for coming by."

"I'm just sorry I didn't find what you were looking for."

"Yes, but"—he stopped inside the main exit doors, grabbed her arm—"you're absolutely sure there's no safety deposit box he'd neglected to inform me of."

"Milo didn't like safety deposit boxes, you know that," she said. "He thought they were inconvenient. That's why he had the safe installed at Kenninghall. And you've been all through that." Hannah looked past him, through the glass door entrance to the building, and saw it was raining. She started to button her coat. "What was important to Milo, he kept close at hand."

"Yes," he acknowledged, sounding weary. "Milo was consistent in that way."

She stepped toward the doors, impatient to get away. She had a dress to buy. "I'm sorry I wasn't more help."

"So am I, Hannah." He looked distracted for a moment, then held the door open for her. "But we can't be faulted for doing our best, can we?"

Hannah thought his remark strange, but she was halfway out the door, so all she managed was an "I guess not" before being pushed through by the lunchtime crowd.

"Who is she?" The door barely closed behind them before Yates put the question to Anne.

She gave him an irritated glance. "She gave you her name. Hannah Stuart. If you want more info, find out for yourself. I'm not interested in gathering information to forward your love life. You're the detective."

"I'm not a detective," he said by habit. "And it's not my love life I'm worried about. It's Vonecker's." He knew he sounded short, but since seeing those pictures this morning, this investigation of Vonecker had a new dimension. It was personal. Before he was through, he was going to know the brand name of Vonecker's toothpaste.

"While I'm glad to see you're on the job, Yates," Anne said, heavy on the acid, "you're old enough, and no doubt experienced enough, to know that a mouse like Hannah Stuart doesn't rank high enough on the bimbo scale to interest Gerry."

"Just tell me about her, would you?" Yates raised his brows to snag some patience. The word *mouse* applied to Hannah Stuart might be apt, but he didn't like it.

"She's a lucky woman, that's what she is." Anne took Vonecker's chair, started going through his drawers, then slammed them shut in exasperation. "What the hell am I doing?" she asked herself, sitting back and closing her eyes. "This thing with Gerry has put me over the top. Wherever the hell the *top* is."

Yates ignored her. "Stuart," he repeated.

Chapman opened her eyes, shot him a scathing look. "You're a damned dog with a bone, aren't you?"

He waited.

Chapman shook her head and surrendered. "She recently inherited a tidy fortune from one of Gerry's clients. An antiques dealer or some such. A man named Biehle. Milo Biehle. Hannah was his assistant—and mistress—if you believe Gerry. Which I'm not inclined to do at the moment."

Biehle. Biehle. Yates tugged at his earlobe. The name made no instant connection, but it struck a chord. An old one. Yates didn't put any pressure on his memory. He trusted it, knowing it seldom failed him.

"What was she doing here?"

"How the hell should I know, and what's this got to do with dragging me out of a meeting?" She glared at him. "In case you've forgotten, it's Vonecker we're interested in. And a certain shady character by the name of Don Hallam. Remember him? The reason you were hired in the first place? Now will you get on with whatever it is that couldn't wait the fifteen minutes until our appointment, so I can get back to my client."

"One condition."

"Now the man has conditions!" She looked heavenward. "What?"

"Find out all you can about this Biehle guy and Hannah Stuart."

"You're reaching. *Really* reaching. I told you I reviewed all of Gerry's files. There's no connection between that perfectly nice woman and scum like Hallam."

"Maybe not." He shrugged, purposefully casual. "But if it's all the same to you, Chapman, I'll do things my way."

Anne gave him a narrow, questioning look. "You're onto something—*somebody*—aren't you?"

"Don't know." He handed her the photographs. "You tell me." Air gathered and froze in his windpipe, sat there like a slow-melting ice cube as he watched Anne adjust her glasses.

She glanced at the first photograph, the one of Morgan Greff, and said what he expected—and dreaded—to hear. "It's him. That's Donald Hallam."

Hannah pulled into the driveway of Kenninghall and turned the car toward the garage. She braked when she saw a woman on the porch. The rain was coming down so hard now, even with the wipers on high speed, she had trouble making out who she was. She peered through the rain sloshing across the windshield.

No. It wasn't. It couldn't be.

She looked harder. *It was.*

Libby Stuart—her stepdaughter. The step-daughter she hadn't laid eyes on in years. Hannah took a deep breath, shoved the car into park, and leaned back.

Trouble.

Libby Stuart meant trouble. She sighed long, re-minded herself Libby was Will's daughter. And for Will's sake, Hannah would deal with it. For a sec-ond she wondered when and how she'd become so beholden to the dead, forcing the thought aside when she realized how selfish it was.

Libby sat on the top step, obviously waiting, but too far away for Hannah to read her expression. When Hannah saw she'd brought two suitcases, her heart tumbled.

By the time she got to the bottom step, rain dripped from her hair, over her face, and under her collar.

In the days since Milo's death, her universe shifted constantly beneath her feet. She moved about, re-acted, interacted, and had managed to stay in con-trol. But Libby, here? It was too much. She may be on fate's leash, but she could do without the hard jerks.

"Libby," she said. "I'd say 'what a surprise,' but I think shock is the better word." Trite. Banal. But the best she could do. Try as she might, she couldn't manage a smile.

"Yeah, I guess so," Libby said, standing. She'd been smoking, and as she stood, she flicked her cigarette into the rain and stuffed her hands in her jacket pocket. A cheap jacket, Hannah no-

ticed, over-worn with a tear on the zipper's seam.
Times must be bad.

Hannah stepped up beside her. "We'd better go
in. There's no sense standing out here." She glanced
at Libby's two suitcases, wondered what drugs were
in them, how many bottles. "It looks like you plan
to stay awhile." She knew her voice was flat, unwel-
coming.

"For a few days. If you don't mind."

"A *few* days will be fine." Repeating her words,
Hannah gave Libby a direct look. It was best she be
clear with Libby, because if she didn't set limits,
there'd be none.

Each woman picked up a case. Hannah opened
the door and they stepped into Kenninghall's ex-
pansive foyer. The day was dark, so Hannah flicked
on a lamp near the door.

Libby looked around, wide-eyed. "Wow! This is
amazing. You've done okay for yourself."

Hannah didn't answer; instead, she took off her
coat and hung it on the Regency coat stand beside
the door. Libby continued to look around as she
slipped out of her worn jacket.

But while she appeared to be in awe, Hannah
knew better.

She was taking inventory, assessing values, for-
mulating the first of her endless requests for help.
What Hannah wouldn't give, Libby would take.
She would lie, cheat, steal, and then disappear. It
was what she did.

Hannah wouldn't forget the pain she'd caused
Will, the constant drain she'd been on their re-
sources, both emotionally and financially. While
they'd worked and struggled to keep Stuart Antiques

profitable, Libby ran wild. The calls became more
frequent—calls from the police and social work-
ers—Will's anguish deeper. And the loans, to pay
Libby's overdue rent, to buy Libby clothes, to
move Libby to another city so she could find work,
then finally the calls to make bail, pay lawyers, as
drugs and alcohol took her to the streets and
lower.

Will never gave up believing in her, never gave
up hope. Hannah believed her destructive behav-
ior was cruel and selfish and beyond understanding.

The unforgivable offense was her not coming to
Will and Christopher's funeral. *Her own father . . .
Chris . . .*

"I'll make coffee," Hannah said. "This way."

Libby followed her to the kitchen, took a stool
at Meara's island, and waited as Hannah started the
coffee, leaving the kitchen to its silence.

"You don't want me here, do you?" Libby asked
finally.

Hannah was putting coffee in the filter. She
stopped, took a deep breath, and turned, coffee
measure still in her hand. "No, I don't."

"I'm not surprised."

When Hannah made no move to turn around
and finish making the coffee, Libby stood, walked
over, and took the measure from her hand. "Will
you please sit down, just for a minute. I have things
to say. And while you may not want to hear them, I
need to get them said." She looked grim.

They reversed positions. Hannah took Libby's
seat while Libby made the coffee, the only sound
in the kitchen the beat of the rain on the slanted
windows of the sunroom at the far end. The rain

coursed over them, a waterfall, obscuring the view of the acres beyond, acres plump with tulip and daffodil bulbs lying in wait for the spring sun.

Libby didn't speak until the coffee began its slow drip.

"I'm not drinking anymore, Hannah—and I don't use drugs," she said.

Hannah had heard this before. It was the standard preamble before her litany of requests for help. She didn't bother to acknowledge the lie.

"I'm not telling you I'm cured. But I've been clean"—she closed her eyes briefly—"since right after Dad and Christopher's funeral."

"A funeral you didn't choose to attend."

"I couldn't."

"Why? I want to know why." The instant Hannah asked, she regretted it. There was no point in asking Libby for excuses. She'd have a hundred of them, and they'd all be cooked up. As false as her regret.

Libby's eyes dulled. "I guess it's accurate to say I was at a stag party and . . . couldn't get away." Her lip curled slightly, reminding Hannah of the way she'd sneer at Will when he tried over and over again to talk sense into her. That sneer, that selfish, arrogant sneer . . .

Her disgust threatened to blot out reason and Hannah closed her eyes. Still she could see two caskets.

One so small, so very, very small.

And this monster of a woman, this sorry excuse for a daughter, was at a party? Hannah flattened a hand on the island and pushed herself to her feet, willed the tremors of anger to stop.

She couldn't tolerate her here, not for a few days,

not for an hour. "I'd like you to leave." She headed for the door. "I'll get my coat, drive you to the bus station. I have about a hundred dollars in my purse." When her hand was on the doorknob, and without turning, she added, "That's all you're going to get from me. Now or ever."

"Hannah, wait. Please."

Hannah turned the doorknob.

"At least hear me out. Then, if you still want to, you can drive me to the bus stop."

Libby's face was ashen, the curled lip, the bleak eyes replaced by panic.

"Please," she repeated, softer this time. "If I have to beg, I will."

Hannah hesitated, knowing what a talented actress she was, how deftly she could weave a tapestry of deceit when it suited her. *Will would listen.*

"All right." She made no move to go back to her seat, choosing instead to stay near the door. "But the truth. Skip the varnish."

"Unvarnished truth?" Libby said, more to herself than to Hannah, but giving her a desolate stare. "I've had a lot of practice with truth in the past few years. I'll give it to you, Hannah." She leveled her gaze, met Hannah's directly. "But I'm not sure you can handle it."

Chapter 8

"The night I got your message about Dad and Christopher, I was committed to—" Libby rubbed her hands over her denim-covered thighs and raised her eyes to meet Hannah's, her expression a mixture of bravado and shame. "You knew I was hooking?"

Hannah nodded.

Libby stood, started to pace. "That night I had a, uh, job lined up. I was supposed to meet the guy in half an hour. I was stone broke. If I didn't . . . do for the guy, there was no way I could get home. I needed the cash. And I needed something else. I was out of my mind crazy. Sick about Dad and Chris—you've got to believe that—" She looked hard at Hannah. "But even sicker in another way." She sucked in a breath, looked as though it cut her chest bone. "I needed my drug of choice."

"And what was that?"

Again her head came up, her eyes bored into Hannah. "Heroin. The big H."

"Oh, Libby . . ." Hannah, shocked, appalled, hadn't known her abuse had gone so far.

"Yeah, 'oh, Libby.' I'd been using it for about three months. Long enough to know I wouldn't get through the funeral without it. I figured I'd do the john, get the money, shoot up, then catch the next bus home." She closed her eyes. "Nice plan, huh? Junkies are damned good at planning."

Hannah wanted to run, instead she tightened her grip on the doorknob. She couldn't conceive of the situation Libby described and didn't want to. That was Libby's world, not hers. Hannah Stuart's world was tidy and secure, and it took all she had to keep it that way, to eliminate variables. And that's what Libby was, a variable.

When Hannah didn't speak, Libby went on, her voice flat. "I met the guy where we'd agreed, got in his car, and—" She put her arms straight down at her sides, and bunched her fists. "Shit! This is tougher than I thought it would be." Her eyes filled with tears and she brushed them away, squared her shoulders.

Hannah reminded herself how often, how convincingly, Libby had wept in the past—how well those tears had worked on Will. Like magic rain they'd washed away Libby's sins and drowned her father's heart.

"The upshot of this charming tale is"—Libby moistened her lips—"the guy had a different kind of *date* in mind than I did. More of a party, he said. Just him and his buddy. I said, okay, but it would cost more. By this time my nerves were screaming, and—oh, shit, you don't need to hear that—" She turned away for a moment. "The guy took me to a run-down condo somewhere outside the city to meet his friend. Turned out he had more than one friend. Turned out there were five juiced-up pals of his looking for action with some sucker of a whore—and I'd drawn the lucky number."

Hannah's heart slowed in her breast, and she shut her eyes against the vision of Libby—any woman— in such an ugly situation. The helplessness, the defilement.

"Three days later, I crawled into the hall and someone called the cops. I guess they figured a wild-eyed, bare-assed hooker didn't fit the high tone of their roach-infested building."

"Oh, Libby. Libby . . ."

"Yeah, I know. I asked for it."

"No! No one asks for that."

"Not even me? The daughter from hell. The two-bit heroin-addicted hooker who got herself so trashed she was seven days in the hospital before she remembered her father and little brother were dead." Her eyes were black with remorse. "You told me once that, in the end, we all get what we deserve. I've thought about that a lot. Because when I look back, I can see how I'd been aiming myself toward that ugly room—those five guys—from the time I was thirteen. That night, or something like it, was inevitable."

Hannah shook her head, her mind a screen of tragic, brutal images.

"You still believe it? About us getting what we deserve?"

Did she? She wasn't sure. She used to. She remembered that. Work hard. Do the right thing, and life will be good to you. Life—all tied up in a logical, controllable package. A package you could cope with. Comfortable. Explainable. But that was then and this was now. Now she wasn't sure about anything. Had she deserved Milo's loving support, his generosity? No. And Will and Christopher? How did her smug, fat-cat philosophy explain what had happened to them?

"No," she said. "I don't believe that. Not anymore." Now she didn't know what she believed and didn't want to think about it. Life was chaos and all you could do was keep your head down and hang on.

The room fell silent.

"But do you believe *me*?"

Hannah didn't answer. Her heart wanted to believe, her brain wasn't so sure. Right now the only thing she was sure of was she didn't want Libby here—or the discord, raw emotion, and endless problems that trailed her like evil wraiths.

Libby was seventeen when Hannah married her father, only five years younger than herself. She'd been in trouble of one kind or other since she'd turned thirteen. Hannah hadn't expected a mother/daughter relationship, but she'd hoped they'd become friends—and that maybe their friendship would turn Libby from her self-destructive road. She'd wanted that for herself and for Will. It was a fool's wish. She saw that now. Five years separated their ages, but a universe fell between their personalities. Hannah was honest, ambitious, deliberate. Libby? For her the fast lane was too slow; she preferred the center line during emotional rush hour.

She was hyper, unpredictable, and manipulative. On her good days, she was quick-witted, amusing, and a joy to be with, but such times were rare and,

Hannah knew now, only when she wanted something.

Except with Christopher. Chris had adored "Bibby."

Hannah's heart lurched and her vision blurred. She took a breath, moved her thoughts back to Libby, her own naivete in thinking she could make a difference. The kind of change Libby needed to make came from within. Had she made it? Hannah was afraid she hadn't, that her showing up here was only a convenient pit stop.

"Do you believe me, Hannah. I need to know," Libby repeated, her expression stark.

"I don't know." It was the best she could do.

"You're honest, anyway." She straightened her shoulders, but looked disappointed. "But then you always were. I admired that about you."

"I didn't think you admired anything about me— or your father. Except maybe our checkbook."

"Hannah . . ."

"What did you do with the sapphire earrings?" Libby flushed. "I sold them."

"They were my mother's, you know. The only thing I had of hers." She'd worn them on her wedding day.

Strange she should think of them now. Certainly they hadn't been the only items Libby had stolen, or the worst thing she'd ever done. But, no matter what Libby did, Will never gave up believing. "She'll come out of it someday," he'd say. She never did, and after their last horrendous argument, a few months before Will died, Libby walked out; never saw her father again.

"I'm sorry," Libby said. "Truly. I wish I could get them back for you, but then"—she lifted her hands, the gesture impotent, weary—"I wish I could get a lot of things back. Including some pretty major parts of my life."

Hannah stared hard at the woman before her. She was thinner than she remembered, and her gaze was more . . . direct. But had she truly changed?

"A week. You can stay for one week." For Will, Hannah would take the risk, but she planned to keep a close eye on her uninvited guest.

Yates drove straight back to his apartment from his meeting with Anne. His first call was to John Crayne to tell him to take the tail off Vonecker. The second was to his sister, not to tell her what he'd discovered about Morgan Greff, but to pick her reliable brain.

"Stell, how are you?"

"Yates! It's got to be a slow, rainy day in that city of yours if you're calling me. Want to tell me what calamity has you picking up the phone to call your favorite sister?"

"No calamity. And last I checked you were my *only* sister," he amended, adding, "And forget about laying on the guilt trip. You know how to work a phone as well as I do. Or do high-flying hotel owners get their secretaries to place their calls."

"Point taken." She laughed, and to Yates it was a warm hug. It was too long since he'd seen her. He'd remedy that soon. Drive down to San Francisco for a weekend, maybe.

"So, how's business?" he asked. "No, skip that. Let's get to the good part. When are you going to make me an uncle?"

"Maybe in the next millennium. It takes two, remember? For now, I'm a dedicated single. Just like big brother. So don't count on me to carry on the family bloodline."

Probably just as well, Yates thought, all blood-lines considered.

"But I can't believe you're calling to inquire about my child-bearing prospects. What's up?" He heard the shuffling sound of paper.

"Can't a brother just call to say hello?"

"He can, but he usually doesn't."

Yates chuckled. "You're right. I've got a question for you."

"Now why doesn't that surprise me?"

"Didn't you recently renovate a room in the Lord William? Do it in a bunch of old stuff?"

"Antiques, Yates. Very expensive antiques." She sighed, but he sensed her good humor. "And the 'room' you're talking about is the Diplomat Suite. It encompasses the whole top floor of the hotel."

"I'm impressed."

"You should be. That reno cost a bundle."

"You mean my MBA sister blew the budget?"

"Big-time, but it was worth it. Be a good boy, and I'll let you see for yourself. You can use it the next time you're in town. That's a bribe, in case you missed it. Not that a cretin like you will appreciate it, of course. I can still see that office/apartment of yours—excuse me while I shudder."

"What's wrong with my apartment?" He looked around.

"Not a thing if your idea of home is a warehouse-sized room with three pieces of metal furniture and a futon. Which brings me to the question, since when did you get interested in hotel renovations?"

"Since this afternoon. I heard a name and couldn't place it—"

"And we both know what havoc that plays with that steel trap memory of yours."

"Right. As if you're any different. The guy's name is Biehle. Milo Biehle. An antiques dealer of some kind. I was wondering if you knew anything about him."

"Why would you be interested in Milo Biehle?"

"You know him, then?"

"Anyone serious about antiques knows him. Although only big money actually deals with him. He's an independent dealer, very exclusive. His own collection is priceless. I bought a couple of pieces through him when I did the Diplomat Suite. Extremely knowledgeable and a very nice man, as I recall."

"A nice *dead* man. He died a couple of weeks ago."

"I'm sorry to hear that. Like I said, a nice man." She paused. "But you still haven't told me why you're interested in him."

"I'm probably not. His name just turned up on the edge of something I'm working on and I'm checking it out."

Yates leaned against the window sash and looked down into the street. All he saw was tops, unfurled umbrellas and car hoods, glistening with rain. Soon the streetlights would come on. He tried to convince himself he'd answered the nagging question about the familiarity of Biehle's name, but it wouldn't sell. He told himself it *must* have come from Stella sometime when she was talking about the hotel. Where else could it come from? He remembered her enthusiasm when she started the renovation project, her escalating stress level as it progressed. The subject had dominated their infrequent phone calls.

He had no idea why he asked the next question.

"Did you meet his assistant, Hannah Stuart?"

"Only by phone. She handled the paperwork on the sales. I talked to her a couple of times. But that was months ago. I don't really remember—excuse me a second."

He heard a muffled conversation and she came back on the line, sounding rushed. "Duty calls, Yates. Is there anything else I can help you with?"

"Who says you helped?"

"Ungrateful wretch. Get down here, will you? And soon? Your suite awaits."

"Will do, if you promise to take a couple of days away from that pressure cooker job of yours and show me around."

"Absolutely! Oh, and before I forget. There's some talk . . . rumblings really, about my running for mayor. Early yet, of course."

Yates heard the restrained excitement in her voice, knew how much this meant to her. How much she deserved it. "That's great, Stell. It's what you've always wanted. I'm happy for you."

"Thanks, big brother. Many a slip between the cup and the lip as they say, but I've got my fingers crossed."

"Consider that doubled. And keep me updated, okay?"

Yates clicked off and continued to stare into the street below. After he finished grinning, thinking about having his sister as mayor of San Francisco, Biehle's name poked at him again.

There was something else. Some other connection. He could feel it. He went back to the sofa, sat and stared unseeingly toward the window he'd just left.

Greff—posing as Don Hallam—was Vonecker's client.

Biehle had been Vonecker's client.

Coincidence? Maybe. But he didn't trust coincidence—and he couldn't shake the feeling Biehle's name was familiar, not as one of Stella's suppliers, but as a shadow from what he called his other life.

A life Morgan Greff had destroyed.

He should walk away from this case, leave Anne to wipe up Vonecker's slime. Yates settled his score with Greff long ago, and he sure as hell didn't relish reliving the experience. He doubted Stella would, either. He hadn't mentioned Greff's name, because he knew what she'd say. "Leave it alone, Yates. Leave him alone. It's a no-win situation." Stella, always the pragmatist, always counting the odds.

She'd change her mind in a heartbeat, if she knew the filthy business Greff was hip deep in. *Allegedly in,* he reminded himself. If there was one thing he knew, it was that he didn't know enough. Maybe Vonecker had been falsely accused, maybe he was innocent as a lamb. Which would make Greff innocent, too.

Innocent. Greff.

Never having heard the two words in the same sentence before, Yates tested them on his tongue. Ice cream and deep fried snake came to mind.

He pulled an earlobe—to loosen some serious thinking.

Before he did anything, he'd check out Biehle. And Hannah Stuart was the place to start.

* * *

Wilson Bone pulled his white, 'ninety-two Dodge van up to the cheapest pump in the gas station. He topped off his tank, then pulled one of the twenty-gallon, red plastic containers from the back and filled it with the higher octane. He'd fill another at the next station. Another at the next, and so on. As the gas splashed into the container, he inhaled, took the fumes deep.

Gas. A nice garden variety stew of flammable hydrocarbons. Available anywhere. No fancy explosives you either needed to steal or sign for. No trace.

"Need some help with that, sir?"

Bone looked up to see a kid with the name Bruce *scrolled on his shirt smiling at him and nodding at his red container.*

"I thought this was self-serve." That's why he chose the damn place. He calmed himself, told himself it didn't matter. He was a long way from the job. By the time he reached Seattle, his trunk would be full of gas and not one ounce would have been purchased in Washington State.

"It is"—he gestured in the direction of the second set of pumps—"over there. These here are full service, but no problem. Cost ya a bit more per gallon, though."

"Hey. I'm pumpin' the shit myself. No way I'm payin' extra."

"You gotta pay the pump price. This here one is ten cents more a gallon. It's on the computer." Bruce said the last as if God Almighty had personally etched it on a stone tablet.

Bone glanced at the two prices. Shit! He'd have to be more careful. This little error was puttin' him four bucks over budget. He hated that. Hated when things didn't balance. If he wasn't on a job, he'd tell the dumb bastard

what he could do with his damned computer. But he wasn't
into making memories for the kid. He'd make up the four
bucks. Skip lunch, maybe. He'd balance somehow.

"Okay." He forced a smile. "But it wouldn't hurt if you
guys made your signs so a guy could read 'em."

Bruce nodded disinterestedly. "Will that be cash or
credit card?" he asked.

"Cash." Bone hung up the pump head, screwed the cap
back on the gas container, and dug out his wallet. He
counted out thirty-seven dollars and sixteen cents.

"Thank you, sir."

Up yours, Brucey baby. Bone got back in the van and
slammed the door.

When he pulled out of the station, he headed north.

On Saturday night, Hannah was dressing for
her dinner date with Morgan Greff when Libby appeared at her bedroom door.

"Want some company?" she said

She didn't but . . . "Sure."

Hannah navigated their shared space warily, kept
at bay the memories Libby's presence invoked.
Uneasy and confused by her being here, Hannah
still couldn't figure out why she'd come, what she
wanted. She disliked being suspicious, but couldn't
help herself.

In the days since Milo's death, Hannah had de-
veloped a comfortable routine, a new life pattern.
If she stayed within it, was disciplined, she'd be
okay. Everything would stay together. *She'd stay to-*
gether. She might be the new Queen of Repression,
but it was working. Soon Milo would be just another painful memory buried under the structure
of habit and day-to-day chores. Talking about him

tonight with his cousin, Morgan, was all she could handle. She dropped her earring.

Libby picked it up. "You're nervous."

"No. Just clumsy," she lied, taking the silver earring from Libby's outstretched hand.

"You look nice." Libby assessed Hannah more closely, smiled. "Better than nice. What's the occasion?"

Hannah stood, smoothed the plain gray dress over her hips. "I have a dinner engagement."

"Anyone special?"

"Not really. Just a cousin of Milo's from out of town." Even as she said the words, Hannah wasn't sure how close they were to being true. For one thing, she didn't know where Morgan came from—and her use of the word "just" as a qualifier smacked of an emotional cover-up. Certainly something about Morgan Greff felt special, and she *was* looking forward to dinner with him.

Libby wandered around Hannah's room, whistled softly. "You know, everything about this house is so incredible. And even in the rain, Washington is beautiful. Must be a great place to live."

Hannah tensed. *Here it comes. She's making her move. She wants to stay.*

Libby must have sensed her unease. She smiled. It was the smile of her father, slightly crooked and teasing. "Don't worry, I'm not moving in. I have a job, remember—you even called to confirm it."

Hannah didn't answer, unless her hot—and surely red—face did it for her. Subterfuge and deceit weren't natural talents of hers. But when Libby had told her she worked as a counselor for a drug and alcohol center in Portland, she had called to confirm her story.

"You don't need to look so guilty. If I were you, I'd have done the same thing. You have no reason to believe I've come here without an, uh, ulterior motive."

"No, I don't," she said tersely, unwilling to let down her guard.

"Actually, I kind of like having my references checked. And having some to give, for that matter. Who did you speak to?"

"Someone by the name of Tom Colwood." Hannah turned back to face the mirror, apply a touch of coral to her lips. Libby stepped up behind her and Hannah couldn't help but note their differences weren't only in their personalities. Libby's thick, honey blond hair and olive skin were in steep contrast to her own dark hair and pale complexion. Libby had always been a beauty. Too beautiful for her own good, Will always said.

"What did he say?"

Hannah turned to face her, but hesitated before repeating Tom Colwood's words, as if saying them aloud would make a chink in the armor she'd forged against her unwelcome guest. "He said you were one of the most valuable counselors he had."

"Good old Tom."

"He didn't sound very old to me."

This time Libby blushed. "He's not, actually."

"He also said he couldn't run the place without you."

"Not true. Tom could end three civil wars on a bad day and not get winded doing it."

Hannah was intrigued. "You like this . . . Tom Colwood, I take it."

"Uh-huh. But more than that, I owe him. He was my original sponsor. Without Tom, I'd probably still be turning tricks on dirty sheets with a rig in my arm." She winced. "Jeez . . . sorry, I'm not used to, uh, watering down my words."

Before Hannah could answer, the doorbell chimed. Her stomach fluttering oddly, she turned back to the mirror to apply some last-minute color to her cheeks. She *was* nervous! As prickly and unpredictable as a teenage girl facing a first date.

"Want me to get it?" Libby asked.

"Please. Tell him I'll be right down."

When Libby left the room, Hannah gripped the edge of her dresser and worked to quell the mixture of excitement and trepidation arcing through a body accustomed to no more emotional exercise than a bout of depression during the solitude of a long walk.

She sat back from the mirror and took a calming breath. Dinner. That's all it was. In a couple of hours she'd be back at Kenninghall and everything would be as it always was.

Chapter 9

Yates didn't know what to expect when the door opened, but it wasn't a hot blonde wearing wallpaper jeans.

"Hi, I'm here to see Hannah Stuart?"

She gave him the once-over. "Lucky Hannah."

Before he got his mouth open, she said, "Come on in." She stepped aside and Yates took his first step inside Kenninghall. The size of it made him whistle.

"This place is something, huh?" She grinned.

"Yeah, definitely something."

"This way."

Yates followed, man enough to enjoy the view of that plastered-on denim she was wearing.

He was told Hannah Stuart lived alone, that the only other person on the estate was the housekeeper who lived in a small cottage behind the main house. When Anne had filled him in on Biehle's business and what little she knew about Hannah, she'd nearly convinced him there could be no connection between the antiques dealer and Greff—and certainly not one between him and Hannah. But the name Biehle still nagged. He intended to ask Hannah Stuart directly what, if anything, she knew about Morgan Greff. It was the shortest distance between two points, and there was no reason he could see not to take it.

And he wanted to see her again. He hadn't forgotten the jolt when they'd shaken hands.

"In case you're wondering," the woman in front of him said over her shoulder, "I'm taking you to the library—if I can find the damn thing. Hannah will be down in a minute." She opened a door, peered in. "This is it."

Yates followed her into a room with floor-to-ceiling books on three walls—most of them behind glass—just off the entryway. He stood in the center of the room and looked around, while she went to a serving table behind one of the two love seats near the fireplace.

"I'm Libby Stuart, by the way."

"Hannah's sister?"

"Nope. Daughter."

He knew he looked baffled and she laughed again.

"Stepdaughter. Hannah was married to my father."

"Uh." He nodded.

"You know, the only thing this castle lacks is a butler, so I'll have to do. Can I fix you a drink?" She tilted one of the bottles and read the label. "Scotch?" She looked at him and grinned. "Very good, very expensive scotch."

"Sure. That'll be fine."

She poured and brought it to him.

"Won't you join me?"

"No, the bottle and I parted company a few years back. But thanks anyway." She sat on one of the love seats and looked up at him.

He sat on the edge of the one opposite her and drank some of the scotch. She was right. Damn good.

"So, you're Milo's cousin."

"Not that I'm aware of."

"But I thought—"

Just then Hannah walked into the room. She frowned when she saw him, as though she were struggling to remember. His ego took a direct hit, and was only slightly salved by her next words.

"You're the man from Gerry Vonecker's office." She stared at him. Her pale blue eyes were startling in their clarity. A pretty woman. *A very pretty woman.*

She waited.

"Yes. Yates Lang. Sorry if I've interrupted something. I was hoping you'd have some time to talk for a few minutes."

"Actually I'm waiting for someone, and he's due any moment." She took a few steps closer. "I thought you might be him, actually."

The doorbell interrupted.

"I'll get it," Libby said, jumping up.

"What is it you want to talk to me about, Mr. Lang?"

"Yates," he corrected, uncomfortable with the formality. Her expression was puzzled and she looked tense, as if his presence here made her uneasy. "I wanted to know if—"

"*This* is the cousin," Libby announced triumphantly, stepping through the doorway. An impeccably dressed man trailed her into the library, then stepped to her side. His gaze instantly settled on Yates.

Yates's brain imploded, and his blood drained to his sneakers. His grip fused to the cool glass in his hand.

Greff.

If Greff had any reaction to seeing him standing in Hannah Stuart's library, he gave no sign. Not surprising. Because no one was cooler—icier—under pressure than Greff. And no one was a more adept chameleon. The man changed colors, sides, and personalities to suit his needs.

It was a particular talent of his, as Yates knew from firsthand experience. Greff called it his major asset.

He nodded at Yates, gave him a cool smile. "Yates . . . Lang, isn't it? It's been a long time." He didn't offer his hand, nor did Yates.

Yates forcibly relaxed his grip on his glass. "Yeah, a long time." *And the son of a bitch was still smiling, still flashing those Chiclets as though he had a right to be alive.* Yates's throat constricted; his face felt like carved stone. He had to get out of here—fast. Greff might be able to hide under a slick facade; he wasn't so talented.

The two women stared at the men. Libby concentrated on Greff, her gaze speculative, while Hannah stared at him. Yates didn't know why, but that pleased him. When neither he nor Greff spoke, Hannah took up the slack.

"You two know each other?" She looked at Yates.

"Used to." He put down his glass. "I'll leave you to your plans, see myself out."

Greff's gaze stayed with him, smug as hell.

Yates shot him a look, before turning his back.

Yeah, I'm running, you bastard, because if I don't, I'll break your bloody face.

Hannah touched his arm as he passed her. "But you said you wanted to ask me something," she said. "And I'm sure Morgan won't mind waiting for a few minutes."

They were on a first-name basis, for God's sake. What the hell was going on here?

The internal question stopped him cold, and a few misplaced neurons fired. Damned if he didn't have the answer he came for. Hannah Stuart definitely knew Morgan Greff, but how and why? No way was this woman involved in the shit business Greff was in. The questions nettled his brain like thorns. He had an idea. A lousy one, but it would have to do. "No, I wouldn't want to keep you from your plans just to talk about selling a car."

"Car?"

"Anne Chapman told me Milo Biehle was a collector of sorts, had a few classics. I thought you might be interested in selling one."

"I hadn't thought about it." She looked uncertain.

"Would you? If the offer was good enough?"

"I don't know."

"How about I come back tomorrow. Say around ten? We could talk about it then." He pushed, sensed he had to.

"Fine. Ten will be fine."

"Tomorrow, then." He turned to go, and his gaze collided with Greff's. The air between them thickened with distrust and suspicion. Yates saw the challenge in Greff's gaze, remembered the words he'd spoken so many years ago. Even now they seared his mind like a fresh brand. "You're a loser. Like all the damn Langs. A shit-for-brains, pudding-for-balls loser. And don't ever take me on again, because next time I'll fuckin' bury you. That's a promise."

He strode toward the entryway, his back prickling under what he knew would be Greff's patronizing gaze.

That was sixteen years ago, Greff. My balls are a lot harder these days.

Outside, he walked down the steps, stopped on the gravel path leading to the house. He looked back. Through the window he saw Greff accept a drink from Hannah, watched as she touched her hair in that peculiarly feminine way that said a woman had the hots for a guy. He fought the urge to go back in there and pop out a few of those man-made ivories the asshole called teeth. Instead, he shook his head, burrowed deeper into his leather jacket, and headed to his car. He was disappointed.

He hadn't taken Hannah Stuart for a fool.

Fifteen minutes later, Hannah and Morgan were at the door of Kenninghall.

"How do you know Yates Lang?" Hannah asked him as he helped her on with her coat.

"Old business. Unpleasant business. Definitely not the topic to start our evening with." He squeezed her shoulders, leaned forward until she could feel his warm breath against her ear. "An evening I've been looking forward to."

Hannah's hands fluttered up to her collar, and

she took an awkward step forward out of his grip. "I think we'd better be going. The reservation is for eight o'clock, isn't it?"

He seemed amused. "I've made you uncomfortable."

"No, not at all," she said, far too quickly, her fingers working ineptly with the top button of her coat. The truth was she didn't know *what* he made her feel. Other than unexpectedly off balance. She was accustomed to walking an emotional tightrope, but one straight and taut—not slack and swinging in a wind gusting stronger by the second. But her unease wasn't Morgan's fault. He was Milo's cousin. Family. He was merely being courteous. She wouldn't read more into his kindness than that. She forced herself to look at him. "Shall we go?"

"Yes." He touched her cheek, ran his finger slowly along her jaw. She jumped. Instantly hated herself. "And I promise not to touch you again unless"—he smiled down at her—"you invite me to."

She started to speak, but realized she had nothing to say. There was something vaguely sinful in Morgan's overt charm. And she was enjoying being cajoled and prodded out of her familiar cocoon. She was still looking at him when Libby came out of the library.

"Sorry. I thought you'd gone," she said. She smiled at Hannah and glanced toward Morgan. Her smile died.

"We're just on our way," Hannah said, finally closing her coat button.

"Have a nice time," Libby said, taking the first step on the staircase.

"We plan to," Morgan answered, his hand already on the doorknob.

"And Hannah?" Libby added.

"Yes."

"Be, uh, careful. Okay?" She stopped on the step, stuffed her hands in the pockets of her jeans.

Hannah sensed a warning of sorts. Morgan frowned.

"Careful of what?" Hannah asked, aware that she, too, was frowning. "A quiet drive to a local restaurant along deserted country roads?"

Libby tossed a cascade of blond hair over her shoulder. Hannah knew the gesture was a nervous one. "I guess I'm still too much of a city girl," she said.

Hannah, perplexed, stepped through the open door Morgan stood beside.

"I'll wait up," Libby yelled.

Morgan closed the door behind them so Hannah had no chance to answer. He chuckled as they walked to the car.

"I feel like the town bad boy taking the minister's daughter on her first date." He opened the passenger door for her and waited while she got in. "Is she always like that? So protective?"

"I wouldn't know. I haven't seen her in years." Hannah settled her coat around her knees. Protective was not a word she would use to describe Libby, unless you put the word *self* in front of it.

Morgan, one hand on the car's roof, the other on the open door, gave her a dazzling smile. "Not that I blame her. If you were a relative of mine, I'd look out for you, too. And I am somewhat of an unsavory character, you know. At least Miranda thinks so."

Hannah looked up. His jaw was in shadow, and the porch light accented his eyes, their reassuring spray of lines embedded in vital, youthful skin. If there was an unsavory side to Morgan Greff, it was attractively packaged. What Hannah saw was mystery and a welcome, mature strength she could relax into, a confidence garnered from years of living. Will had that; so, in his own way, had Milo. In another twenty-five years, would she be as comfortable in her own skin? Or was it something unique to the male species?

"Perhaps you need to try again with Miranda," she said.

"Maybe I will." He closed the door, walked around the front of the car, and got in the driver's seat.

When he was turning onto the main road, he gave her a sideways glance. "By the way, how did *you* come to know Yates Lang?"

"I don't. Not really. I met him briefly when I visited Milo's lawyer in Seattle. Gerry says he's a forensic accountant."

"That fits." Morgan's mouth firmed and he nodded.

Hannah went on. "Apparently he does business with one of Gerry's partners."

"How would he know about the cars?"

"Milo's passion for vintage cars wasn't a secret."

"I see," he said, his gaze back on the road. "And will you sell him the car?"

"Possibly." She'd have to do her homework. She knew nothing about the cars or their value. They'd been Milo's pets, his personal passion. They'd never been part of the regular business inventory.

Morgan looked at her again, his expression stern. "I'm not usually one for giving advice, but be cautious. Lang's not a man to be trusted."

"Care to tell me why?" she asked, curious but

not surprised by his comment. It was obvious the two men didn't like each other.

He paused, seemed to think on her request, then shook his head. "Can't. It would betray someone's confidence."

She respected that.

He went on. "Just tell me you'll be careful around him, both from a business perspective—and personally." He reached over and squeezed her hand as if to accent his concern.

"I'm not sure I know how to be anything but careful," she replied.

"Then you're a wise woman," he said.

Hannah turned to stare at the night-darkened fields rushing past the car window.

Odd.

Morgan's warning bumped solidly into her own perception of Yates Lang. A perception that, until now, she hadn't known to be so positive. She didn't know anything about him, really, but she liked him. Maybe she'd been living in her cocoon so long her instincts were rusty. She closed her eyes and leaned her head against the fine leather headrest.

No doubt she'd be smart to take Morgan's advice when it came to Yates and be on her guard.

"Enjoy yourself?" Morgan asked, settling back in his chair and taking a small drink of water. Hannah noticed he was a moderate drinker and had declined after-dinner liqueur.

"Very much. Thank you. It was a lovely dinner," she said, and mellow with good food and candlelight, she added, "Milo and I rarely went to restaurants. He preferred to eat in."

"What about you? What did you prefer?"

"I was happy with Milo's decisions, and besides, Meara is a wonderful cook."

"Is she?"

"Yes, she is."

"And what does she do best? Italian? French? Japanese? Indonesian? Hamburger Helper?"

Hannah had to smile. "If you're looking for a dinner invitation to Kenninghall, Morgan, you're not very subtle."

He laughed. "I wasn't trying to be." He reached into his pocket, took out a fine leather wallet, and removed a credit card. He dropped it on the bill. The waiter arrived and whisked it away as if it were perishable. "I think I'd enjoy another dinner with you—especially at home where you'd be relaxed."

Hannah didn't answer. Instead she asked the question that had nagged her all through dinner.

"I thought you wanted to know about Milo. But you haven't asked me a single question. Why?" She folded her napkin and rested it beside her empty water glass.

"I didn't ask any questions because I didn't need to. You told me what I wanted to hear, in fact," he chided gently. "You didn't talk about much else."

"I'm sorry if I—"

"Don't apologize." He reached across the table and lightly clasped her wrist. "From what you've told me, my cousin was a lucky man who led a pretty decent life. His mother adored him. He was successful in his business, and he had the respect of his associates." He held her hand now, stroked the back of it with his thumb in an idle, sensual gesture. "But more than that, he had you."

His eyes met hers directly. "And I'd say having you would be as good as it gets for any man."

Hannah's tongue knotted until there was no hope of intelligent comment, but Morgan's gaze didn't waver. And he didn't let go of her hand, even when she tugged on it. It wasn't much of a tug, she admitted, and she was secretly glad he didn't let go. His grip was strong and steady. That it hinted of possessiveness, she didn't mind, because other than a few I'm-so-terribly-sorry handshakes and Meara's harshly cold shower, Morgan was the first person to touch her since Milo's death.

"You're beautiful and you're smart. That's a potent combination." His voice was low, intimate, as his thumb massaged the back of her knuckles.

She tugged harder, and he released her hand, but slowly, as if reluctant to let her go. His fingernails lightly scraped across her palm before contact was broken.

Heat from his casual caress swirled up her arm, and her neck warmed to discomfort. Her response to Morgan Greff stunned her. It was as if her body had uncoupled itself from her mind.

My God, when had she become so physically needy? Her blood, agitated by puzzlement and fear, pumped erratically. If she stood, she'd probably fall over.

Grateful to see the waiter coming toward their table, she reached for her bag. "I think we should go. Libby's waiting for me." Dear God, she sounded addle-brained and completely illogical. Where was her composure? That "marvelous cool" that Will had always teased her about and Milo had counted on.

"Are you angry?" he asked.

"Angry?"

"I broke my promise," Morgan said. "I touched."
He smiled at her as he completed the credit slip
for the bustling waiter. What cool she didn't have,
he had to spare, it seemed.

When the waiter left, he asked, "Should I apologize?"

She met his eyes, saw the challenge there: sexual,
arrogant, and uniquely masculine. It was a challenge offered in a game he'd be expert at. A game
of whispers and steamy midnight promises. But
with Morgan, she suspected, the game involved
more muscle than heart.

The game of sex.

Hannah hadn't played it in a very long time. But
she remembered . . . how you could lose yourself in
it. Forget.

"No. Don't apologize." She spoke quickly, rushed
to get the words out. "Come to dinner at Kenninghall."

He took her hand again, played with her fingers, smiled. "Hamburger Helper?"

She laughed, actually laughed. "I think we can
do better than that."

He kissed her fingertips. "I can't wait."

Chapter 10

It was close to midnight when Morgan dropped her off. Under the dim light of the porch, he took her face in his hands, kissed her slowly, carefully, as if she'd crumble under his hands. She almost did. And he held her. Locking her in his arms, he nuzzled her hair.

"I want you, Hannah," he murmured against her ear.

She stepped back. Too fast. Things were moving too fast. Her senses were in overdrive. "Morgan, I—"

"It's okay. I understand." He held her hands, bent to kiss her forehead. "I can wait—at least until after I've tasted Meara's cooking. After that"—he grinned, dropped his hands—"no promises."

"It's . . . been a long time for me." She felt like an idiot.

He touched her face, his own cool and confident. "Then when it happens, it'll be special—for both of us."

"Come on Wednesday. Will that be okay?"

"Perfect. I'll see you then."

When she closed Kenninghall's door behind her, she shut her eyes and leaned against its heavy oak. She felt very much like a pendulum in a faulty clock. She was hanging up her coat when she heard Libby.

"Did you have a good time?" she asked, leaning against the open door to the library.

Hannah's attention went to the glass in her hand. It looked like orange juice, but she couldn't be sure. "Yes," she said, her tone crisp in an effort to deter further conversation. Again she glanced at Libby's glass.

What was left of the evening's glow dimmed, faded to gray. The warmth was gone, replaced by old memories, suspicion.

"Dinner good?" Libby asked.

"Very."

"Would you like a drink?" She lifted her glass. "There's juice or I can make coffee."

"Why?" Hannah was angry suddenly, frustrated that Libby was here, reminding her of . . . things she didn't want to be reminded of.

"Why would I make coffee?"

"That's not what I was asking, and you know it."

"Okay. What were you asking?"

"Why are you being so obliging, Libby? So friend-ly. Ever since you arrived, no matter how much distance I try to put between us, you keep trying to cozy up. You're up to something," Hannah lifted her hands. "And I want to know what."

"Is that how you see it? Me being 'up to some-thing'?"

"Yes." She compressed her lips and stared at her

stepdaughter. "So I'll ask you again. What are you doing here? What possessed you to show up after all these years?"

Libby nodded back toward the softly lit library where a fire crackled on the grate. "Can I answer it sitting down?"

Hannah crossed her arms under her breasts, shook her head. She didn't want to sit down, and she didn't want a soul-searching conversation. She wanted a straightforward answer, not to grapple yet again with the damaged relationship between herself and Libby. It was too much like shadow-boxing. She never was any good at sifting the lies from the truth, so what was the point? But she had asked the damn question—when what she really wanted to do was go to bed and think about her time with Morgan.

"Please. Let's sit for a minute. We need to talk. It's important."

Hannah thought they'd talked enough, but she caved—she always did—and followed Libby into the library. She perched on the edge of the sofa across from where Libby sat, determined to leave at the earliest opportunity.

Libby drew in a breath. "At first I thought it was because of step nine," she said.

"Excuse me?"

"I didn't get clean and sober alone. If it hadn't been for the twelve steps, taken one at a time, I wouldn't be here today, and I sure as hell wouldn't be drug and alcohol free. Nine is about making amends to people you've hurt, harmed in some way. I always knew you qualified big-time, but I just never had the guts to face you."

"So, why now?"

Libby drank the remainder of her juice. "A couple of phone calls. One about four years ago, the other last month."

"Go on."

"Four years ago, a woman called me. A headhunter, she said, doing a background check on you because you were applying for a job with a client of hers, an antiques dealer. Routine procedure, she said."

"Applying for a job—" Hannah stopped midsentence. She hadn't applied for a job in years, and four years ago, she'd already been living and working with Milo for a year. What Libby said made no sense at all.

When Hannah made no effort to finish her sentence, Libby continued. "She was really chatty, asked about your work history, Dad, how long you'd been married. Did you smoke, drink? What kind of person you were. Stuff like that. Sounded legitimate enough. Although looking back on it, I can see that a lot of the questions were a bit personal." Libby frowned then smiled faintly. "But as I was newly clean and wallowing in guilt at the time, I was anxious to say all the right things. When she hung up, I was left with the warm, fuzzy feeling I'd helped you get a fancy new job with what the woman called a 'noted antiques dealer.' Later, when I found out where you were, I assumed it was Milo Biehle who'd done the check."

"Why didn't you call me?"

"Why would I? And if I had, would you have talked to me? Four years ago?"

Hannah thought a moment. "No. Probably not."

"That's what I figured. Besides, there wasn't anything weird about the call. Like I said. It sounded like a standard reference check."

"You said you got another call. More recently."

"Three in all. The first one in June, the last maybe six weeks ago." She looked warily at Hannah, tensed. "I was asked to come here, but he said not to come until he was . . . gone."

Hannah's mouth slackened. "Milo! You're saying Milo called you?" If Libby had said an angel had trumpeted her here, she could not have been more surprised. But Milo calling—it wouldn't process.

"He told me he didn't have long to live, and when he was gone, you were going to need someone. I guess you don't live right, because I was the best 'someone' he could come up with. He didn't want you to be alone. Sounded like a nice guy."

"I don't understand it. Milo knew we were . . . estranged." Maybe she hadn't gone into the details of her and Will's relationship with Libby, but he certainly knew they weren't, and never had been, close.

"Yes, he did, and he wanted to be real sure I wasn't the old Libby. When he mentioned he'd had me thoroughly checked out before he called, I remembered the call from four years ago. Made a crack about it, about him being a cautious kind of guy." She paused. "He said he didn't know anything about that call, but that he wasn't surprised that I'd got it. Someone was always watching him, he said, and everyone around him."

"That's insane. We led a quiet life here. Why would anyone be interested in either him or me? None of this makes any sense at all."

"Sense or no sense"—Libby leaned forward, her dilated pupils catching and reflecting the light of the fire, her expression earnest—"he said he had enemies. Dangerous enemies. And that after he was gone, those enemies would be yours. Said they'd gather 'like buzzards'—his words. He said you'd be in 'perilous water'—his words again. That you'd need a friend." She stopped, frowned. "And after meeting your date tonight—Mr. Sam Slick, I totally agree with him."

The sky glowed.

The night air, alive with wind, sent sparks by the millions into the cold, black heavens. Wasted glitter. It was beautiful, awesomely, heart-poundingly beautiful.

Bone, mesmerized, lay on his stomach in an adjoining field. He ignored the screams of dying animals, the frantic yells of the farmer, until he saw him run into the burning barn. Fool.

No good. It wouldn't do him no good. That barn was goin' down and nothin' on this green earth would stop it.

And soon.

He'd checked it out last night. The barn was old, poorly built, and stuffed with hay. Bone had known it would be a good burn, and he was right. Though he would have liked it quieter. What the hell good was all the hollerin' anyhow? The place was an inferno. One beautiful fuckin' inferno. No one could put it out. Wilson Bone's fires burned to the ground. Always. Right to the damn ground.

And night fires were always the best.

*　　*　　*

Yates got up early Sunday, spent the morning with black coffee in hand, soaking up everything he never wanted to know about vintage cars. A man who drove a good old made-in-Detroit Chevy, with no bells, no whistles, he'd never paid much attention to cars, new or old—until now.

After an hour or so with some classic car magazines and the *The Complete Encyclopedia of Motor Cars,* he figured he knew enough to get by. A few buzz words and some knowing nods baffled the best of them.

For the balance of the morning, he concentrated on Biehle. The big news was discovering a family connection between Biehle and Greff. Cousins, the blonde said. Somewhere along the line he must have heard Greff mention him. That would account for the bell in Yates's head that had gone off the minute he heard the name. But Biehle was dead.

So why in hell was Greff sniffing around Hannah Stuart?

A black felt pen lay at his right hand. He picked it up and started to chain the links, writing bold cursive over car notes already committed to memory.

Vonecker: Biehle's lawyer—and now Hannah's lawyer. In business of the very dirty variety with Greff aka Hallam and Zanez.

Greff: Already in bed with Biehle's lawyer and currently angling for the same position with Hannah Stuart.

Yates had no doubt of that. Unless the bastard had undergone a morals transplant somewhere along the line, it would be standard procedure. And if he was looking to pull back the sheets, he had a reason.

Greff had a reason for everything.

He looked at what he'd written. None of it made any sense. He tossed the pen back on the coffee table, cursed, and reached for his coffee. He was going nowhere at warp speed, but he couldn't shake the feeling, his best bet was to concentrate on Hannah Stuart.

Greff was. That was good enough for him.

He looked at his watch, almost eight. If he was going to make La Conner by ten, he'd better hit the shower and then the road.

The phone rang. He considered ignoring it but decided it might be Crayne, whom he'd given the unenviable task of tracking the elusive Tenassi. Maybe he had something. He clicked on the receiver.

"Yates Lang, is it?" The voice was low and bell clear. "Interesting choice of names."

Greff.

Every cell in Yates's body quivered to alert. Although he wasn't surprised by the call; Greff always took the offensive. "Better than some I've heard. What do you want?" he asked, not liking that his palms were starting to sweat.

Greff chuckled. "Me? Nothing. It's been a long time. Just a friendly call."

"Why don't I believe that?"

"Maybe because you're too smart for your own good and always have been."

"A compliment? Thanks. Now what the hell do you want?" Yates started to relax. There was always the chance this call would tell him something. If he didn't blow it—get his blood up.

"What were you doing at Hannah Stuart's last night?"

"I could ask you the same question."

"You could. And I'd tell you it was none of your business."

"Exactly."

"But then, as usual, I hold all the aces," Greff said, silk in his voice, iron in the words. "I can be as unaccommodating as I please. You can't."

There was no mistaking the threat. Greff preferred his path smoothed by fear.

"How's Stella?" he went on, not missing a beat. "Still the high-profile businesswoman and woman-about-town in San Francisco? I should look her up sometime. Last I heard, she's thinking about the mayor's job."

Score one for Greff, a direct hit. Always way ahead of the eight ball. "That's what the woman says," Yates said without inflection.

"High-profile job, politics. Media breathing down your neck night and day. Got to be squeaky clean to play that game." Yates heard him take a drink. "I heard about poor Ellie. Too bad."

"Yeah, I can tell you're ripped up about it."

"Ancient history."

"For some." For others it was a hole in the heart that would never close.

Greff went on, his voice harder, his words clipped. "Now, how about I ask you again, real nice this time. What were you doing at Biehle's last night?"

So much for 'poor Ellie,' Yates thought, his heart a stone behind his ribs. She'd given this asshole her love, her mind, and her fortune. Now she was 'ancient history.' And anything he said in her defense would cause Greff to heap further abuse on her.

When he didn't speak, Greff added another

question. "Have you got something going on with that woman?"

Yates rubbed his nape, considered his next words. This was no time for a misstep—but he sure as hell wasn't going to let the bastard see him sweat. "I was doing exactly what I said I was doing, trying to buy a car. A 1937 Cord, to be exact. Shocked the hell out of me when you showed up."

Silence. Yates thought of a snake, flicking its forked tongue, alert for threat.

"Since when did you get interested in vintage cars?"

"It's been a long time. I'm interested in a lot of new things." *Like what the hell you're up to.*

"And how did you find out about these particular cars?"

"I do the odd contract for a law firm in Seattle. I heard about the estate through them." This was one of those times when a dash of truth served better than a dollop of fiction. Unless he missed his guess, Greff had already checked him out with Vonecker.

Silence. Yates visualized Greff's mind working, making connections, judging risk, then deciding on the best course of self-interest. Greff's intelligence was all keen analysis and rapid action. If it hadn't been, he'd be dead by now—or serving a life sentence.

"Then get the car and get the hell out of my way. I have business with Hannah Stuart, and I don't plan on having any two-bit P.I. mess it up. Clear?"

Yates's gut twisted into a knot and pulled. "You're always clear," he ground out. He'd let Greff think he'd back off. Let him think whatever was good for Yates. Two could play that game.

"Good," he said, then paused. "How are you, anyway?" The question was gruff, awkward, its intent misfiring along the hard edges of Greff's voice.

The knot in Yates's gut tightened painfully. Old memories surged up—and he shoved them down, back into the murky ditch where he saved everything to do with Greff. "You've said what you had to say. You can skip the small talk."

More silence. Longer.

"I guess," Greff said finally. "Truth is, we never were any good at it."

"We were never any good at anything."

"Yeah."

Yates heard a click, stared down at the dead phone in his hand. His heart still beat in his chest, his breathing fell to its normal rhythm, and his hands were as steady as a dead man's.

His mind was an empty black hole.

"No. We never were," he repeated, knowing with absolute certainty they never would be.

Hannah hesitated outside Milo's bedroom.

It was time to open the letters. After what Libby told her last night, past time. Milo said she was in danger. But from what? And why would he choose Libby of all people to warn her? He couldn't begin to know what she was capable of. Danger. What kind of danger? Libby didn't know. Hannah rubbed her forehead, wanting to erase this new reality from her life. Libby said when she'd asked Milo for specifics, he'd told her Hannah would know soon enough, and she'd know what to do.

The answer had to be in the letters.

She opened the door, stepped in, and walked slowly to the bureau. Her hand shaking; she felt for the hidden latch that opened the narrow drawer and removed the envelopes. It was the third time they'd been in her grasp. She turned them over in her hands, ran her index finger along the seal of the first envelope bearing her name.

She closed her eyes, heard Milo's voice. *"When you read these, you'll hate me."*

Never! She could never hate the man who'd come for her, brought her, ill and desolate, to Kenninghall, then asked nothing of her other than to be with him. "Grieve," he'd told her. "And when you're done, we'll build you a life, Hannah. I'll take care of you, always. I promise." And she had grieved. Reeling between rage and guilt, she'd foundered into a depression so black and dense it encased her. Its circle of pain so tight she could scarcely breathe, let alone eat. When she thought of anything, it was death and the end of the blackness. But Milo pulled her back, prodded her to move, to do, to think. He kept his promise, and eventually she'd rallied, started to help him in his work, and lead what Milo had called "her half-life."

She put the envelopes in her sweater pocket, closed the secret drawer, and walked across the hall to her room. Her desk sat under a high window from which gray light seeped into the room. She set the other envelopes to the side and reached for her letter opener, using its sharp point to pierce the first envelope with her name on it.

My dearest Hannah:
   If you're reading this, I'm gone. I'm selfish enough

*to hope you miss me, but I don't want your endless
tears. You've cried enough—as have I.*

*It seems life set us both on paths we'd rather not
have traveled. And each of us has fought a battle
with demon guilt. A battle neither of us appears to
have won. I write this letter sick with it, because,
sadly, I must ask you—the dearest person in my
life, and the last one deserving of this ugly task—to
tie up one loose thread in my tattered life. There is
simply no one else I can turn to.*

*When you read the contents of the other envelopes
your feelings for me will change. I can only hope
your concern for Miranda will overcome your revulsion and allow you to honor this last request. I
offer no excuses for what you are about to read;
there are none. I've spent my life trying to atone for
what I did that long-ago summer evening. If I have
succeeded, I will be in God's keeping, if I have not . . .*

Remember always that I truly loved you, Hannah.

Milo

Hannah's hands were clammy, and something
cold and freakish slithered over her heart. She
fought the urge to stand and run from the room,
from this very house, and fixed her attention on
the second envelope.

"Oh, Milo." She covered the letter with her hands,
then rested her forehead on her knuckles. "Whatever it is, why didn't you tell me yourself? Why
these frightening letters?"

She didn't want to open the other envelopes,
but if Libby wasn't lying, if there really was danger,
it meant Kenninghall was at risk. And that left her

with no choice. She had to do something, other than be the coward she was.

She lifted her head and picked up the letter opener, tucked its sharp tip under the fold of the second envelope, but her hand shook and the opener slipped from her trembling fingers. She picked it up, again inserted its point firmly into the envelope—

A car pulled up to the front of the house.

She looked out her window in time to see Yates Lang get out of his car and walk unhurriedly to her front door. She'd forgotten her appointment with him, and he was at least twenty minutes early.

In spite of Morgan's warning she be careful in her dealings with Yates, she was grateful for the distraction—the need for delay. She took some deep breaths to calm herself, slipped Milo's first letter back into its envelope, and slid all the letters into her sweater pocket.

She headed downstairs, the weight of her world swinging like lead ingots against her hip.

Chapter 11

The front door of Kenninghall swung open, and Yates looked down at Hannah. Clad in jeans and an oversize black sweater, she looked tired and pale. Nothing like the woman he'd seen last night. But then, that woman was going out with Greff. He had a way of making women shine when it was important to him.

"You're early," she said.

He couldn't tell from her tone whether it mattered or not. After his conversation with Greff, he couldn't wait to leave the apartment. He'd needed the long drive to think, to plan. "I can come back."

"No. It's fine." She stepped back to let him in. "Would you like a cup of coffee?"

He was drowning in the stuff already. "Sure."

He followed her into the kitchen. Huge. He scanned. Hanging copper pots. A sideboard loaded with dishes. Fireplace with a couple of wingbacks in front of it. A long table dominated the room.

The whole place, except for the chairs, looked medieval. Not a fridge, stove, or oven in sight. Clever.

She gestured to a stool at the table and he took it, watched as she poured two cups of coffee at a side counter.

Other than her tinkering with the coffee, the house was draped in silence. No TV on. No radio. Nothing. And there were no road sounds. Where he lived, in downtown Seattle, the noise seldom stopped. This place was eerie.

She made no effort at conversation, nor did she smile. Yates figured she was either used to the unearthly quiet, or so preoccupied she was unaware of it.

He gestured with his right hand, his intent to encompass the house. "I have the feeling I've stepped back about a hundred years."

"Close. A hundred and nine. It was built by a businessman from Seattle. He was English, so he copied the eighteenth-century English country style." She spoke the words as if she'd said them a thousand time.

He struggled on. "It's in remarkable condition."

"It's been completely restored."

"By Milo Biehle? The man with the cars."

"Yes. When Milo bought it, it had been empty for years."

"And you? Did you help with it?"

"Not really. I came . . . later."

When she didn't offer more, he asked, "How many rooms are there?"

"Forty-three." She carried two coffees to where he sat, placed one in front of him, then sat opposite him, and held her own mug as if to warm her hands. When she continued to look past him as though he weren't there, he was tempted to snap his fingers in her face.

"Lot of work to keep up, I guess."

"Yes. It is."

Inwardly, he groaned. He wasn't exactly a rap artist, and damned if the woman wasn't acting like a puppet without a master. Then she surprised him.

"Would you like a tour?"

"Great." Yates knew his enthusiastic response was more gratitude for her giving him extra time than seeing the house. He needed to get to know this woman and that meant spending time with her. It wasn't going to be easy.

"Milo was very proud of Kenninghall."

"With good reason, by the looks of it."

She glanced around the comfortable kitchen, her expression wistful. "Yes. He loved showing it."

"You miss him."

For the first time, she lifted her gaze to meet his. "Very much," she said. "He was my best friend. Death doesn't change that."

Yates figured death changed everything, but he kept his mouth shut. For a moment it looked as though she might cry; instead, she smiled faintly. "Sorry," she said. "I still get emotional when I think about him."

"Sure." He drank some coffee. The woman was hurting. It was obvious, but emotional landscapes of the female kind, he didn't navigate well. He thought about Greff, how easily he'd take advantage of this kind of pain, turn it to his advantage. If Yates was smart, he'd do the same. Ever since he'd discovered Hallam and Greff were one and the same, he'd had one goal. Keep an eye on the bastard, and make sure Anne Chapman's investigation didn't result in charges.

"You can take your coffee with you if you'd like," she said, nodding at his cup.

"No," He pushed the coffee cup aside. "I've actually had my quota already."

"Me, too." She stood. "Let's go, then."

They were on the third floor.

Yates had lost count of the bedrooms on the second and third floors; the place was a maze of them. There were two music rooms, one for private study, one for performance, and a host of other rooms he couldn't imagine any use for. And every one of them was packed with antiques, most of them draped in white sheets. Kenninghall, except for the lived-in areas, was a giant warehouse. Yates knew nothing about antiques, and the number of them in the house overwhelmed him, but he recognized quality when he saw it. Stella would go nuts in this place.

Hannah answered his questions politely, explained the nature of Milo Biehle's clientele, small and exclusive, how he traveled all over the world for his pieces. And when asked, she could describe any one of them in detail, value, origin, and history. Yates was intrigued—with Hannah Stuart. And he couldn't figure out why. If there was a word to describe her, it would be bleak. Her soft voice was husky, but monotone. She seldom skirted a smile.

They were starting down again when he stopped at an odd, arched door at the end of the third-floor hall. "What's in here?" He turned the handle. Locked.

For the first time in the half hour or so they'd been touring the house, Hannah hesitated, stared at the door as if it were the first time she'd laid eyes on it. He saw her swallow hard.

"Sorry. Am I out of bounds?"

She blinked. "No. Not anymore. It's a chapel. Milo's chapel."

"I see." He didn't see at all. He thought private chapels had been left back in the Middle Ages.

"I've never been in it. Milo never told me not to. I just never felt right about it."

"And now?" He gave her a look of what he hoped was encouragement and tried not to look as interested as he was—in anything and everything to do with Biehle.

Her gaze met his, then he lost her. It was as if he'd evaporated, and her mind had shifted to more important things. She frowned, but as quickly as it creased her forehead, it was replaced with a look of purpose. She turned her back on him and walked down the hall. Stopping at a narrow rectangular table, she ran her hand between it and the wall it abutted. When she pulled out a key, she turned it over in her hand—as if undecided again.

"No," she said, almost to herself. "I don't think Milo will mind if we take a look."

The key turned easily, and the door opened to a windowless room about twenty-five feet long and fourteen feet wide. A single lightbulb dangled from a ceiling wire. The room was uncarpeted and, in contrast to the rooms Yates had just walked through, ghetto stark. No art, no decoration of any kind, just one straight-backed wooden chair sitting in front of an altar, its surface covered in candles of all shapes and sizes. The top of the altar was lumpy with wax. Two rough, benchlike pews sat against each wall, and a brass incense burner hung from the ceiling about a foot above the table.

"What's that smell?" Yates asked, sniffing the air. Woodsy, sharp, with a little bite.

"Sandalwood. It was Milo's favorite."

"Did he spend much time here?" Yates asked. He walked to the altar, wondering what kind of religious nut sat in a room like this burning incense.

"Yes." She came from behind him, and they stood side by side looking at the altar with its mass of burned candles. Hannah reached out to touch a spire of wax. When it broke off, she drew her hand back. "He came here every morning and every night. I can't remember a time he missed. That's why I knew where the key was. I'd seen him retrieve it many times."

"And he didn't change the key's hiding place?"

"No reason to. He knew I'd respect his privacy." She reached across the candles and picked up a framed photograph from the center of the altar. She turned it toward the bulb's dim light and her brow furrowed.

"Something wrong?" he asked.

"Not wrong. Odd." She ran a finger over the figures in the photo—a family of three smiling happily for the camera. "This is a cheap frame from a drugstore or a photography shop and—"

"Uh-huh?"

"The picture looks like the one that came with the frame."

"There's one way to find out. Let me see that."

He turned it over and slipped out the cardboard backing. She was right. A flimsy, badly-colored print came with it. He put the unit together again and handed it to her. "Maybe he intended to put a picture in it and never got around to it."

"Maybe," she said, not looking as if she believed his opinion likely. She stroked her index finger over the images, then carefully centered the frame on its tripod stand. After looking at it for a few moments, she rubbed her arms as if she were cold, although the room was, if anything, overly warm. "If you've seen enough of the house," she said, "why don't I get a jacket, and we'll look at the cars." She didn't wait for him, just turned and walked out of the room.

Something had upset the lady.

Before leaving the chapel, Yates took one last look around. One thing was certain, Biehle was one strange dude.

Hannah walked with Yates to the six-car garage and opened the side door, tried not to think about the disturbing room on the third floor. When she turned on the lights, Yates whistled softly.

"Now this is something," he said, running a hand over the polished front fender of the old Rolls Royce.

Hannah didn't answer, but she followed the path of his hand with her own. She was glad she'd had Meara's nephew come and dust off the cars so they'd be ready for viewing. Milo would have wanted that.

When Yates moved off, stopping to admire each car in turn, she stepped back and stuffed her hands in her pockets. Her fingers closed over the letters, and she had the insane urge to crumple them and throw them in the nearest trash, or better yet, burn them. She wondered again about the chapel, and her spirit chilled. She'd always known Milo was a spiritual man, that he meditated often, and she'd assumed the chapel was for that purpose. But the bare walls, rough-hewn pews, and unadorned altar confused her. Nothing about it—other than the sandalwood—was to Milo's usual, more excessive tastes. And the picture—

"This is a real beauty," Yates said, standing in front of the 1937 Cord.

Hannah shoved the letters deeper into her pocket and thoughts of Milo deeper into her mind. Again she was grateful Yates was here as a diversion from her unwelcome thoughts. She stepped up beside him.

"You're interested, then?"

"I'll say . . . If the price is right."

"I'm sure we can work something out." Until now, Hannah had been undecided about selling any of the cars, but Yates's enthusiasm made up her mind. She'd always believed treasures from the past should be with people who cared about them, and it seemed that Yates did. When he'd first looked at the Cord, his eyes held none of the chilly cynicism she'd noticed when they'd met in Vonecker's waiting area. Instead, they were filled with appreciation, an almost boyish excitement. Despite Morgan's warning about him, she couldn't see harm in selling the man a car. It was just business. Her business, she realized again, still slightly shocked by it.

"Hannah, are you there?" Libby called from the door.

"Yes, I'm here, what is it?"

"There's a call for you. Mrs. King?" Libby came to stand beside them. "She wants to know if you still have that Sheraton display cabinet Milo showed her last year."

Hannah turned to Yates. "Will you excuse me?"

"No problem."

"I'll keep him company," Libby said.

When Hannah finished her call and the necessary paperwork, it was close to noon.

She found Yates and Libby sitting at the kitchen table, eating sandwiches and drinking from tall glasses of milk. They were talking quietly as she entered. Hannah poured herself a cup of coffee and joined them.

"Did you know Yates was a private investigator, Hannah?" Libby asked.

For no reason she could think of, Hannah's hand trembled when she set her mug back on the table. He glanced at her shaking hand, looked away.

"More of a consultant," he corrected. "I work mostly for corporations and legal types, do background checks, some forensic accounting, that kind of thing."

"What's forensic accounting?" Libby asked.

"Boring stuff. You wouldn't be interested."

"Try me." Libby smiled at him. When he smiled back, Hannah's stomach sank. So, they liked each other. Not her concern. Men had always liked Libby—too much and too easily for her own good.

"Okay." Yates leaned back in his chair. "In the case of suspected fraud, for example, it would be a combination of investigating and accounting. You get the enviable job of backtracking through a company's books as well as interviewing their employees. Once you've done that, the trick is to come up with an ironclad report that will stand up in court."

"And you do this for Gerry's firm?" Hannah asked.

"On occasion." He stood then. "Thanks for the lunch, but I'd better get going. When I find a place to stay, I'll call, give you the number. When you've decided on the car price, you can let me know."

"You're staying in La Conner?" Libby stood and pushed her chair under the table.

"Until Thursday. There's another car I want to look at, and I've got to spend some time with a client whose office is just north of here. Figured I could do without the Seattle commute while I was there." He flexed his shoulders and pulled his jacket from the back of his chair. "Maybe you could recommend a place?"

Libby looked at Hannah, her eyes a question. Hannah knew exactly what she was thinking. Kenninghall had rooms enough to host a small convention. It would only be good manners to ask Yates to stay here.

But while she hesitated, Libby spoke. "Why don't you stay here? There's tons of room."

To his credit, Yates turned to Hannah. "I doubt Hannah needs a houseguest quite yet."

"No, it's fine. Your staying here makes sense," Hannah said, still uncertain how she felt about it. "The garret room on the third floor would be good, I think." She stood.

Yates looked down at her. "Thanks. I appreciate

it. Now, can I ask another favor?" His gaze held a hint of amusement.

"Of course." Hannah's chest tightened oddly.

Yates grinned and stuffed his hands in his pockets. "Mind if I spend a little more time under the hoods of those beautiful ladies in the garage?"

Unaccountably, Hannah blushed. "Not at all." She brushed some loose hair behind her ear, then headed for the door. Once there she turned back, ill at ease suddenly. "I should tell you that, uh, Morgan Greff will be coming for dinner Wednesday. You're welcome to join us, but if you'd rather not . . ." She waited for his reaction, saw his eyes darken.

Then he shrugged, the gesture both nonchalant and stubborn. "I'll pass on that. Thanks."

His words and his body language said there was a piece of shared history between these men, and it wasn't pleasant.

Connections, Hannah thought, how complicated they were; Yates and Morgan didn't like each other, Yates liked Libby, Libby didn't like Morgan, and Hannah didn't trust Libby. It made the brain hurt. But in spite of it all, she looked forward to Morgan coming to Kenninghall for dinner. She didn't want anything to spoil that, not Yates's opinion or Libby's.

Again she fingered the letters in her pocket. She would leave them until later, when she was alone and could think clearly. She owed Milo that.

Yates's thoughts churned all the way back to the garage

Greff. Here. Damn it to hell!

Considering his idea was to keep Greff in the dark until he figured out what was going on, Hannah's cozy little dinner party wasn't going to help.

Greff was going to love seeing Yates trot upstairs to bed.

He cursed again, would've done it aloud if it weren't for Libby being there. She'd insisted on walking with him to see the cars. And she'd been looking at him strangely ever since he'd told her what he did for a living. She'd been sizing him up, and he couldn't figure out why.

There was nothing sexual about her interest— he'd have picked up on that. It was more a stew of puzzled frowns and internal nail-biting. Yates was curious, but patient. Sooner or later she'd let him in on it. He hoped it would be worthwhile.

The minute the garage door closed behind them, she leaned on it and said, "Are you on a, uh, case right now, Yates?"

"No," he lied, opened the driver's side door on the '37 Cord and peered in at the worn leather bench seat. He really did love this car! Up close and personal, it was a beauty. He looked up. "Think we can have some light?"

She hit the switch near the door, and he saw she was chewing on her lower lip.

"Why? Got a job for me?" He ran a hand over the leather backrest, determined not to look at her.

He waited.

"It's about Hannah. There's something wrong, and I don't know what to do, how to handle it. I owe her so much, but—" She stopped. "She'd probably kill me if she knew I was talking to you about it." She raised worried eyes to his. "But you are a professional, aren't you? Code of ethics? Keep things confidential? That kind of thing."

"Most of the time."

She gave him a frustrated look.

"Kidding, just kidding. As a matter of fact, I take what I do damned seriously. So, if you've got something you want to say, say it. It won't show up in tomorrow's *Enquirer.*"

"Hannah is in some kind of trouble," she blurted out. "Danger, actually, and it has to do with Milo's death. And unless I'm wrong, it also has to do with this Greff character who's sniffing around her." She pushed herself away from the door. "I'm guessing about that last part. So far he's done nothing other than show up at exactly the right time. But . . ." Confusion settled in her brow.

"But?" he prodded.

She walked up to him, joined him by leaning her backside against the car. "This might take awhile."

"Okay." He settled back, gave her his full attention. "I'm not going anywhere. So shoot."

"How much do you know about Hannah?"

"Nothing. Other than she's just inherited Biehle's business, and she's got some damn fine cars for sale."

Libby looked straight ahead as if the beginning of her story was at the end of a long road. "Dad was a widower for ten years when Hannah came along. I was seventeen when she married him. She was twenty-two—Dad was fifty." She clasped both her hands together in front of her. "Hannah and I never hit it off. Mostly because of me. Sex, drugs, and rock and roll—the story of my life." She gave him a sideways glance. "I'm a recovering addict, you know." She said it calmly, as if she were telling him she was an Irish Catholic.

Yates nodded. There wasn't really a response to that kind of declaration. And he was busy imagining a twenty-two-year-old girl marrying a guy twenty-eight years her senior.

"About the time they got married, I was going seriously off the rails." She stepped away from the car. "We tried, Hannah and me, for Dad's sake and Christopher's—"

"Who's Christopher?"

"Hannah's son. My half brother. He was two when—let's not go there right now, okay?"

"Your call." Yates sensed pain, but figured her ramble would take her where she wanted to go eventually.

"Anyway, I couldn't keep it together, and by the time . . ." She drew in a heavy breath, then let it out.

Yates watched and waited.

"By the time of the . . . murders, I was wrecked, verging on becoming the usual by-product of drugs, human waste. When Hannah called—"

"Back up. Murders. What murders?"

"Dad and Christopher's. They were gunned down in a robbery attempt on the antique store he and Hannah owned. Five years ago. The kids, a couple of teenagers, according to a witness, were never identified. Dad died instantly. Chris lasted a week."

"Jesus," he said. "I'm sorry. It must have been hell."

"Yeah." Her look was grim, darkly humorous. "But lucky for me I was anesthetized. Not so lucky

for Hannah, who spent a week watching her little
boy die and only left his side long enough to bury
my dad."

"Where were you during all this?"

"You don't want to know, and I don't particularly want to tell you."

"Fair enough."

"But what I really don't want is for anything bad
to happen to Hannah." She stopped. "And neither
would Dad. He loved her. Called her the woman
with the million-dollar smile." Libby's voice broke.
"She made him happy for the first time since Mom
died. And I—"

He crossed his arms.

"I screwed it up big-time. I resented everything
about her. Her ambition and drive, the way she
was always so organized, working in the shop, looking after Christopher. I even hated the way she
smiled and constantly joked with my dad." She
laughed harshly. "But no matter how much of a
bitch I was, she took it. Kept trying to make things
right."

"And now you want to make things right for her."

"Yes. And for my dad. I know it's too late, but it's
all I can do."

"And what makes you think she's in danger?"

"Milo told me." While Libby told him about the
strange phone calls from Biehle that had brought
her to Kenninghall, and her suspicions about
Morgan Greff—based on what she called her "very
experienced" gut when it came to men—Yates listened in silence.

"And what exactly do you want me to do about
it?" he asked when she stopped.

"You said you do background checks. So can

you do one on Greff?" She rubbed one hand over the back of another. "But the thing is, I don't have any—"

"Money?"

She looked sheepish, nodded. "I can't pay you. At least not right away."

"That's okay. I'll see what I can dig up. And while I do that, you keep an eye on Hannah."

"I will." She kissed him lightly on the cheek. "Thanks, Yates."

"Thank me when I've got something. Now you'd better go back in the house or Hannah will begin to wonder what's going on." He wasn't about to go into his own shared history with Greff. No point. And nothing she'd said indicated a link between Biehle and Greff other than the cousin thing. And there was no way Greff was sniffing around for money. Biehle's holdings would be small change for Greff. So, what was he doing here? What did he want from Hannah Stuart?

He sat in the Cord a long time. He needed information, and he needed it now. Trouble was, he didn't know what the hell he was looking for. And he was running out of time.

And judging from what Libby told him, so was Hannah.

Chapter 12

At six o'clock, Yates, showered and shaved, paced the carpeted floor of Kenninghall's third-floor garret room. The house was its usual eerie quiet, and there was neither a TV nor a radio in his room. Nothing at all to distract him from his thoughts. He guessed Hannah was in the room below his, because he'd heard a shower, and he knew Libby was in La Conner and wouldn't be back until dinner.

For about the millionth time, he went over what Libby had told him this afternoon. He rubbed his neck, and his stomach tightened into a complex knot of confusion and . . . what the hell, he might as well call it as he saw it. Pity. It had been a long time since Yates had felt anything for anyone. He just didn't get close enough to let it happen. But he felt sorry for Hannah Stuart. To lose a husband and son that way . . . He didn't want to think about it.

The shriek rent the room, rising from the floor as if from Hades itself. Yates's breath stopped and he stared dumbly at his stocking feet. Another scream, this one a high-pitched howl of pain.

Hannah!

He yanked his bedroom door open, heard it crash shut as he bolted down the hall, grabbed the rail for purchase, and took the steps two at a time. When he got to her door, he didn't stop to knock.

She was crumpled in the corner near the window, her moans punctuated by gasps for breath. Her eyes were glazed. She started to pant. He knew she was hyperventilating, and that if he didn't do something, and quick, she'd pass out.

He grabbed her by the shoulders and pulled her to her feet, shook her roughly. "What's wrong?" He shook her again.

She blinked to focus, looked at him. He'd have bet a bundle she didn't see him. She gulped for air, breathing in gasps and spasms. She didn't fight him, but her body was rigid as if she were braced against a freezing wind.

He pulled her to him, stroked the back of her head. "It's okay. It's okay. Shush now."

Without warning, she jumped back, eyes wild, one hand pushed hard against his shoulder as though to ward him off. "No," she screamed. "No, it's not okay. It will never be 'okay.' " She closed her eyes, her every breath shallower than the last. "Can't you see? It was a lie. Everything. He made my life a lie. He made me care . . . for him"—she spat out the words—"a murderer. A child killer."

"What are you talking about?"

Crazed eyes lifted to his. "They have to be told, you know. Everyone has to be told. It can't wait. No." She lifted her left hand. It was shaking, clasp-

ing some crumpled paper, her grip on it so fierce
the bones of her knuckles jutted out like broken
teeth. "And I have proof. I'll get them. This time I'll
get them. All of them. Murderers. Child killers."
She smiled, an ugly smile. Paired with her wide-
eyed glare, it was a lunatic's grin, fearsome and fa-
natic. "I've got proof, you know. This time I have
proof. I'll get them, get them all."

Yates had no idea what she was talking about,
but he didn't need any more clues to tell him she
wasn't in her right mind. He reached for her, determined to get her and whatever was going on
here under control. She tried to dart past him, but
he was too fast for her. She struggled, wild-eyed
and raving, under his firm grip. He didn't let go,
and then with a suddenness that stunned him, she
collapsed in his arms.

Hell!

He took a deep breath. She was a dead weight.
He dragged her as gently as he could to her bed,
settled her on it, and put a cover over her. He put
his ear to her mouth. She was breathing easier
now; he decided to let her be. He couldn't help if
he didn't know what the hell was going on, and
any idiot could see the papers in her hand held
the key. She still held them in a witch's grip, so he
sat on the edge of the bed and pried them out of
her fingers, opening one at a time.

He took another look at Hannah, brushed some
stray hair off her forehead, and started to read. In
less than ten seconds, his breathing was as frenzied
as Hannah's had been.

* * *

Greff clicked off the phone, and with no hesitation clicked it on again. Redialed. If the woman didn't pick up, he'd—

"Hello."

"Lena." The surroundings of his luxurious hotel suite faded at the sound of her voice.

He heard her pull in a breath, let it out. "Morgan. What's going on?"

"If you'd get your tight little ass back here, you'd find out, wouldn't you?" He sat on the edge of the hotel room bed, suddenly tired. Hell, he was probably getting some kind of bug, the stress he was under. He heard a muffled sound coming through the phone. Voices? If the bitch was cheating on him, he'd damn soon know about it. "What was that?" he asked, running a hand over his taut abs, suddenly feeling a distinct burning in his gut. He was getting sick. Probably a damn ulcer.

"My cat."

"What cat? You don't have a damn cat."

"I do now. Got him yesterday and he's absolutely perfect. Sleek as sin and dark as hell. Just like you, baby." She laughed. "I adore him."

"Yeah, and what are you going to do with him when you head back Stateside?"

"I'll leave him in the hotel room. Someone will take care of him."

"That's some kind of adoration you've got going there." He swallowed a stomach enzyme and chased it with water. "It's time you came home. Make a reservation."

"I figured next week sometime. I've got a couple of meetings set up. With those buyers I mentioned?"

"Forget the buyers, Lena." Christ, didn't the woman listen to a word he said?

"One more score, then——"

"We have to take care of Vonecker."

Silence.

"You hear me?" Greff said.

"I heard you." She lowered her voice. "Where? When?"

"Soon."

"How?" He caught the excitement in her voice. His Lena loved this kind of shit. She was probably getting wet just thinking about it.

"Random act of violence. They happen."

"And who——?"

"I'll take care of him myself. Less risky that way." The last thing Greff wanted was to sign on some contract idiot, create another possible knot in his noose.

Lena went back to business. "We need him, Morgan. What the hell are we going to do now?"

"We don't need anyone. Not anymore."

"Ah, yes . . . The retirement plan. I keep forgetting."

He heard her nail clicking on the handset. "You have a problem with this?" he asked.

"No. Whatever you want. You know it'll be fine with me."

"Yeah? Then what I want is for you to bring it on home, sweetheart. We've got business to take care of. First we get our hands on those letters, then we head for the Caymans." He rubbed his stomach. "For good, Lena. For goddamn good." He turned off the phone, rubbed his stomach again. Damn pills hadn't done a thing. He hurt like hell.

He stared at the phone in his hand. *Come home, Lena,* he said silently. *I need you. The damn walls are closing in on me.*

Abruptly he stood. Had there been someone tapping his brain at that moment, he'd have to kill him. Need? No way. Pent-up juice, maybe. And the Stuart woman would take care of that. Morgan didn't do *need*. What he did was *stress*. His problem was a dead cousin and a few scribbles on paper.

Then he thought about the cops, peering through microscopes at Vonecker's battered brain, picking fiber from his coat, wading through his damn blood looking for clues. Not that he'd leave any, but . . . shit, a million guys had said that before, and they were all on death row. Maybe it was a mistake, doing the job himself. He paced. He'd thought it less risky that way, but maybe he was wrong.

What the hell was wrong with him? Worrying like a rookie. Lena said he was getting paranoid. Maybe she was right. He stuck out his chin, rolled his head around his shoulders. Loosened up. Hell, there wasn't anything here he couldn't handle— he was at his best when he was cornered, always had been.

He padded across the dense carpet and headed for the shower, his third for the day. He turned the water on hot enough to scald and stepped in, felt better immediately. He'd have the damn letters soon enough. All he needed to do was keep himself—and Miranda—alive until then.

And fuck Hannah Stuart.

All Yates had to do was destroy the letters. With them gone, Hannah had no proof and Greff was safe. Home free. Yates damn near brought up his lunch at the thought.

Greff always made it home free.

But Jesus! Murder? Let him get away with murder?

He folded the papers, rubbed his index finger along the furrow in his brow. There had to be another way. But right now he couldn't see it. All he could think about was Stella. She deserved her shot, but if Hannah followed through, made Milo's story public, there'd be no chance of that.

"Give those to me." Hannah snatched the letters from his hand. He'd been so preoccupied with them, he hadn't noticed her coming to.

She sat up and stuffed them in her pocket. Damn it, he should have been quicker.

"Are you okay?" He forced a coolness in his voice he didn't feel, took in her sheet-white face, her trembling hands. Her stare when she looked at him was glacial.

"You read the letters," she stated.

He nodded.

She got off the bed. He stayed sitting on its edge. She started to pace, then stopped and turned to look at him. "You know this man."

He knew she meant Greff. He nodded again.

"Did you know he was a murderer?"

"No." And that was the truth. When they'd parted company years ago, Greff was strictly white collar, in the business of laundering money and busy covering his ass ten ways to Sunday. But then Yates hadn't known he was bringing young girls in from Asia either. None of which changed a damn thing. He had to get control of the letters. Then he'd figure out how to handle things.

"And you," he said. "You had no idea of Biehle's involvement."

"Did I know I was living with a child killer, you

mean?" Her eyes were round in her face, burning coals against her ashen skin. The eyes of a zealot. "You think I'd be with a man who'd do that, gun down a family for a few dollars and some beer? You think I could live with him knowing that?" Her voice rose went shrill. For a moment he thought she'd cry. She didn't.

"According to his letter to you and his confession letter, Biehle didn't kill anyone. It was Greff who had the gun. Greff who pulled the trigger. Biehle was—what?—fourteen?"

"My God! You're making excuses for him. I can't believe it."

"What are you going to do?" he asked. It seemed as good a time as any to get a hint of her intentions.

She pulled the papers from her pocket, waved them at him. "I'm taking these to the police. What do you think I'm going to do."

"What about Biehle's mother, Miranda? She'll have to know."

She raised her chin. "I don't care."

Yates got up from the bed, walked over, and gripped her by the shoulders. He lowered his head to look into her blazing eyes. "I think you do. She's an old woman. Why spoil her last days?"

She started to speak. Stopped. Her face a mixture of hate and confusion.

"Read the letter again," he suggested, buying time, trying to think of a move. "Now that you're calmer. Then make your decision."

"It won't change my mind."

"Just do it." He took the letter from her hand and walked her over to her bed. "Sit down, and take it slow." He pressed her down to a sitting position on its edge. She gave him a stubborn glare. "We'll read together." He sat beside her, took the letters from her hands, and smoothed them across her lap.

Dear Hannah:

I have a story to tell you and it is a painful one. It is the story of the event that shaped my life, robbed me of all self-respect, and rendered me unworthy of love, family, and friends. I have often thought had my life been different—unmarred—you and I might have had more between us than friendship. But I knew you could never love a man who was the mirror image of those who took away the lives of your beloved Will and Chris.

For I, like those brutal cowards, am a murderer.

These are my sins. Sins for which it is impossible to atone. Sins which can never be forgiven by anyone other than God. And given my decision to not confess my crime, I suspect even his forgiveness is unlikely. I go into the flames with no hope of understanding, either by God, or yourself.

But even in this dilemma I must ask your help.

On August 23, 1963, my cousin, Morgan William Greff, and myself, Milo Fredrick Biehle, shot and killed a family of three. The family, whom I later identified from the newspaper reportage (clippings are included) was named Ramirez, and included Julio, his wife Mirana, and their infant son, Joseph. In my defense, I did not go into the store with a gun, nor did I fire one. That grisly task was carried out by Morgan. Why was I there? I have asked myself that a thousand times. And the only answer I can come up with is my stupid, illogical hero worship of my cousin, three years older than myself, and every-

thing I was not at the stumbling, awkward age of fourteen. Morgan thought up the corner store robbery, said it would be fun, make a man of me. We would walk in, he would pretend *to have a gun in his pocket, and I would demand one hundred dollars from the till. We wouldn't be greedy, he said, because all we wanted was a few bucks and a couple of cases of beer—and the thrill.*

Morgan liked thrills.

It went horribly wrong.

Mr. Ramirez was not easily intimidated. Not surprising really, when all he faced was a pulpy, sweating, spectacled teenager, stuttering orders and looking as if all he wanted to do was bolt—which was true.

Morgan, according to our plan, was to do nothing but stand back, poke his finger against his pocket, and look as threatening as possible. But when Mr. Ramirez laughed at us, told us to get our "sorry asses" out of his store, and reached under the counter—for what I'll never know—Morgan stepped in front of me and fired. At what seemed precisely that moment Mrs. Ramirez stepped through the doorway behind the counter holding their ten-month-old son. Morgan fired again, and again. In seconds the Ramirez family was dead, blood was everywhere, and Morgan was dragging me out of the store. We ran for what seemed like hours.

And I have not stopped since, my conscience in steady pursuit.

Morgan's conscience remained untroubled. In his warped thinking, he killed in self-defense. Mr. Ramirez threatened him, he said, and he refused to be threatened, ever. Not only did he deceive me by carrying a loaded weapon, he showed absolutely no remorse about using it to slaughter an innocent family. I remember his saying that he felt powerful, as if the killing had energized him, made him more than he was before. He believed if you could kill someone, you could do anything.

Why didn't I step forward? Confess? Pay the price for my crime?

Because of Miranda. You know, Hannah, that my father abandoned me and my mother when I was very young. I have no memory of him. She was left without funds, unskilled, and alone, with the responsibility of a young child. She took a hair-dressing course, turned out to be very good at it, and provided for us by—as she describes it—"cutting a trillion tons of hair." It couldn't have been easy. But she adored me and I her. When the crime was reported in the newspaper, Mother was shocked, disgusted that anything like this could happen in our own neighborhood. Sickened, as was everyone else, to think that someone could kill a family in cold blood, a family that included a "babe in arms."

I could not tell her I was that someone, Hannah. I just could not.

She didn't deserve the pain of knowing that the son she loved, the son she'd worked so hard to raise, was an accomplice to murder. I resolved then to keep my ugly secret until Mother would not be hurt by it—until after she died. I made a vow to God that when that day came, I would tell the whole truth about that August night. But to protect myself, I had to also protect Morgan.

I just never thought I'd go first! Stupid, I know. And now I must entrust the secret to you. I'm sure, given your own tragedy, your first instinct is to turn these papers over to the police. I beg you to wait.

Miranda is nearing ninety—it is much too late to
break her heart.

Letter number three is my detailed confession.
Will it be enough to incriminate Morgan? I believe so—and so does he. You have often commented
on my obsessive note-taking, Hannah. Well, it began
after the murders. I wanted to remember everything.
You could say it was my small way of ensuring justice for the Ramirez family. In my more official confession letter, I have recorded every detail of that
night, giving a full account of my part in the murders, as well as Morgan's.

Morgan and I haven't seen each other in over
thirty-five years, but he is well aware of my plan
and what these papers contain. I saw no harm in
letting him sweat, knowing both my mother and I
were safe as long as he didn't know the whereabouts
of the information. But now that I am gone he will
be desperate—and dangerous. Be assured he will
do everything in his power to ensure my deathbed
confession dies with me.

Again I beg you, Hannah—not for me, but for
Miranda—to wait until she is gone before going to
the police. She is an old woman. I'm pleading with
you not to encumber her final days with the knowledge that her "beloved" son is a murderer. She
surely doesn't deserve the pain.

When you are done reading these pages, I suggest you put them back where they came from.
Morgan has forever been in the background of my
life watching and waiting. When he shows up—
and I'm certain he will—be extremely careful. Your
safest course of action is to feign innocence and
deny all knowledge of the letters.

I know as you read this letter any affection you

might have felt toward me is gone. It is a thought that makes my heart weep. But I am left with no choice. Hate me as you must, Hannah, but please, please *think about Miranda.*

And it must be said. I have loved you, Hannah. In all ways, for all my days.

At fourteen, in an adolescent effort to atone for my crime—my mortal sin—I made a vow of celibacy. I kept that vow. You were the only woman who ever made me regret making it.

It was God's cruel joke, bringing us together by taking away the people you cared about most in this world, Will and your beautiful son, Chris. You were so bright with love, so full of expectations for your life, your family. At first I thought he'd given me an unexpected second chance, that by helping you through your tragedy I could atone in some small way for the deaths of the Ramirez family. But in the end it was a punishment. I came to love and desire the one woman I could never have, never dream of sullying with my love.

Forgive me, Hannah. And I beg you to give the same care and kindness to Miranda as you always so willingly gave to me. Unlike myself, it is a kindness she deserves.

> *Yours in life and in death,*
> *Milo*

Chapter 13

Hannah rested the papers on the bed beside her, and sat still as stone. Reading her letter a second time was worse than the first; shock morphed into something sick, irrevocable.

She had no idea what she was feeling, if she felt anything at all. Her throat was tight, hot with fury and tears. Her stomach was leaden, as if every bite she'd ever eaten lay congealed there. Her head was full of shadows and sharp lights. She couldn't see. She couldn't think. She stared ahead, unblinking.

"Here."

Yates forced a glass of water into her hand. She didn't want water. Her lips were dry-sealed as if they'd never open again.

"Drink it."

She drank, sipping obediently in response to his urgent tone, while her heart rammed her rib cage with the thrust and sway of a wrecking ball.

Thud, thud . . . it pounded, laying waste to five years of meticulously constructed defenses.

Thud, thud . . . smashing through, razing the dense wall of grief that surrounded the bone, blood, and bile that was her life.

A lie. All of it—a lie. Herself the biggest liar of them all. Stupid, weak beyond forgiveness.

Her hand shook and water sloshed onto her skirt. She grasped the glass with both hands, held it tight to her knees.

Milo, a murderer! The man she'd loved as a brother, admired as a man. She'd given her life to him, willingly placed it in his soiled hands, no questions asked, no expectations laid. In doing so, she'd betrayed Will and Christopher. Her stomach contracted as though punched.

She'd entrusted her soul to a killer so she wouldn't have to think or take control of her unpredictable emotions. And she'd allowed Milo to use her grief, her weakness, to appease his own guilty conscience.

She'd been a fool, a stupid, subservient fool.

"Hannah, drink the water."

She stood, threw the crystal glass across the room with maniacal force. It shattered against a seventeenth-century armoire. Her breath came in short uneven gasps. She willed it to level. "I don't want water," she stammered, the words like ice shards in her throat. "I want my . . . I want my . . ." She flattened her palms against her temples, squeezed to hold the remains of her sanity in place. She didn't know what she wanted. That was her goddamn problem! If she could have screamed, she would have; instead she moaned, then swallowed, constricted the muscles in her throat until she could scarcely draw a breath.

"Maybe you should sit down." Yates put a hand on her shoulder.

She lifted dry eyes to meet his. He looked nervous, ill at ease, but his big hand was warm, the pressure firm.

Hannah hadn't been touched in a long time, not since . . . *she'd kissed Morgan Greff.* Oh God! Her stomach heaved; she was going to be sick. And she was freezing. Still she couldn't make herself move. She heard Yates murmur a curse.

"Come here." Yates tugged her toward him, held her close. "This has to be tough for you," he said. "And I'm not the best at consoling women, but right now I'm all you've got." He put his hand at the back of her head, pulled it to his shoulder, and stroked her hair. "Take a minute or two. Get it together."

Hannah, wracked by the effort to hold back tears, and stiff as an oak, fisted her hands in his cotton shirt and held on. She'd take his offer of a minute—because what she did not want to do was cry herself a river. She was done with tears.

Yates edged her back toward the bed. "All you need is time to think. To assimilate." He released his embrace, slid his hands down from her shoulders to her hands. Holding them loosely, he said, "Why not lie down for awhile."

Hannah pulled her hands from his, straightened her fingers until they hurt, and shoved them in her sweater pockets. "Lie down? That's about the last thing I want to do. Among the rest of the mess in my mind is the ugly fact that I've invited Morgan Greff here—to Kenninghall."

"Yes, you have," he said calmly.

An image of their cozy dinner came to mind, him holding her hand, her letting him. Was no one who they appeared to be? Panic made her voice rise. "You read the letter, the man's a killer. He shot down a family in cold blood."

Yates took a step back, gave her an unreadable look. "It wasn't your family, Hannah."

She gaped at him, for a moment too stunned to speak. "You know?"

"I know some." He didn't add the obligatory I'm-so-sorry that she'd come to expect. His eyes said it as his gaze held hers. He touched her cheek.

She turned her face away. "Who told you?"

"Libby."

"She had no right."

"They were her family, too. So I don't expect she'd agree with you on that." He tilted his head. "But I'd like to hear it from you."

"Why should I tell you anything?"

"Tell. Don't tell. It's all the same to me. I figured—us being in this together—some sharing of histories might be a good idea."

"Together?" she echoed. "Why would you think that?" She looked up, into his cool, intelligent eyes. She'd have to be wary of this man, was her fleeting thought before he took a couple of steps away from her. "What's any of this to you?"

"We both read Biehle's letters. We both have information that could put Morgan Greff away for the rest of his miserable life. And we each have a reason to hold off before doing that."

"I don't understand."

"I wouldn't expect you to. There's some explaining I need to do." He walked to the window, turned his back to her, and stared down at the driveway. "But the main thing is, we need to get our acts together before he comes to Kenninghall."

"He won't be coming to Kenninghall. You don't think I'd—"

"I don't think you have any choice in the matter. He'll come to Kenninghall invited or uninvited. The smart thing to do is let the dinner invitation stand," he said, turning to face her. "Right now he *suspects* you have access to Biehle's confession, but he can't be sure. Best you leave him in that limbo as long as possible. Once he knows you've read it, you're a threat." He crossed his arms, leaned casually against the window sash. "He'll react badly to that."

"I don't care how he reacts. I'll do what I have to do."

"I'm sure you will, but right now, you don't have to do anything—other than use your head."

"Did I miss something here, because I don't remember asking for your opinion," she said.

"Free to damsels in distress."

"I'm not—"

"Look, we're in this together, like it or not." He left the window and walked toward her.

"You keep saying that, so I'll say—again—I barely know you. And I can't imagine why I should take your advice about anything."

"We can fix that. Let's take a walk, get some fresh air. I'll tell you my story, and you'll tell me yours." He took her hand, tugged gently. "Come on, I think better when I'm moving."

So did Hannah. And she did need to think—first about how to tell Miranda, and then about the steps she'd need to take to make sure Greff paid

for what he done. She needed everything organized. "I'll get a jacket and meet you downstairs."

Yates went to the door; his hand on the knob, he
turned. "Would you like me to keep those letters?"
He gestured with his chin to the papers on Hannah's
bed. "It might be safer."

Her gaze shot to his. "No. I'll deal with them."

"See you downstairs then."

When Yates was out of sight, Hannah crossed
the hall to Milo's room and put the letters back in
the hidden drawer. That done, she turned, leaned
against the bureau, and surveyed the room. She
didn't see the freshly installed four poster—Milo's
Scrooge bed—she saw a deathbed and remembered . . . night after night waking up, rushing to
the cold, gleaming metal cradling Milo's failing
body, terrified this night would be the last, the
endless pills, pain, and relentless assault of his disease, her aching sense of loss when he'd died.

Fool!

Dear God, Milo, how could you—

It was as if a clammy hand were squeezing her
heart. Tighter and tighter until it wrung out all
warmth and affection. The last vestige of love. Given
the vacancy, something grim and ugly took its place.

She couldn't touch Milo now; he'd never pay for
what he'd done. But Morgan Greff would. She'd
make sure of it.

She turned her back on the mythic deathbed
and walked out of the room. She'd hear what Yates
had to say, but nothing would keep her from doing
what she had to do. The murder might be forty
years old, but the need for retribution was now.

Back in her room, she slipped on a jacket, then
went downstairs to meet Yates. He was already out-

side, sitting on the top step of the porch, hands clasped between his knees, staring at some distant horizon. His expression was deeply melancholic. Caught by the afternoon wind, dark strands of hair swirled over his face; he seemed oblivious to them.

A porch board creaked, and he got to his feet with an athlete's grace. "Better button up. It's not warm."

"I'm fine. Let's go." Hannah was through being the passive receptacle for other's instructions— whether it was to button up, drink up, or shut up. A fact Yates Lang was about to find out.

For a time they walked in silence. When Hannah couldn't take it anymore, she stopped, turned, and confronted him. "You wanted to talk?"

He stuffed his hands into his windbreaker pockets. "Yeah."

Silence.

"Well, talk then." Hannah's directness surprised even her. But it felt good. It felt right.

He rubbed his temple. "Having trouble getting started."

She shot him a look, knew she looked annoyed, didn't care.

"Let's keep walking." He strode off.

After a second or two, Hannah followed.

When she caught up with him, he began, "I'm not exactly who you think I am."

She stopped again, shook her head. "It seems *no one* is who I think they are." She stared at him, hard. "So . . . who exactly are you, Yates Lang?"

"I *do* work for Simpson, Chapman, and Vonecker." He said this defensively, as if a partial truth would be enough salve for the lies to come.

She waited.

"But I didn't come to Kenninghall to buy a car."

"Go on." The rising wind blew her long unbound hair across her chin. She brushed it aside.

"There's a good chance your Morgan Greff is involved in the importation of young women . . . children for the sex trade." His words were clipped, dropped like hot stones, as if he couldn't get them out of his mouth fast enough.

And they stunned Hannah. "He's not 'my Morgan Greff,' " she mumbled, denying what she could, trying to grasp the rest. "The sex trade? Children?"

"Yes. The evidence is strong—but not conclusive. Yet."

She felt sick, as if the dirty business Yates talked about was manure and she was hip deep in it. "All the more reason for me to get the letters to the proper authorities—sooner rather than later. Kill two birds with one stone."

"No. What you'd be killing would be any chance for us to find and charge all the other people involved. Greff might be put away, but the rest of them would carry on. Which would mean more shiploads of kids handed over to perverts to be used as . . . God knows how they use them."

Hannah's stomach clenched. "Who exactly is this 'us' you're referring to?"

"Anne Chapman and myself. She hired me because it looks as if her partner, Vonecker, is heavily involved."

"Gerry Vonecker?" She felt her eyes widen. *So he was after the letters. He needed to protect Greff.* Even Milo's lawyer wasn't who she'd thought he was.

"Yes." Yates gripped her by the shoulders. "So what I'm asking you for is time. I know Greff should be put away. Hell, he should be put down. But he's more than a murderer, he's a man who trades in human flesh. Kids. He's the worst kind of scum." Yates glanced away, then back. "But he's not the only scum in the pond. These operations involve networks of pedophiles. With some time and luck, we can get them all."

"How much luck? How much time?"

"A month, maybe two. If we're *lucky.*" He smiled but it was so slight, gone so fast, she might have imagined it. His mouth set to grim when he added, "The luck part is my job." He dropped his hands from her shoulders. "All you have to do is play dumb about the letters and keep him guessing. As long as you do that, you'll be safe, and I'll have the time to nail him." He stopped. "And if it's all the same to you, I'd like to hang around Kenninghall until this thing is sorted out."

"You're assuming I'll wait."

"You'll wait, because you don't have a choice. This isn't about you, or a forty-year-old murder. This is today. It's about kids' lives, young girls ripped from their homes and sold to the highest bidder. You're in a position to stop that. Can you live with yourself if you don't?" He didn't wait for her answer. "And on the flip side, holding off will give you time to think about how to tell Biehle's mother. How old is she?"

"Eighty-eight." For the first time since reading the letters, her brain kicked her emotions aside. The image of her telling Miranda bloomed fully formed in her mind. It wasn't pretty. Miranda's heart was weak. This news could kill her.

Her brain couldn't take any more. Why wasn't anything ever simple? Instead there was confusion upon confusion. She didn't want to wait, like some grim reaper, for Miranda to die before exposing Milo and his killer cousin, but she didn't want to hurt Miranda. She absolutely didn't want to be responsible for shiploads of children. But . . .

Someone had to pay. No one paid for Chris and Will. No one. Ever.

She set her mouth in a straight line. "I'll wait," she said, "but not forever. And I'll want to be informed on everything you find. Everything. No more lies. I've had enough of them for a lifetime."

He looked away, then back, stuck out his hand. "Deal."

Hannah took his hand, held it, and looked him in the eye. "And Yates?"

"Yeah?" He tried to free his hand, she held on.

"Promise me you'll get him."

Yates glanced away, then back, his face shuttered. "I'll get him, but only if you can keep it together. Can you do that?"

Could she sit across a table from Greff, sip soup with him as if nothing had happened? She thought of the special dinner dress she'd worn when Greff had taken her out. She thought about how she'd primped, how brutally wrong she'd been in her assessment of him. Dear God! She wanted to vomit. A darkness settled over her. She didn't have an answer for Yates, because she didn't know what she'd do—without someone pulling her strings. She'd forgotten who the real Hannah Stuart was and what she was capable of.

"It's time for dinner," she snapped. "Meara's cooking early tonight. Let's go. You can eat with us."

"That an invitation? Or an order?"

"Both. Either. What does it matter?" She stomped off.

"Whoa, hold up there."

Hannah turned to see him standing a few feet away, either annoyance or worry lined up across his forehead.

"You didn't answer my question. Can you handle it?"

"What?"

"An evening with Greff, knowing what you know. Can you handle it and keep your cool?"

She decided to bluff, snorted with no concern for elegance. "You're talking to a woman who's been playing dead for five years. That's about as cool as it gets. I can handle it." She marched off, leaving him in the middle of a country lane, impatient to reach the quiet of Kenninghall, the safety of her room. She needed a clean line of time in which to think. Nothing in her body felt right except . . . the rage. It sat hard and deep in her stomach, a fixture now, cast in steel and marble.

Yates watched Hannah walk toward Kenninghall, first quickly with straight shoulders, then more slowly, more inward. He wondered what was going through her head. Whatever it was, it sure as hell wouldn't be good.

The early evening brought a light fog in off the ocean. It settled in gray black patches on the roof of the big house, made it look like one of those Transylvanian castles used in old horror films. Goddamn place was so big, so full of stuff, a man could scarcely breathe. Damn fire trap.

And there was Hannah, a woman transformed. In an afternoon, she'd morphed from church mouse to avenging angel. Not pretty. But logical. She'd been sucker-punched. Yates knew life had a way of doing that, and from there on, it—and you—were never the same again.

And he was destined to lay another one on her—when he destroyed the letters. Without some kind of proof, it would be her word against Greff's. In that scenario, there wasn't a chance she'd win.

Yates stood in the center of the road, rubbed his temple. He felt like shit. For a man who liked to be left alone, who liked his women in small doses and gone before sunup, he felt too much concern for his black-haired, sad-eyed, very reluctant hostess.

He didn't know what he hated more, having to save Greff's useless hide, or deceiving Hannah. There was something about her—even stiff as steel, as she'd been when he'd held her in his arms earlier, she'd felt good and awfully vulnerable.

He started to walk. Halfway along the forever driveway leading to the monster house, he heard the front door slam. The avenging angel hadn't bothered to wait for him.

He took the steps two at a time. When he reached the front door, he walked in without bothering to knock. He needed another shower, time to think about this new low in his life.

But more than either of those things, he needed to figure out how to let Greff get away with murder.

Chapter 14

"Whatcha got all that gas back there for?" Mary or Marie or whoever said.

"None of yer damn business." Bone knew he shouldn't have picked her up, but hey, when a man needed a bit, he went out and bought it. Not that Bakersfield, California, had much to offer. But then who the hell cared. She was a dime-store hooker, and she'd do—then she'd be dead. So her seeing the gas didn't mean shit.

"Well, it stinks is all."

"Life stinks."

"Now that's the truth."

He pulled the van into the vacant spot directly in front of his room. He never took a room unless he could park right out front. That way he could keep an eye on things. He didn't want anyone messing with his stuff, poking around.

He opened the motel room door and walked in. Maizie—or whoever—followed. The cheap motel room smelled as if it had been hosed down in nicotine.

Bone tossed his bag on the floor near the TV, then

pulled the drapes closed to shut out the afternoon light. He turned to the woman.

"Get 'em off."

She started to peel, do this kind of striptease thing. Too damn slow. "Don't need a song and dance, just get 'em off and get your ass on the bed."

She rolled her eyes but did what she was told.

Bone looked at his watch, then rummaged through his bag for a bottle of Tylenol. Damn, he had a headache! He went to the bathroom, took three pills and chased them with tap water. By the time he got back, the bitch had done what he said. She was buck naked, stretched out over the sagging belly of the bed, picking at her nails, and waiting for him.

She rolled to her side, covered the good stuff, and gave him a hard look. "Show me the money, honey."

He didn't like her tone, but he didn't want a ruckus either, and whores were damn good at making a ruckus when they didn't get their change. He rifled in his pocket, pulled out a wad of bills, and tossed it on the bedside table. Who gave a shit, she'd never see a dime of it.

"Okay, baby, let's us get the job done, huh?" She rolled to lie on her back again.

"You in a hurry?"

"Nope. I'll stay till the money runs out."

Bone started stripping.

He figured he'd dump her off about fifty miles out of town.

Dinner was in the Kenninghall kitchen, and after opening a few wrong doors, Yates found it.

Hannah and Libby sat at a table by the kitchen window.

A fire was lit in the hearth, but still the large

room was cool. But there was some sound. The
wind, grown stronger in the last hour and now
laced with rain, forced cold drafts down the chim-
ney, making the fire splutter. The glass in the window rattled in concert.

"Hey, Yates," Libby said. "I thought we'd lost
you."

He took one of the empty chairs at the table.
"Nearly did. There's more rooms in this place than
Buckingham Palace."

Hannah shoved food around her plate, acknowledged his arrival with barely a glance, looked gloomy
as hell. Women! A couple of hours ago, she was
ready to take on the world; now it looked as though
it had taken her.

"And how would you know that? You been
there?" Libby asked.

Good thing Libby was here to make conversation. "England, yes. Buckingham palace, no. Just a
vivid imagination. What about you?" He asked
Libby the question, but looked at Hannah. No response. None.

Libby's gaze followed his. She looked perplexed,
then pushed her chair back. "I'll get you a plate—
unless you don't like roast chicken?"

"Who doesn't, but don't bother. I'll get it myself." Quicker than Libby, he got to his feet and
headed to the long oak table. The food was set out
buffet style. He loaded his plate and went back to
the table, watching Hannah as he did so. She was
right; she was good at playing dead. But it was an
act that wouldn't fly when Greff showed up for
dinner. She'd have to do a whole lot better than
this.

"Looks good." He put his plate on the table, decided to try some small talk to draw her out. "Who's the cooking wizard?"

When Hannah didn't answer, Libby did. "Meara McCoy. Hannah said she was Milo's housekeeper and cook for fifteen years." Libby glanced nervously at Hannah. "Isn't that right?"

Silence.

"Hannah?" Libby said again, this time looking worried.

Hannah looked up from her plate, her eyes blank. She stood abruptly. "Excuse me. I'm not feeling well. I'll see you in the morning." She walked out of the kitchen, still holding her napkin.

When Libby started to get up, Yates grabbed her arm. "Leave her."

"She was weird from the moment she sat down," Libby said, taking her seat again. "What's wrong?"

Yates wasn't about to fill Libby in on the day's events. No use giving her knowledge that would add her to the endangered species list. "She's had some unsettling news."

Libby went still. "What kind of news?"

"Nothing that can't be handled."

"I was right, wasn't I? She's in danger, isn't she? Like Milo said she'd be."

Yates nodded. Damn, he really didn't want Libby involved in this. Everyone who knew increased the odds of the whole mess going sideways. But he owed her some honesty. "Yes. But it'll be okay. You don't have to worry."

"Not worry!" Libby looked stunned. "Of course I'm worried. I want to help, and to help I need to know what's going on."

"No, you don't. It's the last thing you need. But"—he smiled, tried to lighten things up—"you better get used to seeing my mug around here. Because I'll be here a while."

Her face was a picture of consternation. "That's good, but I—"

"Let it go, Libby. Like the twelve steps tell you to. How does that prayer go . . . accept the things you cannot change?"

"Always had trouble with that one." Her eyes narrowed. "How'd you know about it anyway? Firsthand?"

He shook his head. "Second, close enough to respect the sentiment." He picked up his fork, started to eat.

"Give me a clue at least."

"No." Maybe he shouldn't be, but Yates was surprised by how stubborn she was. "You're better off out of it."

"I didn't hire you to not tell *me* things." She looked irritated as hell.

"You didn't hire me," he said. "No money, remember."

She assessed him a long time, dragged a scarlet-tipped nail back and forth across her white napkin. "Okay," she said, not looking happy. "I'll keep my nose out of it—but you'll tell me if there's anything I can do, right?"

"Absolutely."

"And you'll let me know when everything's okay."

"Done. And don't worry about Hannah. I'll take care of her. But tonight I think she's best left alone."

"Right, Yates. Anything you say." He didn't miss the sarcasm.

But left alone *only* tonight, Yates amended silently, picking up his fork, because if Hannah was still doing her imitation of a gravestone when Greff showed up for dinner, he'd pick up on it, know immediately something was wrong. Neither of them could risk that.

He'd talk to Hannah tomorrow, figure out some way of getting her back on an even keel.

Gerry Vonecker slipped out from under the red satin sheets and sat on the edge of the bed. A soft grumble from behind him made him smile, and he turned to run an appreciative hand over the curve of hip under the rich bedding, a young, firm hip that went a long way to making him young and firm, too. He hadn't felt this good in ages, and he sure as hell hadn't gotten this hard in ages.

His smile widened as he dressed, but he was careful not to wake the sleeping girl. If she woke up, she'd start talking. That would ruin everything. The unripened body was one thing, but the unripened mind he could live without.

He left some cash on the bedside table and a note telling her he'd be back tonight. He'd hang on to this one for a while longer, he thought, glad she'd learned at least a little English. Not that he wanted her to get too smart.

Yes, she'd do until the next shipment, due at the end of the month. That thought, and the time, six a.m., reminded him he'd better head for the office, do a second run-through on the *Naarmu* import papers. At this hour, he'd be the only one there, able to work uninterrupted, and there was no chance of Hallam showing up. Truth was, the guy was making him nervous—all the more reason to double-check the paperwork.

When the door closed behind him, the pretty young girl in the bed sat up, pulled the sheets up to cover her budding breasts. She cursed under her breath, the words an incomprehensible whisper. She looked at the money. Spat. Then looked at the phone.

Outside, the morning air was raw, and Vonecker pulled his collar close to his neck. From the doorway, he glanced up and down the street. He didn't expect to see anyone this early, but it paid to be careful. There were a couple of semis in loading bays up the block, but this section, a row of warehouses recently converted to upscale apartments, was deserted. He shrugged deeper into his coat, walked the few steps down the street, and turned into the alley where he'd parked his car. From a few steps away, he hit the unlock button on his key chain.

His hand was on the car door handle.

The voice came from behind him. "Hey, Vonecker, I've been waiting for you."

He swung around—in time to catch the crowbar full force across his face. His cheekbone cracked and crumpled, and a rush of cold air enveloped his exposed, hanging eyeball. He slammed back against the car and slid down to the pavement, inhaling his own blood. The next blow splintered the crown of his head.

He didn't have enough time for a last thought.

* * *

Starting at eleven a.m., Yates went looking for Hannah. She didn't show up for breakfast and hadn't been seen since last night.

Meara wasn't worried, and told Yates Hannah was known for taking long, early morning walks, that she'd probably be back before lunch. But Meara didn't know what he and Hannah had learned yesterday, didn't know how a few words on paper had messed her up. He'd checked and all the cars were in the garage, so she couldn't be far.

"Meara's right, Yates. Hannah was always going off on her walks even . . . since back then. She might have walked into town. Maybe to do some shopping. Why don't you check there. I'll go across the fields out back," Libby suggested, and by her tone, he figured she caught some of his worry.

"Good idea."

He drove into town, slowly toured the few short streets that made up the touristy La Conner shopping area. Yates didn't expect to find her looking into shop windows or flashing a credit card. He didn't know Hannah well, but he'd bet his last nickel she wasn't the type to shop away her problems—particularly this one.

Back at the house, he started a door-to-door search of Kenninghall. No small task when it involved all forty-plus rooms.

He found her in the last room he checked. Milo's chapel, at the other end of the hall from his own garret room on the third floor. She sat in the one straight-backed chair that faced the simple altar and had on the same clothes she'd worn last night, meaning she probably hadn't slept at all, or barely.

The chapel was cold, and there were no candles burning. Through the round stained glass window set high in the pitched ceiling, light seeped in to make a puddle of colors on the hard shine of the bare floor.

If Hannah heard him open the door, or the creak of the hardwood when he entered the room, she gave no sign. With no attempt to tread softly, he walked to one of the narrow benches at the side of the room and sat down. She remained in place, inert, in utter silence, both hands resting loosely on her knees, her gaze steadfast on the drugstore picture of the smiling faux family.

Her face was chalk white, etched in pain, her eyes hollow. Something his mother once said crept into his mind. About demons. Fear and guilt, she called them. They come in the night, she'd told him, to draw their cruel pictures on soft faces.

Last night, obviously, they'd visited Hannah.

Gone were yesterday's tears, the chilling rage, the hard demands for justice. Today, in this silent chapel, all he could see was desolation and bleak despair. What was left of Yates's battered heart beat hollow in his chest, because he knew there'd been a time in his life when he'd looked exactly the same. A time when a truth forced a new reality, one no one could have predicted.

When she spoke, it startled him.

"I had a family once," she said, her words flat and without inflection, as if she were a child reciting a poem—as if the words had to be said but had no meaning. "Long ago and far away . . . like in a fairy tale. But they're not real anymore."

He didn't respond, sensed none was required.

"I had a husband named Will and a son—a beautiful son—named Christopher. A good husband and a beautiful son. Like them." She raised her chin in the barest gesture toward the photo. Her eyes were dry. "They're dead, you know."

"I know."

"And I killed them."

"Hannah . . ." Yates shut his eyes a moment, rubbed his forehead, couldn't find words, knowing if he did, they'd be useless.

"Oh, I wasn't the one who held the gun"—she blinked slowly and took a shallow breath—"pulled the trigger, drew their blood. But selfishness can kill, too. And that's what I was . . . selfish. Thinking about Hannah." She lowered her head

"You're not respons—"

She lifted one hand from her knee, as if to hold his words back, but the effort proved too great, and she let it fall limply back in place. "I had a head cold. A common, garden variety head cold." She shook her head, still didn't turn to look at him. "So I insisted Will take Christopher, go to the shop, and pick up the receipts and tapes for the month's end accounting—so I wouldn't have to go in the next morning."

She turned, met his gaze. Her eyes were red rimmed, burned to dry, as though she hadn't blinked for hours. "Will didn't want to go, said he'd bring the books home with him the next night. He and Chris were 'busy,' he said. They were building cars. I can still see them sitting cross-legged on the living room carpet, laughing, fighting over the hundreds of colored pieces of building tiles between them."

She rubbed the back of a hand across her eyes. "I didn't listen. 'Take him with you,' I said. 'It'll take less than an hour.' " She pulled in a breath, seemed to hold it forever. Yates knew she was thinking about how that hour had turned into a lifetime. Again the chapel filled with a funereal silence. He caught the faint scent of sandalwood. The smell drifted in and out of the rooms in the house as if it were the perfume of a restless ghost.

Hannah let out the breath, closed her eyes. "I *insisted* my family go to their deaths."

Yates got up from his narrow seat and crossed to where she sat, limp, completely spent. He knelt in front of her, took her hands in his. She looked down at him, but he wasn't sure she saw him. He squeezed her hands.

"You've heard this before. Probably a thousand times. But you have to learn to believe it. *It wasn't your fault.*"

She gripped his hands, tight, and her words when they came were awkward and forced. "Two boys . . . two cruel, heartless boys . . . they slaughtered my family for thirty-nine dollars and some vintage bar towels. How do I forget that? If I hadn't been so selfish . . ."

Yates didn't know where to go with this. He knew she needed to let it out, that it might do some good, but he also knew there was such a thing as too much grief—and if a person crossed the line, they'd never be the same again. Hannah was on that line.

"You weren't selfish, you were sick. Let the guilt go, Hannah. It's a waste of time. It won't bring your family back and it won't bring—"

"Justice?" Her eyes were vacant, her short laugh hollow. "I've given up on that. They never paid. Probably never will."

She pulled her hands from his and stood. "Those two boys killed my family, ran down an alley, and disappeared. Like evil spirits. They came, did their terrible work, and evaporated." She touched the picture on the altar, picked it up. "Just like your Greff, and Milo, when they did their killing."

It was his turn to protest the "your Greff" phrase, but he said nothing. Because in some ways Greff was "his," bound to him by pain, mistakes, and an ugly shared history Yates worked hard to forget. None of which he planned to explain to Hannah.

"What was Milo thinking, I wonder. When he came into this room night after night and prayed at his altar." Her voice was hard again. "Did he think about the family he killed? Or was he only concerned with making himself feel better?"

"Maybe both. He put himself in the wrong place at the wrong time. He was a kid who made a lousy choice."

Hannah sneered. " 'A lousy choice.' You mean like buying a pair of shoes that pinch your toes?"

"No. That's not what I mean and you know it." She was getting angry again. That relieved him. Anger was good—if he could control it.

"I was living with a killer. I can't get past that. Someone exactly like those boys who took the lives of my husband and son. How do I reshape five years of memories? How do I rewrite the part of a man I called friend into *fiend*? How do I take back my life? Do I even have one?"

He paused, suddenly uncomfortable. "Where are we going with this?"

"I wish I knew." She ran a hand through her long, tangled hair. "If there's an emotion I *haven't felt* since yesterday, I can't name it. And to be honest, I'm still a mess. I feel like"—the look she gave him was fearful, accented with a weak smile—"a sack of rockets on a campfire."

"You'll be okay," he said, sounding more confident than he felt.

"I know I said I could handle it, but I've thought about it, and I'm not sure I can. Pretend, I mean, that everything is the same as it was . . . when he kissed me at the door." She wiped the back of her hand across her mouth.

Yates felt as if that bag of rockets she'd mentioned went off in his gut. He shut down the vision of Greff's mouth on hers, squared his shoulders, and took a step away. "You have to face him. There's no other way." If there were, he'd come up with it. He didn't want Hannah breathing the same air as Greff.

"No, there isn't." Wearily, she put the framed photo back on the altar. "Somewhere in this mess I call my mind, there's a drop of logic left. On some level I know that life is for the living—and it's for sure the kids on those terrible boats don't deserve what Greff and his sick friends have planned for them." She finally turned and looked at him directly, lifted her chin. "So I'll do what needs to be done. Don't worry."

Yates was worried. Big-time.

He'd made a mistake, hadn't realized how close Hannah and Greff had become—during one dinner. No way could she handle him. The best thing to do was cancel.

He was about to tell her that when there was a knock on the door. Hannah went to open it, and Libby looked past her shoulder and into the chapel.

"Wow. A church! I thought this place was always locked."

"It's a chapel," Hannah corrected.

Libby stepped in. "Whatever it is, it's amazing." She took a moment to look around, then focused on Yates. "Someone called Anne Chapman called for you. She said it's important, that if you don't call her right away, she'll replace you with a Doberman . . . said you'd get her meaning."

Yates came damn near to smiling. Thank God for the Chapmans of the world, all black and white, and straight talk. "Thanks." When it appeared Libby planned to wait for him, he added. "I'll be down in a minute."

"Oh," she said, looking at him then Hannah. "Gotcha."

When she was gone, he said, "About the dinner with Greff, beg off. Find a reason to cancel."

"That's a pretty sudden change of heart, isn't it?" She frowned.

"I've reconsidered. I don't think you're ready. I'll come up with another way."

"No. There is no other way, and I'm as ready as it gets. I'm not sinking into the background. Not this time." Her mouth was a thin line, her eyes bright.

"You're making a mistake."

"That's something we'll find out."

"Okay, it's your call." He might not like the look in her eyes, but he understood it enough to know she wasn't about to change her mind. He wanted to curse. Instead he turned to leave.

"Yates."

"Uh-huh." He turned back.

"I trust you. You should know that, and you can trust me. I won't let you down."

He saw her breathe deeply, physically pull herself together, watched determination harden her gaze. What was left of Yates's normally high-riding principles hit the dirt with a thud. "Fair enough," he mumbled. He walked out of the chapel, taking his ten-ton conscience and damned bleeding heart with him.

Chapter 15

Yates decided to push the worry of Hannah having a meltdown during her dinner with Greff out of his mind. He'd got her into this, he'd damn well get her out—in one piece.

He dialed Chapman's private line. She picked up on the third ring. "You called, Chapman?" he said without introduction.

There was a pause. "Oh yes, Mr. Johnson, I did. But I'll have to call you back. Will you be by the phone?"

"It's Yates, Anne." Hell. What was wrong with the woman?

"I know who you are, Mr. Johnson, but I'm tied up right now. I'll get back to you immediately I'm through."

"You've got company."

"Uh-huh. That'll be fine. Just a few minutes." She hung up.

Yates stared at the dead phone in his hand. Anne Chapman doing the silent bit was a whole new experience. But given he had some time, he decided to make another quick call.

"John, Yates here."

"Hey. I've been looking for you. Don't you ever check your e-mails, answer your phone?"

"Not lately. What've you got?"

"Not much, other than an update on Tenassi. She's in Spain. Marbella, to be exact. And her ticket has an open return. Looks as if the lady plans to be gone awhile."

"If that changes, give me a call. I won't be home, but I'll watch for messages."

"Okay, but if you want the goods on Tenassi, I wouldn't turn down the chance to work on my tan—all expenses paid, of course." Yates heard his smile, his deep intake of nicotine.

"You'll have to be content with those *tanned* lungs of yours, buddy. Tenassi's low on my priority list right now."

"When I hang up, I'm going to get myself a real client, one with deep pockets and a semi full of Marlboros."

"Hell of a plan. See you, Crayne." Yates hung up and the second he did, the phone rang again. Out of habit he picked up immediately. So did Meara. When she realized it was for him she hung up.

"Chapman?" he said.

"Vonecker's dead," she said without preamble. "The police just left."

"When? How?"

"Early this morning. In an alley not too far from Pike's Market. The how? Not subtle. A crowbar that did a first-rate job of smashing his skull."

"Shit!" Yates rubbed his chin, which reminded him he hadn't yet shaved.

"Yeah. Shit," she repeated, then paused.

"So I'm guessing the cops don't see this as a run-of-the-mill mugging?" Yates added.

"He had his wallet, cash, and credit cards. The keys to his Mercedes were in his hand. So, Yates, it looks as if you're getting your blood and guts case after all. But I have to say I feel sick about this."

"Nobody likes seeing someone catch his last ride that way, but there wasn't anything you could have done to stop it. The guy was keeping some very bad company." A thought bloomed in Yates's mind. Hell, this could get Anne Chapman off the case. "But this does let Simpson and Chapman off the hook. Chances are Vonecker's nasty sideline went down with him."

Chapman's voice was as hard as a judge's bench. "I don't see it that way. Those ships are still coming, Yates. Still bringing their cargo of misery to our corner of the world. And I want them stopped and every one of the lowlife creeps involved behind bars—or worse."

"You want me to stay on it, then."

"I started with you; I'll finish with you. Just do your job, Yates. Bring me what I need, and I'll take it from there."

"You're one tough lady, Chapman."

"I'm a determined one. So if you don't come up with what I need, I'll find someone who can." She hung up on him before he could answer.

"Shit!" Yates said again.

Wednesday evening, Hannah looked through her closet without enthusiasm. When her hand touched the new dress she'd bought to have dinner with Morgan Greff, she yanked it off the hanger and stuffed it in a garbage bag. She'd throw it out tomorrow.

She brushed her hands off on her bathrobe and reached back into the closet to select a pair of slacks and a sweater, tossed them across the bed. Both were as old as the house she stood in, but they had the advantage of being black and not being too big, as were most things in her closet.

There would be no primping tonight. But she wouldn't let Yates down—even though she'd rather do anything than have this dinner. She picked up her brush, drawing it roughly through hair still damp from her shower, then applied light makeup.

Somehow she'd keep those rockets of hers in the damn sack. If Yates were coming to dinner, it would be easier, but he wasn't. So it would be Greff and her. Alone. She'd get through it—if the vile man didn't try to touch her. If he did, she wasn't sure what she'd do.

She pulled the brush through her hair again, stopped.

But I liked being touched by Yates.

Confused by the out-of-nowhere thought, she brushed harder, faster. Until another thought came. How lean and hard his body had felt, when he'd pulled her to him, flush and tight, after she'd read the letters; his big hand holding her head to his chest, his beating heart. Even in her fog, she'd sensed his discomfort, his edginess, as if he wanted to run. But he hadn't. He'd simply held her.

Her brushing faltered when she realized she'd never been even close to a lean strong body like Yates's, a body much like his sharp mind—taut with energy. Will had definitely not felt like Yates,

and other than one misguided teenage relationship, Will was the only man Hannah had ever been
intimate with.

He'd been fifty when she married him—a good
man, but one who'd preferred his books and antiques business to physical activities. Much like
Milo . . . She shuddered. No doubt it was the simi-
larities that made them such good friends. Both
men had willingly stepped into her life to take care
of her—and she'd let them. Was she starting to de-
pend on Yates?

She tossed the brush on her vanity table. *No
damn way!*

There was something coiled and resistant in
him, as if he were unreceptive to connections of
any kind. Even when he'd held her, stroked her
hair, there was an aloofness about him. Funny . . .
how she had so many impressions of Yates, considering they'd been ignoring each other for three
days now. Not smart.

She should pay more attention, start using her
head to make judgments, not her stupid . . .
needs.

She trusted him; she'd been honest about that,
but considering her record, that didn't mean
much—coming as it did from the same woman
who'd put her faith in Milo and kissed that ser-
pent, Greff.

There was a tap on her half-open door, and
Meara poked her head in. "I'm about to set the
table. Will I be setting a place for Libby, or will it
just be yourself and the gentleman?"

Libby! She should have thought of her before.

"Yes, Meara, please set a place for Libby." For the
first time since her arrival at Kenninghall, Hannah

was glad Libby was there. "And, Meara, would you put us in the main dining room, please?"

"You're spoofin' me!" Meara's eyebrows shot up. "There's dust covers on most of the furniture in there."

"Leave them."

Meara started to protest, but apparently thought better of it. "You're sure now?"

"Yes. The dining room is perfect."

"Then the dining room it'll be—though it's cold as a nun's toes in there." She looked at Hannah as if this final reminder would make her reconsider. When Hannah said nothing, she shook her head and added, "Oh, and I'll be leavin' before dessert service, if it's all right? It's Scrabble night at Miranda's, and I've got some work to do if I'm to break even after last week."

"That'll be fine, and thank you for working so hard tonight."

"Ah, but it's a pleasure to have company coming. Dining room or no. This old place"—she lifted her head as if to encompass the whole of the estate—"can use a wee bit of fun."

The word fun sounded so incongruous when applied to the evening ahead, Hannah couldn't do anything but nod. When Meara was gone, Hannah dressed quickly and headed to Libby's room, three doors from her own.

When Hannah arrived at her door, it was ajar. When she poked her head in, Libby was ending a call. "When will I see you then? . . . Okay. Good enough." She noticed Libby, flushed. "Uh-huh. Me, too," she said into the phone, before hanging up and nodding at Hannah. "Hi, this is a first."

It was the first time Hannah had visited her in

her room. "Sorry to interrupt, but have you got a minute?"

"Sure." She lifted her hand from the phone. "That was Tom Colwood." She got up from the bed where she'd been sitting. "Checking up on me, I guess."

"Does he need to?"

"No. Not today," Libby said, giving Hannah a slight smile. "And today is what matters."

"You miss him?" Hannah asked the question because she didn't know where to start.

"Yes, I do. Very much." Her smile faded. "But I don't think you came here to inquire about the state of my love life—or extend an olive branch."

"Not exactly."

"So? What do you want?"

"I'd like you to join Morgan Greff and myself for dinner tonight." Hannah dropped her eyes. She hoped Libby wasn't going to ask for any kind of explanation, because she didn't want to lie, and she couldn't risk the truth.

Libby looked at her for a long moment, her gaze intensely speculative. "You want a chaperone," she said. "What about Yates? Won't he be there?"

"No. And I don't want Greff to know he's at Kenninghall, so I'd appreciate it if you wouldn't bring up his name."

"I see."

"I seriously doubt that you do." Hannah, who'd stepped a few feet into the room, turned toward the door, then looked back. "Will you come?"

"Greff won't be happy."

"No, he won't."

Libby looked pleased. "Then I'll come."

"Thank you," she said, and felt better already.

"Dinner's at eight in the main dining room." Hannah might not be able to avoid this dinner, but now at least it wouldn't be one-on-one. Despite her shaky emotional state, she would take control if it killed her.

"Hannah," Libby called as she stepped out the door.

"Yes?"

"You're smart to keep your distance from that guy. To tell the truth, I was worried. I thought—" She stopped.

"Thought what?"

"That maybe you two had a . . . thing starting."

Hannah laughed without mirth. "You know what, for a minute or two, so did I." She walked down the hall back to her own room.

Greff arrived at seven-forty-five, with a fine bottle of wine and an armful of flowers. The perfect guest.

Meara answered the door and showed him to the library. She was all smiles. "I'll tell Hannah you're here," she said.

"Thank you, Meara, but I'm early, so tell her not to hurry." *She'll be five minutes, tops,* he told himself, settling into the sofa facing the fire. Women never made him wait. Hannah Stuart would be no exception.

Thirty minutes late he was pacing the room, nursing a drink he'd fixed himself from a tray and decanter set on the coffee table, and trying to keep his cool.

Ten minutes after that, Hannah entered the room. Not rushing. He tried to ignore the knot of irritation in his throat.

"Morgan, I'm sorry I'm late. I hope you've been comfortable."

No explanation, no excuse, he noticed. "Yes, I've been fine. Meara looked after me." He hoped the last sentence didn't sound accusatory. He took her hands, raised one of them to his mouth and kissed it. "You look wonderful."

"Thank you," she said, dropping her gaze, but leaving her cold hands in his. "But you must be hungry. I know I am. Shall we go in? We can . . . chat there."

"Wherever you lead, I'll follow." *She's nervous again,* he thought, and the idea of that made him feel better, erased his annoyance. The evening would go exactly as he planned.

She pulled her hands from his. "I thought you'd enjoy seeing something of Kenninghall, how Milo lived. So I asked Meara to put us in the dining room."

"Perfect." He forced his usual smile and looked around as if he were impressed. "This place is so unique. I'd love to see all of it one day."

"Yes, of course," she answered, and led him out the library doors to a room across the entrance hall. She opened double doors to reveal a dining room the size of a damn football stadium. "My God," he said, looking around. Old Milo had done okay for himself. The room had to be at least forty feet long and the dining room table didn't look much shorter. It sat at least twenty. The room was poorly lit by two chandeliers that hung high at each end of the table, and filled with furniture, most of it under white dust covers.

"It is large, isn't it?" She walked quickly to the far end of the table and took the seat at its head, then gestured to the one on her left. "Please," she said. "Sit down."

Morgan had given his two seconds of interest to the room; now he focused on Hannah. She was white. Not pale. White. Something was wrong. He didn't have time to think what before a side door to the dining room opened and Libby Stuart walked in.

"Morgan, nice to see you again." She took the chair to Hannah's right.

What the hell . . .

Greff had counted on a quiet dinner for two, not some damn family get-together. He nodded in Libby's direction, looked at Hannah, and raised a brow in question. She gave him a slight smile and looked at Libby. "I'm glad you were home tonight. You'd hate to miss Meara's roast beef."

"Yeah, some cancellations are good news." With that cryptic remark, Libby looked over his shoulder and smiled as the housekeeper arrived with the first course and started fussing around the table.

Morgan leaned closer to Hannah. "I thought we'd be alone." He managed to sound cool and disappointed, rather than pissed off, which was what he was.

"Yes, well . . . Libby being here is kind of a surprise to me, too. I thought she was going out." She lifted a shoulder and dropped it again. As a casual shrug, it failed, serving only to show her tension.

He sat back in his chair, listened to Libby engage Hannah in some stupid conversation about the right way to ship tulip bulbs. Hannah carried on with her as if the subject was actually important. She was avoiding him. No fucking doubt about it. Morgan drank some wine, swirled the red liquid in his glass, and forced back the anger rubbing like a file against his rib cage.

Hannah was a cautious woman; he knew that from the night he'd kissed her. And considering she hadn't been sleeping with Milo, probably a sexual basket case. No damn doubt she'd explode before first base—

That's what she's afraid of.

Morgan had his answer and relaxed. She couldn't hide behind tulip talk or her stepdaughter's skirts forever. As for that explosion on first base, he'd make sure of it. The night was young; he had plenty of time.

He looked at Hannah, gave her a brilliant smile. "Wonderful soup. Your Meara is a genius," he said, then turned to Libby. "And it's a good thing you were able to join us, Libby. It'll save me making a fool of myself, trying to talk about antiques."

Both women looked at him, but it was Hannah who spoke, looking at him curiously. "What would you like to talk about, Morgan?"

He leaned in and put his mouth to her ear, close enough to see his breath ruffle her hair. "You, Hannah. I'd like to talk about you."

He pulled back in time to see her face redden, a hand flutter to her neck where a second ago his mouth had been close enough to kiss her. She swallowed and looked away.

She was jumpy all right, but she was also hot. Morgan knew arousal when he saw it. He went back to his soup.

Yes, the night was young. All a man needed was patience—and a slow hand.

Chapter 16

Yates wished to hell he could be a fly on the wall. He'd give anything to know what was going on in that dining room. Instead he'd stayed in his third-floor room and paced, feeling like a castrated bull.

He wasn't worried about the police connecting Vonecker and Greff, although it was a complication he didn't need. He was worried about Hannah. Until the letters, he'd never figured him for the violent type. Murder. He still couldn't wrap his head around that.

He tried to convince himself that Greff—like Milo—had been a dumb kid out for thrills, not kills, and that something had gone bad. Murder didn't fit Greff's way of doing things. He was smooth, cunning, and sly, a master manipulator. White collar and clean hands to the bone. Murder was dirty business with a high degree of risk. It didn't fit Greff's M.O.

Yates stopped pacing; he hated the direction of

his thoughts, his sick attempt to downplay, ratio-
nalize Greff's miserable life—the murder of an entire family. He knew the truth. Greff was a
murderer and an importer of children for the purpose of sex. And the murder of that family hadn't
been his last, because he'd killed Yates's mother,
too, as surely as if he'd pushed her off a cliff.

The room closed in on him. He needed fresh
air.

Downstairs, they'd be at dinner for hours. He
hoped to hell Hannah would hold up. He was a
rat, letting her go ahead with this dinner, but he
had to keep Greff on ice until he got the letters;
they were his only chance to get the upper hand.
He'd wave them in Greff's face, tell him to shut
down Zanez and get the hell out of the country.

He'd have what he wanted; he tried not to think
about what Hannah wanted. Needed.

He made another circle of the room, rubbed
the back of his neck. He had to get out of here.

He'd find some back stairs, go out, take a walk.
Anything was better than making ruts in the carpet for the next two hours.

Hannah used every ounce of her willpower not
to fly out of her seat and escape. She tried to relax,
force herself to a calm she was far from feeling.
She should have listened to Yates and canceled.
This was a disaster. There she went again, believing everything would be all right so long as she
went along with someone else's judgment call.
Same old Hannah.

Same old doormat.

But what she hadn't factored in was revulsion.

She was sitting at a table with Satan, a man who'd murdered a family and was in the business of selling little girls.

"Excuse me," she said, the words coming from her mouth so abruptly they surprised her. "I'll only be a moment." She tossed her napkin on the table, rose to her feet, and left the room before either Morgan or Libby could speak.

She headed for the stairs, passing Meara on her way to the dining room with the main course. "Are you all right, Hannah? You're pale as a ghost."

"A headache. I'm going for a pill. Take the food in, Meara. I'll be right back."

At the top of the stairs on the second floor, she collided with Yates.

"What are you doing here?" she asked, and hoped her rubbery legs and trembling shoulders didn't transmit her growing sense of panic. "I thought you were going to stay out of sight."

"And I thought you were entertaining Greff," he whispered, his voice tight with concern. He grasped her arm, tugged her away from the stage that was the top of the stairs and down the dark, shadowed hall.

"I am . . . entertaining him." Hannah managed to keep her voice low—even though what she wanted to do was scream. She pulled away from him outside her bedroom door. "I, uh, have a headache. I was coming to get a Tylenol." She opened her door and walked in; Yates followed silently. "And besides, Libby is with him."

"Libby!" He cursed under his breath. "He didn't come to see Libby. You're the one he kissed, remember. You're the one he's after."

"I can't do it!" Her voice rose, and she wrapped

her arms around herself to keep what composure she had fenced behind her rib cage. "I just can't."

"A couple of hours. Keep it together for a couple of hours, and that's it."

Her eyes were wide and dry; she slumped against the foot post on her bed. "He's evil. And I keep thinking . . . I almost—" She stopped, unable to bring herself to admit she'd fantasized having sex with him. It said too much about her. She put a hand over her mouth.

Yates stepped in front of her, took her hand from her face, then grasped her shoulders. "You don't need a pill. You need this."

He took her face in his hands, touched his mouth to hers. Hannah's breath stalled and her senses narrowed, focused on the rough velvet of Yates's mouth. No longer conscious of the oak post against her back, the room of expensive antiques, or the dim light casting gray shadows into every corner, she could only stare in a state of bizarre apprehension at the man in front of her. This wasn't right. Made no sense. Again he brushed his mouth over hers. Her eyelids drifted closed and suddenly there was nothing, no one in the universe but him.

Fear stole from her lungs, evicted, replaced by heat and longing.

When Yates stepped back the barest inch, took his mouth from hers, Hannah hung suspended, until his hands slid down to her shoulders. "Or maybe this," he murmured, his eyes dark. Crushing her to him fast and hard, he took her mouth without apology, wrapping her in an embrace so deep, so complete her knees buckled. Yates gripped her waist, then her hips, held her against his lean body—and Hannah let him, pushed her own heat to his, unable to get close enough. She slid her hands up, into his thick black hair, fisted them there. His hair, heavy silk, slipped between her fingers, defied her grip.

Closer, she had to get closer.

She felt him harden, heard him exhale roughly.

Closer. Closer. She tipped into him, moaned.

"Jesus!" Yates took a step back. In the stillness of the room, his breathing was heavy and erratic.

Cool air flowed into the space between their bodies, and Hannah put her hands behind her, gripped the post.

Yates stared at her as if he'd never seen her before.

Hannah stared back, because she had neither the will nor the strength to move her eyes. "Why did you do that?"

Yates met her questioning gaze. "I thought I was doing you a favor."

"Excuse me?"

"Look, that came out wrong." He took another couple of steps away, rubbed his jaw. "I wanted you to forget about Greff . . . him kissing you. I figured—"

"You figured your kiss would erase his."

"Something like that."

"So you're saying it was a motivational technique, then? A keep-the-woman-on-track kind of thing?" Embarrassment warmed Hannah's neck. He'd felt so good . . .

"I'm sorry. Bad call."

Hannah didn't answer—maybe because some part of her hated that he'd apologized. She let go of the bedpost and strode to the door. Since Milo died, she'd been dragged like a half-sunken ship into other people's lives, other people's problems. If this was what Milo had meant by "coming to life again," she wanted no part of it. Everyone with their own agendas and using her to attain them; Greff wanted the letters, Yates wanted Greff, Libby wanted—God only knew what Libby wanted.

Her head spun trying to figure everything out.

She wished they'd all go away, play their sick games in someone else's head, and leave her alone. Even though most of her problems were her own fault. She should've taken control, decided for herself what she needed, what she *wanted* in her life—not let others . . . fix things for her.

Well, there was one thing she wanted, and she would do it right now. She'd go downstairs, play her part and get Greff out of Kenninghall.

"I'm going back downstairs," she said, feeling cool as a winter window. "If you want to sneak out, take the stairs at the end of the hall. They go straight to the kitchen. You can go out the back door."

She went out and closed the door behind her. Oddly, she felt much more in control than she had in weeks. It felt good.

And Yates's kiss? He might have intended it to erase Greff's, but she couldn't help but wonder who would erase his.

Hannah arrived back in the dining room in time for the main course. She gave her headache excuse and sailed through the rest of the dinner—an Oscar-caliber performance. When she again thought of Yates's soul-searing kiss, she pushed it until it fell off the back of her mind.

She'd been used by Milo, stolen from by Libby, courted by Satan himself, and now manipulated by Yates. She didn't know who to hate, who to love, but most of all she didn't know who to trust. Which meant the smartest thing to do was trust no one.

She would help Yates stop Greff's ugly business, and then she'd take her own justice, for the family Greff and Milo had murdered—and her own. That done, she'd have the long halls and silent rooms of Kenninghall to herself.

After dessert, Libby left the room to take a phone call, and Hannah was surprised to hear Morgan say, "Much as I hate to cut this evening short, Hannah, I'd best get going." She tried not to let her relief show; she'd been afraid she'd have a hard time getting rid of him.

He went on, "We'll have to do this again sometime. Perhaps when you're next in Seattle?"

"Of course. That would be wonderful." She even smiled. He didn't need to know it was delight because he was leaving.

He got up from the table, went behind her chair, and leaned close to her ear. "Will you walk me to my car?" he asked, pulling out her chair and offering her his hand.

Hannah's stomach lurched. Where was Libby? She had no choice but to take his hand. She dropped it as soon as she was on her feet. "I'll get your coat."

He followed her out of the dining room.

Hannah went to the large hall closet. "I'm so glad you came, Morgan." She retrieved his coat, handed it to him, and walked—careful not to pick up her pace—the few steps to the door.

"So am I. A great dinner and great company.

Thank you." He draped his coat over his arm, opened the door, and put his hand to the small of her back, using a gentle pressure to guide her to the porch. Outside, the night was bitter with cold and the wind carried it like a weapon.

Hannah shivered. "I'd better go in."

Morgan slipped his coat over her shoulders, then gripped the lapels to trap her in its folds. Hannah's heart thundered. "I don't think—"

"No, don't think. Feel." He held the lapels of his coat closed with one hand and brushed her wind-blown hair away from her face with the other. "That's what I've been doing all night. I haven't been able to take my eyes off you." His lips followed his hand, brushed over her forehead.

"Morgan—" Panic clotted in her throat.

"Shush now. Hear me. I want you, Hannah. I want to kiss you." He stroked her cheek, moved his hand down to clasp her throat—first lightly, then with increased pressure. Her pulse jumped under his thumb. "Touch your breasts," he whispered against her hair. "Take them into my mouth and play wicked games with their hot, hard tips. Then I want to taste you—all of you. Your lips, your skin . . . your juice." He smiled down at her, smooth, confident. "Will you let me do that?" He pulled the coat lapels tighter; in the porch light his eyes were black.

Hannah froze, her mind a blur of terror. She tried to pull back but the coat held her fast. She had to think. His mouth was coming down to hers. She stared at it, fascinated, rapt . . . brainless.

She dropped her head so quickly, his lips bounced off her hair. "This isn't a good idea." Words tumbled around her skull. Desperately she tried to catch a few. "I, uh, mean, we barely know each other."

"That's what makes it good." He was unmoved by her evasions. "Sex with a stranger is more exciting."

"I don't think so." She pulled back, harder this time.

The lapels of the coat closed like a noose around her neck. "Then how about sex with a dangerous stranger?" He slipped a hand under the coat, squeezed her breast, thumbed her nipple. "Does that turn you on?"

He brought his mouth down on hers hard.

Hannah struggled against his unyielding mouth, sealed her lips against his probing tongue. Pushing and shoving, she managed to get her hands out of the front of the coat. She pounded on his chest. "Stop it!"

"You don't mean that." He moved his wet lips to her throat.

"I think the lady means exactly that." Yates stepped under the porch light.

Surprise loosened Greff's grip on the coat, and Hannah stumbled back, her throat opening to choke on the clean night air pouring into her constricted lungs. She resisted the urge to bolt for the door. Yates took the few steps necessary to stand beside her.

"Yates," Greff said. "I didn't expect to see you here. Still looking at cars?"

"Uh-huh. Hannah and Libby were good enough to offer me a room for a few days. And what bachelor would turn down Meara's cooking." He looked perfectly relaxed, hands in his pockets, windbreaker open to the wind.

Greff shifted his attention to Hannah, his expression hard. "You never mentioned you had a houseguest. You should have invited him for dinner."

Hannah opened her mouth, but before she could speak, Yates said, "I was out. Just got back."

Hannah was angry again. She didn't need anyone making up her lies. She could do it herself. "And I didn't get the impression you and Yates were friends." She took off Greff's coat and threw it at him.

Greff paused, flicked his gaze between Yates and Hannah. "Lang and I are much more than friends."

Hannah saw Yates tense, his jaw set like concrete.

Greff shrugged into his coat. "We're . . . the best of enemies. That's an accurate description, wouldn't you say, Yates?"

The two men, both with dark hair, and almost the same height, eyed each other. The air thickened with malice.

Yates didn't move. "Close, although I'd skip the word 'best.' "

Morgan laughed, then turned to Hannah. "Thank you again for dinner. It's been an *educational* evening." He lifted her chin, held it viselike until her jaw ached. "And I think you should change your mind about the sex. Must be getting bone dry down there." He let her go.

Hannah gasped and stumbled back.

Yates, his face like thunder, took a step toward Greff, and not so much as glancing at Hannah said, "Go inside. Now."

She hated the authoritative tone in his voice, hated more that she hadn't handled Greff on her own. But neither of those thoughts changed the fact that she wanted to get as far away from him as she could—as fast as she could.

She needed a blisteringly hot shower and a rub-down with a stiff brush and antiseptic.

Chapter 17

"Walk me to my car," Greff instructed Yates, buttoning up his coat.

"Why?" Yates didn't move, but every muscle, sinew, and sense in his body shot to high alert. Between him and Hannah, they'd blown it. He knew Greff; he had their scent.

"We need to talk." He started down the stairs. "But not here."

"I can't think of a thing we need to talk about."

Greff stopped on the bottom step, turned. "I can. Because I believe you and the ice queen read Milo's mail."

"I don't know what you're talking about."

"You know, considering who your father is"—he raised his voice, glanced at the door—"you should be a better liar."

Yates cursed.

Greff grinned. "Ah, so you haven't told the bitch about your illustrious sire."

"No. I tend to avoid that confession."

"Good. That's the best news I've had all night."

Morgan started down the steps toward his Ferrari. Yates glanced at the closed door, then followed. He figured Hannah had bolted to her room, but it would be safer off the porch.

Greff stood beside his car door, made no move to open it. "You sleeping with her?"

"Not your business."

"Damn right it's my business, because you're going to get me those letters."

"I don't know anything about any letters."

Greff's look was skeptical. "You're lying. Like the Stuart woman lied all through dinner." He looked disgusted. "Usually I don't let my dick get in the way of business, but tonight it did. The woman was like water on a hot griddle. I thought—never mind what I thought. But I see it now, she's read the letters"—his expression hardened—"and so have you. Why else would you be hanging around. Still out to get me, huh?"

Yates kept his mouth shut, tried to think.

Greff shoved his face to within inches of Yates's. "Well, get this, if those letters get out, they'll put me away for the rest of my life—and ruin what's left of yours."

"Judging from the hot news from Biehle's death-bed, that's exactly where you belong."

"So the Stuart bitch does have them." Greff looked relieved. "I figured it, but wasn't sure. And you've read them."

"Yeah, I've read them. Added a whole new dimension to that amoral character of yours. So tell me, *Dad,* have you missed *any* of the seven deadly sins?" Yates leaned against the car, crossed his arms. "And I should make it clear that nothing this side of hell would make me happier than to see you looking out from behind steel bars."

Greff smiled. "And for that 'satisfaction' you're willing to stand by and watch that sweet sister of yours take a fall?"

Yates tensed, puzzled by Greff's choice of words. Greff being on the planet was a threat to Stella, but this sounded more specific. "Say again."

Greff's cold gaze fixed on Yates, calculating and unswerving. "It seems to me that our Stella was the last person with Ellie when she died. That right?"

Yates's blood chilled in his veins, but he took the hit, waited.

"Must have been tough, giving Ellie that final needle."

"You son of a bitch." Yates ground his teeth. "If you damn well reached up, you still wouldn't touch bottom."

Greff let out a heavy breath, and when he spoke again his voice was lower, less contained. "Look, Yates—or whatever the hell you call yourself—I don't want to mess with Stella, and I don't want to mess with you. All I want are those fucking letters."

"And if you don't get them, Stella finds herself under investigation for our mother's death?"

Greff picked an imaginary piece of lint from his cashmere coat. "She was the one looking after her. She was the one getting her the stuff. God knows, I know how that works."

"It was methadone, for Christ's sake. Not drugs. And she was doing great until she—"

"Did a little purchase on the side?" Greff shook his head. "One thing about addicts, they're predictable."

Yates took a breath. Why the hell was he even

talking about this—with Greff, of all people. "You should know, you started her on the stuff."

"She made her choice."

"That's it? That's how you see it."

"That's how it was."

Yates shook his head. "You're a soulless bastard, Greff—with a convenient memory. You know damn well you made that choice for her. You brought the stuff home, you encouraged her to take it, and you fed her addiction until you got what you wanted." Yates locked his hands in his pockets; if he hadn't, they would have been fists in Greff's smug face.

"She never said no."

Yates stared at the man who'd fathered him. "You don't feel a goddamn thing, do you? Not guilt. Not regret, nothing."

"You want to live in the past, son, you do it." He paused, and if so much as an eyelash flicked in remorse, Yates missed it. "Me," he finished, "I don't go there."

Yates envied him that.

Yates was fifteen when he found out about his mother's addiction. The dark family secret. Everybody had one.

But this one was tough to believe. Everything seemed all right. No bad withdrawal scenes, no tears and recriminations, just a quiet feeding of addiction only money and the privacy of the very rich could provide. When Yates was old enough to raise concerns, his mother got angry, denied everything, and Greff told him to mind his own business; he was handling it, weaning her off the stuff.

With no way into the problem, Yates opted for a

way out. He went to college, came out with a CPA, and went into the family business. That's when he figured things out. His father was managing his wife's addiction all right—but he'd also initiated it to get control of her family business, which he'd morphed into a major money-laundering operation.

Yates confronted his father, threatened to take what he'd learned to the police unless Greff sold the business and paid his mother what it was worth. With no alternative, Greff caved.

Yates took his sister and mother, now sick and desperate for treatment, to San Francisco. The three of them had stayed tight until his mother's death two years ago.

Ironically the Lang business was shipping. Apparently Greff had gone back to his roots.

"Look, it's a waste of time talking about Ellie," Greff said. "She's gone. Game over. Life goes on and all that shit."

"The philosopher speaks."

"Get me the letters." Greff paused. "A million should make it worth your while—and I'll leave the Stella thing alone."

"First, there isn't a bribe big enough. Second, Stella had nothing to do with Mother's death and you damn well know it."

"What I know and what I want others to believe are different things." His features flattened and his voice dropped. "This isn't sixteen years ago, Yates. I'm calling the shots this time. So don't make the mistake of underestimating me. Get me the letters. That piece up there"—he gestured toward the upper floors of the house with his head—"she's ripe, hasn't been serviced in years. Bed the bitch. You'll have some fun, and I'll get what I want. Then we can both move on."

Yates's normally clear mind went blank, then black. What Greff said sickened him, but he thought about Tracy and all the other nameless women in his life. He hated the fact that the scenario his father painted was one he was all too familiar with. It disgusted him that in this way he'd been his father's son.

Hannah didn't deserve either one of them.

It was time for Yates to play his hand, sooner than he would have chosen, but Greff gave him no choice. "I'll get the letters, but there's a string."

"I'm listening."

Yates pushed away from Greff's Ferrari, stepped closer to him. "You shut down Zanez Shipping's dirty business, and you leave the country."

Greff's eyes narrowed. "How do you know about Zanez?"

"Through Vonecker." Yates figured that was as good an answer as any.

Greff looked resigned—and angry. "Should have guessed that asshole would slip up."

Yates ignored the comment. "Do we have a deal?"

Greff smiled fleetingly, as if at some private joke, and didn't say anything for a long time. "All these years and you're still trying to shut me down." He shook his head. "But then you've always been a self-righteous son of a bitch."

"And you've always been an ego-driven, amoral bastard. I repeat, do we have a deal?"

"Sure. Why not?" He said it casually.

"Another thing."

Greff's face darkened. "Yeah?"

Yates leveled his gaze, felt his jaw harden, and added, "Leave Hannah Stuart alone. She's unstable. She could blow it for all of us." He glanced back at the house. "She's determined to turn the letters over to the cops. If it weren't for the old woman—Miranda—my guess is you'd already be behind bars." A few lies, a little truth.

Greff opened his car door, got in, and lowered the window. "Get the letters. You do that, and I'm history. You, Stella, the Stuart woman will never hear from me again. But get this and get it good— if you don't come through, I'll do it my way, and it won't be pretty."

Yates watched him drive off, his eyes on the car until the taillights faded into the distance. He didn't move, set in place by anger, disgust, and a painful but useless regret about the father who never was.

As a kid there'd been some kind of love; he remembered that. With kids, love came packed as standard equipment. Love—and trust. Yates shook his head. That had to be some kind of cruel joke. What kids should come with was suspicion and a loaded handgun. That way they'd have a fighting chance against men like his father. And the perverts waiting for his shipments.

". . . never hear from me again." That's what Greff said, and that was exactly what Yates wanted—for him, and for Stella. Not that it would make anything right. The price was too high. He looked up to the second floor, where a shadow came and went across Hannah's window.

The one thing Yates did *not* intend to do was seduce Hannah Stuart to get the letters. He wasn't taking any damn moral high ground here, or trying to spite Greff. It was about boundaries. His.

And it was that kiss.

No way was he going to repeat that. Hannah Stuart, with her midnight eyes, sad soul—and lushly welcoming mouth—scared the hell out of him.

He walked back into the house.

As he did so, a curtain rustled closed on the far end of the second floor.

Hannah heard the car start up and drive away, and after a minute or two heard the door close behind Yates. She listened for his footsteps on the stairs, planned to intercept him there. When he didn't come, she put on her robe, went to the corridor railing, and looked down into the foyer. A sliver of light came from the library.

She hesitated, but not for long. Yates and Greff had talked for at least half an hour. She had a right to know what it was about, how it would affect her and Kenninghall.

Yates was pouring himself a glass of scotch from the decanter on the coffee table when she walked in. He looked up, didn't seem at all surprised to see her. He was always so irritatingly cool.

"Would you like one?" he said, tipping his glass in the direction of the crystal decanter.

Hannah was about to say no, but changed her mind. "Yes, I think I will. Thanks."

He poured her two fingers and handed it to her without a word. Hannah took the glass, perched on the arm of a worn settee, its tapestry fabric from the early twentieth century, and switched on a Tiffany shaded lamp. It warmed rather that lit the room. Still Yates didn't speak.

"I suppose you expect an apology."

He frowned at her. "For what?"

"Me. Messing up tonight."

"You didn't mess up." He took a swig of scotch.

"I did. I should have known better. Greff's not an easy man to dupe."

Hannah rubbed her throat with her left hand. "So he knows, then. That I've read Milo's letters."

"He knows."

Hannah processed this information, assessed the danger. A lump of dread settled in her stomach. "Then he'll be back."

"Not for a while."

"I don't understand. Those letters will put him in jail—probably for the rest of his life. Of course he'll come back." Her voice rose, and she set her glass on the table. "And it's my fault. I should have held myself together. Damn!" She rubbed her arms, suddenly cold, awash in images of gun-toting villains laying waste to Kenninghall's treasures in search of Milo's letters. It was too hideous to contemplate.

"He won't be back, not for a while anyway—because I promised to get him the letters."

Hannah's jerked her head up. "You what?"

"As a delaying tactic, it was the best I could come up with." Yates gave her cool look. "You have any better ideas, I'm happy to hear them."

"But why? And how did he think you could get them? You don't even know where they are."

He eyed her under hooded lids. "He thinks I can seduce them out of you."

Hannah felt her face warm. "He said that?"

"It's how he operates. He doesn't see any reason it wouldn't work for me."

Hannah kept quiet. She'd dice her tongue before admitting Greff might be right.

Yates went on. "And he offered me something else. Money."

"How much money?"

"Does it matter?" He eyed her curiously.

"Yes, it does."

"A million dollars."

Hannah closed her eyes; now her visions were of Yates picking every lock in the house, slivering old oak, gouging ancient bureaus. "That's a lot of money." She gave him a straight look, picked up her drink. "Enough to make a man do almost anything."

"Almost." He drained his glass, set it on the mantel.

Hannah didn't know where to go from here. One thing was certain: this nightmare she'd been living in since Milo died wasn't about to end anytime soon. Oh, she could make lists about what vases to buy, which ones to sell, and for how much. She could plan her day around invoices and bills of sale, but figuring out what to do about a man like Yates Lang simply wasn't list material. Dear God, but she was tired of being confused, tired of every day bringing new people, new revelations. New emotions.

"I'm not going to take his money." Yates walked over to where she'd sat heavily on the sofa, untouched drink in hand. He stood over her. "And I'm not going to seduce you. If that was my plan, I'd hardly have advised you of it in advance, would I?"

His eyes, when she looked into them, told her nothing, and she let out a weary sigh. "If you don't mind, I think I'll reserve judgment on that." Damn it, she was too tired for suspicion and guile, too numbed by the events of the evening to differentiate between truth and lies. She lifted the glass to her mouth, drank too much, too quickly. The burn of the scotch made her eyes water.

"Give me that," he said, nodding toward her glass, then taking it from her hand. "Let's go for a drive."

"A drive? It's after eleven."

"They close the roads around here?"

"No, but—"

"Forget the buts. We both need to get away from this place for awhile. We'll take the '37 Cord. You owe me a test drive at least. It does run, doesn't it?"

"Yes, but—"

He took her hand and pulled her to her feet. "No buts, remember. Why don't you get changed, grab the keys, and meet me in the garage. There's not much chance of either of us sleeping tonight."

He was right about that. "What if . . . *he* comes back?" Her grip tightened around his hand, quick and involuntary.

"He won't. You're safe for a few days at least."

Safe from Greff? Maybe. Now all she had to figure out was if she was safe from Yates, but she decided it would be better to ride around La Conner beside him than lie in bed sweating with suspicion—or that other unnamed feeling she'd had since he'd kissed her. "Okay."

"Good."

Meara stuffed her ten dollars' worth of winnings in her handbag and straightened the collar on her tweed jacket, smiling at Miranda and Claire as she pulled her felt hat down and over her ears.

"Ah, and it's thankin' you I am for a wonderful

evening." She patted her purse, unable to resist a gloat.

Claire laughed. "I'm guessing by how thick you're laying on the Irish, Meara, that it's the cash rather than the company that's made your evening so wonderful."

Laughing, Miranda pushed her wheelchair closer to Meara and offered her hand. "And sure I'll be getting my money back soon enough, me darlin.' "

"Miranda!" Claire protested. "Do not encourage the woman. Your *Irish* is even worse than hers." She leaned close and planted a kiss on Meara's cheek. "And I'm still not convinced that 'zedonk' is a real word."

Meara chuckled, plump with her winnings and good will. A fine evening, it was.

With a couple of "See you next weeks" exchanged, she closed Miranda's door behind her and started her walk home.

My, but the night was a cold one. A frost tonight, for sure. The sky was clear as glass with a brilliant moon and pretty puffy clouds, their edges nicely hemmed in dark gray lace. Still, it was a pleasant break from the rain the weatherman said would be with them until the end of month.

Meara snuggled into her warm coat and picked up her pace. She'd make herself another cup of tea when she got home, take it to bed, and burrow into her latest mystery novel. She couldn't wait.

She didn't think about the white van until it passed her. But when she registered how slowly it was moving, she turned to watch it go down the street. At this time of night, on the flat roads around La Conner, you were more likely to see speeders, youngsters out too late with their foot too heavy on the gas pedal. She was surprised to see the van slow even more as it neared Miranda's house, then suddenly pick up speed and head off down the road.

Before she was home, she saw it again. This time driving by Kenninghall. Lost? Maybe.

But she was glad they hadn't stopped to ask her for directions. Those awful vans made her nervous. Weren't they always on TV and in the newspapers, the people in them up to no good at all. If she saw it again, she'd call it in, her being part of the neighborhood watch and all.

But her hot tea and mystery book beckoned, and she thought no more about it.

Chapter 18

"This is like riding a go-cart on a cow pasture," Yates said, maneuvering the old Cord away from the lumpy tar patches that dotted the road they were on. "I guess they didn't go in for springs in the thirties."

Yates was enjoying the ride all the same, and though he hated to admit it, he loved the powerful old car. Unlike today's cars, one tech step away from driving themselves, this baby needed a driver, a man with two good eyes, a firm grip on the wheel, and a quick response to the road ahead. But God help them if they hit a serious bump. If they did, there was a chance this old girl would break into a million parts.

Two minutes later he hit the *serious* bump, and the car shuddered threateningly. "Sorry," he said, and glanced at Hannah, gritting his teeth and smiling at the same time.

"Do you truly like cars or was that a lie, too?"

Like the bump in the road, Hannah's flat, matter-of-fact question caught him off guard. He might be halfway relaxed, but she was hunkered into her heavy coat as if they were dogsledding through the Antarctic. Not that he blamed her; the car was drafty and cold. If the old gal had a heater, he hadn't found it.

"Never thought about them much, but I think I'm about to start." He pushed down on the gas and the old Cord growled forward.

They drove along in silence. When it got to him, Yates said, "Do you want to go back to Kenninghall?"

She sighed. "No. This is a good idea. Let's drive until . . . next year."

"We'll run out of gas." Yates switched lanes to pass a white van cruising ten miles under the limit. "And we wouldn't be gone long enough."

"He scares me, Yates. *Really* scares me."

Yates knew they were back to Greff again. "That's only smart. Greff should scare you." He turned onto a road that led them to the shoreline of the Saratoga Passage, the narrow strip of ocean water that separated the Washington mainland and the fields of La Conner from Whidbey Island. He stopped the car, turned off the ignition.

"But what's even smarter is for you to forget about him for a while," he said.

She put her head back on the seat, pulled her coat tighter around her. "And how do you propose I do that?" She spoke more to herself than to him, as if the idea of expunging Greff from her mind was too difficult to contemplate. She closed her eyes.

Yates looked at her weary face. A face he'd not

yet seen lit by joy or anything close to laugher. He wanted to touch her skin, run a hand along her white throat, tell her everything would be okay, but that wouldn't be true—given her definition of okay was to see Greff put away for murder. Something Yates was determined to avoid.

He put some space between them, leaned his back against the car door. "Try this. He's gone, and he's going to stay gone. And when his current business is shut down, which will be soon, he'll be out of your life forever." That much was true, at least.

Silence filled the confined space within the car. And Hannah didn't look disposed to end it.

"What are you thinking?" he finally asked.

"I'm not thinking. I'm visualizing Greff behind bars. It's a comforting image."

Yates winced inwardly and Hannah slipped back into silence. He left her to it. If he didn't talk, he wouldn't lie.

"I've thought of something else that might make me forget him." She spoke without opening her eyes.

When Yates found his attention riveted on her mouth instead of her words, he looked away, out the narrow, straight windshield of the Cord and into the night. "And that is?"

She rolled her head to look at him, her gaze curious and unwavering. "You could kiss me again."

Yates's chest tightened, and he turned his attention from the view outside the car to the woman inside. Their gazes locked. She looked dead serious.

"Yeah, that made you *real* happy earlier this evening."

"I didn't like the 'experiment' part of it. The rest was—" She stopped abruptly and frowned.

"Don't bother finishing the sentence. I don't want to know."

"The rest of it was okay. Really, it was."

Yates rolled his eyes. "Thanks, I think." He'd have preferred the word spectacular. But he was glad they were off the subject of Greff.

Hannah kept her eyes on him, her frown deepening. "You know what?"

"What?"

"I've never made love to a man under fifty. Is it very different?"

Hell! "You know what?" he said.

"What?"

"Neither have I, so I wouldn't know."

Keeping her gaze locked with his, she actually smiled. He watched it grow from a light turning up of the lips to a full, impish grin that literally poured into his soul. And it was then he knew with no doubt at all, he was in heavy emotional territory with this woman. And he didn't have the vaguest idea what to do about it. He decided to run.

He straightened back in his seat and put his hand on the key in the ignition. It was past time to take Hannah home. She reached over and stopped his hand.

"Don't," she said.

"We should go. It's late."

"It's not midnight yet."

He rubbed the tension in the middle of his forehead. Knew there wasn't anything he could do to ease the tension growing lower in his body.

"You're nervous." She sounded half stunned by it and half amused. "I asked for a kiss, Yates, not a picket fence and a two-car garage."

"And what if a kiss isn't enough?"

She didn't answer, seemed to consider this. When she spoke, her tone was quiet, her words deliberate. "Ever since Milo's death, I've been on an emotional roller coaster. Kind of like that." She gestured toward the water, where a buoy bounced on the night-black ripples. "It's taken all my energy to stay afloat, think things through. But somewhere in the midst of all the . . . turmoil, I started to feel alive for the first time since—"

He watched her, said nothing. She left the thought unfinished.

"But I'm sick of thinking. I want to feel . . . something other than fear, anger and"—she looked out over the dark water—"endless, bottomless guilt."

Yates did something he shouldn't have; he touched her cheek, ran his hand down and under her chin, tugged her face back to face his. "You have nothing to feel guilty for. Do you hear me? Nothing."

"Yeah." The word was flat, and she looked away again.

He was losing her, losing that brief moment of wit and humor. Talking with Hannah was like trying to pigeonhole an eel. He was trying to think of something to say when she spoke again.

"About that kiss," she said at last.

She had his full attention.

"There's something you should know."

"Forget the kiss thing, would you."

Her eyes widened. "There, you see, you're telling

me what to do. Why is it everyone tells me what to do? And why in hell do I keep doing it!"

Yates blinked. Now she was mad.

She took a deep breath and rolled her head. Obviously trying to regain her composure. "Okay, if you'll be good enough to keep quiet, I'll say my piece, and then you can decide whether to kiss me or not to kiss me."

He was fascinated.

"What you should know is that I'll be, uh, using you. Nothing more."

"Using me," he repeated, this time determined to keep her on track. "How so?"

"As I think is perfectly clear, I'm not exactly myself right now. Which means my judgment isn't the best."

"Uh-huh." He sure as hell agreed with that statement. "And this means?"

"This means," she said carefully, "that I don't want any kind of emotional attachment. And I don't think you do either."

"I'd say that's a good judgment call."

Looking satisfied with his answer, she went on. "Then if the kiss does lead to, uh, something more, and we both walk away, neither party will have . . . misgivings."

"You ever had cold-blooded sex before, Hannah?"

"No."

"Well, I can tell you it comes with its own brand of misgivings."

"You'd know all about that, I suppose."

"What? Cold-blooded sex, or misgivings?"

She kept her eyes on him, waited for him to answer his own question.

"Yes," he finally said. "I do. Now, can we get out of here?" He reached for the key again, but she was too fast for him. She had it out of the ignition and fisted in her hand before his was halfway to the wooden dashboard.

"This is stupid. You have no idea what you're doing. What you're asking for." Frustrated, he ran his hand through his hair, glared out the window. This had to be a first. Him saying no to a woman.

He felt her hand fork through his hair where his had just been. Hers was infinitely gentler. When she ran a finger over the rim of his ear, his breathing turned heavy; so did his damn eyelids. And by the time she stroked the evening stubble on his jaw and tugged his face toward hers, he'd already surrendered. Unless there was divine intervention, Hannah was going to get her kiss—and a whole lot more.

He held himself back, tried to think of a way out while all his body could think about was the way in.

"Look at me," she said, her voice quiet.

Unconsciously, he'd closed his eyes to think. Now he opened them, looked at her. He shouldn't have.

He was in her eyes, the way a man dreams of being in a woman's eyes.

This was serious trouble.

He tugged her close, took her face in his hands. "Here's the deal. You give me the keys, I start the car, and I drive us back to Kenninghall. If, by the time we get there, you still think you want some cold-blooded sex"—he stroked her jawline with his thumbs—"I'll see what I can do."

* * *

To Hannah, the bouncing, twenty-minute ride home felt like an eternity. When doubts initiated their brand of mayhem in her thoughts, she resisted them. She didn't want doubts, refused to second-guess the first honest, powerful desire she'd felt in years. She didn't know where it came from, but she knew it was a gift. A gift given her in the here and now of this day.

She'd slid into the confining space of the old car an hour ago, hoping for a mindless run, a break in the tension that had dogged her for days. She'd watched vacantly as the dark cold night rushed by the windows, sensing but not seeing Yates's effort to maneuver the precious car along the patched, uneven country roads with a deft hand.

The car had a distinctive, mesmerizing running sound, an orchestra of metal that propelled it along the road with a strong and comforting roar. The boisterous motor working its own rough magic to displace thoughts of Greff, Libby, and her own endless litany of errors. After a few minutes, she'd closed her mind to all of them, heard nothing but the road and the rumble of the big car.

But she couldn't shut out Yates, his presence only inches away. So close. Touching distance.

She stole looks at his angular profile, etched in shadow against the window and made stark by the light of the moon. And when the scent of him, clean and woodsy, crossed the seat between them, her chest tightened and something snagged in her throat, making her breathing low and uneven. If Yates was aware of her scrutiny, he didn't show it. He remained silent, concentrating on the car's gears and gas pedal to take them past downtown La Conner and along the darkened road leading to the waterfront. She knew he thought she was resting, but she wasn't. She was more on edge—in a totally new kind of way—than she'd been in years.

Her million-dollar man. Would he truly turn down a million dollars to get the letters? Would anyone? She considered this. Yates had told her of the offer, but she wasn't sure what that meant; he'd peppered lies into his truths since his first day at Kenninghall.

But hadn't those lies been necessary? Part of his work. Yates was hired to close down Zanez Shipping and bring everyone involved to justice. He didn't need the letters for that. He only needed time. When he was done with his work, she'd turn the letters over to the police as she planned. Besides, if he took the million, it would make him part of Greff's filthy business. She could not make herself believe he would ever do that.

She'd studied him more, this time more fancifully, tried to figure out whether he was handsome or not. She thought, maybe, in a unique-to-Yates kind of way. High forehead, outdoorsy skin, early fine lines spraying out from the corners of his eyes. Eyes, that when focused on you, did so with a sharp, fascinated intelligence. She had the impression he missed very little of what went on around him.

And that's when they'd hit a bump in the road. And when the car clattered and shook with a vengeance, Yates had first grimaced, then looked across at her and smiled.

She'd looked at his mouth, remembered how it felt on hers—how it brought her body singing toward life, kindled a kind of craving she'd long forgotten.

She wanted that again, wanted to lose herself in the physical, not to forget, but to remember, a place and time when a warm body, deep kisses, and the gentleness of touch could enchant, heal. Yates could give her what she wanted. So she'd asked for it.

She wouldn't back away now, let her unreliable logic feed her a million reasons why it was a mistake. She didn't care. It was sex. Only sex.

And it was one night.

All she wanted was one night in his arms. Erotic oblivion. Trouble was, he didn't seem inclined to oblige.

Yates stopped the car in front of the garage, pushed the remote opener on the key chain, and drove into the empty stall.

When the garage door closed behind them, he made no move to get out of the car and neither did Hannah.

His eyes were dark in the poor light coming into the front seat of the car. "Have you come to your senses?" he asked.

"Yes, I think I have." She opened her door and stepped out. Yates did the same.

"Good." He stared at her across the top of the Cord . . . looking relieved? Disappointed? She wasn't sure. "I'll see you in the morning, then."

"No. I'll see you in twenty minutes."

A totally unreadable expression crossed his face. "I'm not coming to your room, Hannah."

"I agree. It's too close to Libby's. I'll come to yours."

He cursed.

It made Hannah smile. "Invoking the deities won't save you, Yates." She dropped the smile. "What will is an absolute, unequivocal no. I will take that to mean you don't, uh, want me. And that will be the end of it." She waited.

He looked like a man in finger screws.

When Hannah realized he hadn't said no, she turned and walked out of the garage.

Yates watched her leave, locked the car and garage, and told himself to take a walk, cool off, think. And that's exactly what he did.

He walked to the house, up the stairs, and directly into his room. For a minute or two he stood staring at the lock on his door. He could turn it. Make the problem go away.

Trouble was, Hannah was one hell of a problem. He wondered about the chances of her ever forgiving him—if he locked the door, or he didn't.

He decided on the latter. He'd never aspired to sainthood, why the hell start now?

He was in the shower when she came to him, and without a word, she stripped off her clothes and joined him.

In the shower, hot water beating on them and finding no path between their bodies, he kissed her, taking his time, then giving his soul.

If, in his most insane moment, he'd thought of saying no to her, the moment was past. This was the point of no return. If he'd ever been this hard, this damn wanting, he couldn't remember.

She fit into his water-slicked body as if she were part of him, her dark hair plastered to her face and shoulders, her breasts flush to his chest. When he lifted his mouth from hers, she put a hand to his face. Her eyes were large, pupils dilated. Her nipples hard little knots against his chest.

"I think you are," she whispered, and kissed his stubbled chin.

"Am what?" He ran his hands down to her buttocks and shifted his particularly impatient agony against her center.

"Handsome. I wasn't sure until now." She wrapped her arms around his neck, smiled into his eyes.

"A compliment and a dime will get you anywhere."

She looked down at her naked body. "And me without my wallet."

He ran his hand between their bodies, then his finger through the wet curls at the apex of her thighs. She bucked into his hand, gasped against his mouth.

"Honey," he murmured. "I think you can forget about the dime." He fingered her deeply, stroked her until his own need was a white blur in his brain. She leaned into his hand, rocked against him, and tangled her fingers in his hair. He heard her moan, a second before she grasped his shoulders and dug in her nails. Her body grew heavy in his arms.

Hell, not yet.

He reached behind her, turned off the shower, and lifted her in his arms. They hit his bed in a shower-soaked tumble. Yates prayed for patience. She'd been in his arms less than five minutes and he was so wild, so damn hot for her, he thought he'd explode. He rolled onto his back, put some space between them. The cool air of the room replaced the heat of Hannah's body—for about three seconds.

"What's wrong," she asked, and climbed on his

chest. Her nipples nested in his chest hair. Small heated stones.

"Nothing's wrong, if you want this bout of love-making to make the *Guinness Book of World Records* as the shortest in history."

She ran her palm across his chest, kissed where her hand had traveled, and lifted sex-filled eyes to his. "Sounds okay to me." She kissed one of his nipples, nipped it. "After that we can try for the longest."

He smiled through his lust-crazed pain, moved a wet strand of hair to behind her ear. "I've got my-self an insatiable." He kissed her slowly. "That makes me a lucky man."

She smiled back, then as suddenly the smile came, it dropped from her lips. "It's been a long time for me, Yates. You already know that—Greff certainly did."

He put a finger to her lips. "Don't go there."

She took a breath. "I'm not. I'm here. With you. And it's you I want inside me. Maybe too much. But it's the truth, at least."

Yates didn't want to think about truth. He rolled her onto her back, cupped her breast, and rolled its nipple idly between thumb and index fin-ger. He watched her eyes drift closed, her torso shift toward his hand. "Then let's do it, Hannah. Because inside you is exactly where I want to be."

And that was a truth he found impossible to bear.

He readied her, and slipped into her silk. Han-nah's long satisfied moan fell on his senses with the crescendo of a thousand violins. It was as if her whole being constricted, clutched at him.

He plunged deep. Deeper still.

His own body exploding under him, his mind a vortex of undiluted pleasure, a thought tore through his head lightning fast, incapable of capture.

Spilling into Hannah, he grasped for it, its fullness eluding him. Only a question remaining . . .

Why this woman? And for God's sake, why now?

Chapter 19

Hannah did not want to open her eyes. It would be a dream, she was sure of it, and she would find herself cold again—and alone. When Yates moved to shift his weight from her breasts, she held him close, unwilling to lose his warmth, the solidity of his body lying against the length of her own.

Yates let her hold him for a moment, then mumbled something about his crushing her. Rolling to his side, he took her in his arms and softly kissed her temple. If Hannah had known how to purr, she would have. She settled for snuggling closer.

Here in the depth of the night, on rumpled sheets, her body still heated and slick from love-making, she felt renewed. And unafraid.

She turned her head toward the sound of Yates's still-ragged breathing and opened her eyes. He was staring at her, his gaze narrowed, filled with speculation and a darker emotion she couldn't identify. He lifted his head to again kiss her forehead. "You all right?" he said.

"All right doesn't cover it. More like perfect."
She ran her hand along his sleek bicep. Her touch
made him tremble.

Hannah didn't want to talk anymore, didn't want
words to get in the way of sensation. She wanted
him—again. But she'd pushed it this far, pretty
much assaulted the man in the shower; she had to
stop somewhere. The next move was up to Yates.
She sighed and stretched, relishing the feeling of
her breasts flush to the arm he'd rested along her
rib cage.

Yates hardened against her thigh, and when
Hannah smiled at him, he smiled back, a lazy, teasing smile that arrowed straight to her heart. He
cupped her breast, leaned over and kissed its tip, before taking her nipple completely. Hannah let her
eyes drift to a close, gave way to his seductive mouth.

She'd forgotten her body could bring her so
much pleasure. Its reawakening numbed her mind.
Her senses leaped and sizzled under Yates's light-
est touch, like winter rain on a bonfire. But even in
the fire's midst was a deep calm, a gathering of
power. It was as if she'd rediscovered an old—long
forgotten—friend.

Yates stopped, took a ragged breath, and rested
his thumb on the moist nipple he'd been suckling.
"We should talk," he murmured, his expression
stolid, his words toneless.

Her body again bright with need, she mumbled
her response. "Is that what you want to do? Talk?"

He took his thumb from the point of her breast,
licked her nipple as if it were rich cream, then
moved a hand down to where heat and moisture
awaited his probing fingers. He stroked her and
his eyes darkened. "Hell, no," he growled.

Hannah, her body taut and ready, began a slow melt, gave way to his heated touch. Her moan, low, long, and satisfied, said more than a million words.

She heard him murmur in her ear . . . about this being the end of it . . . or him, then her senses shut down to anything outside of Yates's hot, hard body coming down on and into hers.

It was four in the morning when Hannah awoke. With only a sheet pulled over their naked bodies, the only warm part of her was where Yates pressed against her back. Judging from his easy breathing, he was deeply asleep. When Hannah, loathe to disturb him, groped blindly for a blanket, he woke instantly, rose on one elbow to retrieve the quilt for her.

"I should go," she said.

He returned to his position at her back, tucked her close to him. "Not yet." He kissed her bare shoulder. "Not yet."

Hannah thought he fell back to sleep, but a few minutes later, he asked, "Before Milo, before Will and Christopher, Hannah. What?"

At the mention of Will and Chris, grief and tension bound the muscles under her nape into their familiar aching stricture.

As if he knew, Yates shoved her hair aside and kissed her there, then worked the knot in her lower neck with a gentle one-handed massage. "Before Will and Christopher," he repeated calmly.

"An aunt. My dad's only sister," she said, easing warily into the time before her world imploded. "She took me when my dad died. Hard for her, probably. She was close to seventy."

"What happened to your parents?"

"My mother walked out on my dad and me when I was three," she said.

"And?"

"And she never looked back. She died a couple of years later. I was . . . five, I think. I don't really have any memory of her. A couple of pictures, that's it." The place in her heart she'd always held for what she'd come to see as her fantasy mom had become a blurry collage of regret, confusion, and wishful dreaming, difficult to interpret and impossible to explain. How do you explain missing someone you never knew? She moved on. "My dad died of a heart attack. He was only fifty-four. I miss him every day."

Yates rolled her to face him, propped himself on an elbow, and rested his free hand on her thigh. "How old were you when he died?"

"Thirteen."

"Rough." He touched her hair, her cheek.

"Life," she said. "Everybody has one." She didn't want his sympathy and didn't like to talk about herself. What he needed to know, he'd learned in the chapel. Why she'd opened up as she had that day, said the things she'd said, she didn't know. Maybe it was the way his eyes, so green, so unfathomable, focused so intently while he listened, as if every word said was weighed and valued.

"And then?" he urged.

She lifted a brow. "You ask a lot of questions."

He fell back on the bed. "Yeah, Stella says that all the time."

It was Hannah's turn to be interested. "And Stella would be . . . ?" God, she was holding her damn breath.

Yates looked as if he'd bitten his tongue. "My sister."

Hannah waited for him to say more, then asked. "And?"

"And what?"

"Did you fall off a turnip cart or do you also lay claim to a mother, father . . . brothers?"

"Nope. Stella's it."

"What happened to them?"

"Mother's dead. A couple of years ago now." He paused. "Father's . . . gone."

"Gone?"

"As gone as it gets." He rolled back up to loom over her, kissed her suddenly, and a half smile played over his mouth when he said, "Somehow we've managed to get off the main subject."

"Which is?"

"You." He ran his finger between her naked breasts. "Tell me about your aunt."

"Aunt Carolyn was okay. She did what she believed was the right thing, taking in her brother's daughter. But I was thirteen, still grieving for Dad, and not particularly easy to have around. She made rules, I broke them. She made more rules . . ." Hannah took Yates's hand in hers, played with his fingers. "We were never what you'd call close."

"That doesn't sound like you. You strike me as a woman who likes rules."

She knew it was impossible for anyone to visualize that young and difficult *girl*, a *girl* who badly wanted to make her own way but who had no idea how to do it. She barely remembered her herself. "I do. Now."

He waited.

"When I was seventeen—"

"Uh-huh."

"I met Will." She paused to recollect, and was surprised that instead of the usual chill Will's memory brought, she was warmed by it. "Aunt Carolyn was an antique nut, and she always went to Will's shop. I avoided it like the plague." She gave him a faint smile. "All that very uncool old stuff.

"Anyway, he offered me a job after high school—actually I think Aunt Carolyn arranged it out of desperation, when I showed no interest in going to college. Five years later, I married him. It was Will who put me through college." She touched where her heart rested in her chest, and her finger met and hooked with Yates's. Like a loose chain, it bound them when she went on. "I think I loved him from my first day working in his store. He was so . . . confident. So sure and honest."

Yates studied her, his expression deeply thoughtful. "There are good memories, then?"

"Yes." But Hannah hadn't brought them to mind for a long time. She'd been wrong, she realized, to let all the good memories be submerged by the bad. Wrong to let the violence completely destroy the beauty of what she'd had with her husband and son.

Yates continued to study her, but he didn't ask any more questions, and she was glad of it. Hannah had some questions of her own, but for now she was content to lie enfolded in the night's deep silence and Yates's strong arms.

There was always tomorrow.

Bone picked up on the first ring of his cell phone.
"Where the hell are you?"

"Where I'm supposed to be." He gnawed the last bit of chicken from the bone and tossed it at the trash can. He missed. He picked another piece out of the bucket of six.

"When did you get there? And why haven't you answered your phone?" She sounded mad as hell and running hot in the panic department.

"That's two questions. Which one you want answered first?"

"You've got a smart mouth, considering I'm holding the rest of your cash."

"Maybe, but I've got five grand and a set of keys to a van sitting right outside this door. I could split right now. Suit me fine. What about you?"

He heard her sharp intake of breath, a sailor's curse. "Okay, Bone, for now we'll do it your way. But I repeat, when did you get there?"

"Last night. Already did a drive-around."

"And?"

"Don't see no problems. 'Cept some kind of neighborhood patrol thing they got happenin' around here. That'll take some checkin' out. Like I said, no problem. I'll do another drive-around, maybe two, and that's it."

"Good. Just get it done before month's end. You've got my number?"

"Yeah." Christ, this was like talkin' to his old lady when he was ten.

"Call me immediately when the job's done. Hear?"

Bone rolled his eyes, took a swig of beer. "Yeah, I said so, didn't I?"

"And answer your fucking phone from now on." She hung up.

"And fuck you." Bone turned the phone off and tossed it onto the bed beside him.

Christ! She pissed him off. Too bad she wouldn't be in

the damn house when he torched it. That would make
this whole, lousy, ass-freezin' trip worthwhile.

He pushed the on button of the remote, flipped to the
weather channel, and went back to munching on his
chicken.

Hannah stepped into the hall at the same time
Yates arrived on the second-floor landing from his
room on the third floor. It was almost eight o'clock,
late for Hannah, who usually showed up in the
kitchen before seven. But she'd hoped Yates would
sleep even longer.

Give her time to clear her mind.

She wasn't prepared to run into him quite so
soon, or for the wild surge of morning-after heat
and confusion that engulfed her when she saw his
clean-shaven face, caught the scent of his woodsy
aftershave. She'd spent what was left of the night
after leaving his bed pushing him away from her
consciousness. She'd made the rules—no emotional attachments—and she intended to observe
them. They'd had sex, not exchanged vows.

"Hi," he said, settling his unsettling eyes on her.

"Hi, back." Not brilliant opening dialogue, but
obviously the best either of them could come up
with.

"I'm glad I ran into you."

But Hannah thought he looked more preoccupied than pleased. She joined him at the top of the
stairs and they descended together. "I expected we
would," she said.

"Would what?" he asked, still with his I'm-not-
really-here expression.

"Run into each other." She stopped midway on the stairs. "What's wrong, Yates? You look a thousand miles away." Maybe he was having morning-after regrets. The thought rankled.

He stopped, one stair below her, gave her his full attention. "I'm glad I ran into you," he repeated. "Because I didn't want you to think I was running out. I had a call from Anne Chapman. She wants a meeting. I'm on my way to Seattle."

"Is it about Greff?"

"Yes. She has some new information. It may . . . accelerate things."

"I'll drive in with you."

"Won't work," he said, too quickly.

"Why not?"

"Because what goes on between Chapman and me is confidential. There's no reason for you to be there." His voice was curt, dismissive. "She knows nothing about the letters, and for now there's no reason she should. It would only muddy the water."

His rebuff, coupled with the hard set of his mouth, set Hannah back. "I didn't plan on going to your meeting," she said, her confusion resetting to a foolish hurt. "I have an appointment in Seattle today. I just thought we might make the drive together."

He grimaced, cursed under his breath. "Sorry. Overreaction. Of course you can drive in with me."

"I think I'll drive myself." Hannah's own voice was cool. She stepped away from him and grasped the stairs' handrail, not because she was afraid of falling, but because she recognized the cold wind blowing through her chest, chilling her heart, telling her to run and hide. Withdrawal: it had been her answer for everything for five years. It was her familiar, known and comfortable. "There's coffee in the kitchen. You should have one before you go."

"Wait . . ."

She picked up her pace, quickly covered the last of the steps, and crossed the hall to her office, a room entered through the library. When she had both sets of doors closed, she went directly to her desk.

By the time she got there, the impulse to run was replaced by a blazing anger. The arrogance! What did the man think? That she'd cling to him like hundred-year-old ivy?

She heard her office door open. She swung around to see Yates striding toward her. Without a word, he grabbed her shoulders and yanked her hard against his body. His gaze was equally hard when he said, "Sweetheart, you've got to stop running. Learn to stand your ground." Then he crushed her to him and kissed her senseless. He ended the kiss and stood her away from him. "Get your coat. You can do your thing while I meet with Chapman."

She considered the letter opener on her desk, what damage it would do if she plunged it into his ocean-sized ego, but her hands were as weak as her knees. "You know, Yates Lang, I'm not absolutely sure I even like you."

He gave her a half smile. "Get your coat," he repeated, more softly this time, and walked from the room.

It took an effort for Yates to stay in his chair. Anne Chapman didn't try. She stalked around her office like a German shepherd on guard duty.

Yates—now that Vonecker was gone and the firm of Simpson and Chapman's integrity was intact—had been determined to make Anne see reason, drop the Zanez investigation. But so far it was Anne who'd done the talking.

And Yates hadn't liked a thing she'd said so far.

"And you're sure about this information," he asked.

"I'm sure," she said. "First I had another call from my Asian girl—who still refused to meet no matter how expertly I cajoled—then I went back through Vonecker's files and the latest shipping schedule from the Port of Seattle. All the dates meshed. I have no reason to believe the girl is lying." She stopped patrolling her office and faced him. "Zanez has a ship due into the Port of Seattle the first week in November—with its usual cargo of misery—and we have to stop it."

Yates said nothing, his mind on overdrive. If Greff did what he said he'd do, Zanez would be out of business within a month, everything nice and quiet. But if Yates blew the whistle on this shipment, it would be all over the papers, screw up everything. "We have the cops meet the boat, and there's a good chance Hallam and everyone else involved—on both sides of the Pacific Ocean—walks. Hell, he'll just blame the ship's captain, take his pals and his *customer* list, stroll down the dock, and start all over again. You know how these guys work." There had to be another way, and Yates needed to find it, fast.

"I know." She looked tired, sat heavily on the chair behind her desk. "But I also know we can't let those young girls be herded down a gangplank into the nearest brothel."

Yates stood. "We've got a few days. Let me think about it." Yates knew he could think on it for the rest of his life, but he'd only come up with one solution. Get Hannah's letters, wave them in Greff's face, and tell him to do whatever it took to turn the ship around.

"I'll give you what time I can, Yates. But if you don't come up with anything, I'll have to notify the police and port authorities."

"You could drop it," he said. "The minute you make that call, you and Simpson will be in Vonecker's dirt up to your armpits. You'll have a hell of a lot of explaining to do. Vonecker's gone, you could leave it alone."

She stared at him with eyes sharp as glass. "And what about you, Yates? Could you leave it alone?"

He didn't answer. "I'll call," he said, and walked out the door.

Hannah waited for Yates outside HeathBerns, a tiny antique shop tucked away on a side street not far from the Pike Place Market. The shop had recently taken on an estate consignment it wasn't large enough to handle, and the owner wanted Hannah to see if any of the pieces would be of interest to Kenninghall. It was almost one o'clock by the time Yates arrived to pick her up. She was huddled under a postage stamp-sized awning to avoid the rain that had started to fall the minute they'd left La Conner and hadn't let up since.

"Why didn't you wait inside?" He hustled her through the downpour and into his car.

"They closed for lunch a half hour ago. I didn't expect you'd be long, and I was dry enough." She settled her coat around her, and asked, "How did your meeting go?"

"I'll tell you when we get to my place."

"Your place?"

"I'd like to check my messages. Make a couple of calls. It won't take long. Do you mind?"

"Not at all." She was secretly delighted and beyond curious to see where—and how—Yates lived.

Chapter 20

Yates battled Seattle's downtown traffic for twenty minutes, then pulled up outside an ancient seven-story apartment building whose better days had been sometime in the sixties. The balconies off the suites looked more like storage platforms, displaying dead plants, bikes, barbecues, and cheap lawn furniture.

Hannah followed Yates in and watched him greet an old man who sat in the lobby near the elevator with a baseball bat across his lap. He appeared to be the only security, because there was no keypad at the door, and the main doors to the building weren't locked.

In the elevator, they stood in silence until it stopped at the sixth floor. From there Yates led her to some stairs and they climbed to the top floor. There was one door there. Yates opened it.

When she stepped inside, she couldn't believe her eyes. It was one high-ceilinged room, three thousand square feet at least, with windows on three sides. A scatter of glass tile partitions separated living areas.

It was practically devoid of furniture. There was a metal trestle-style desk and a high-back chair, a king-sized bed covered in gray linens, a fifties chrome kitchen set with a red Formica tabletop, and a low-slung, dark blue leather chair and sofa with an oval coffee table in front of it. This grouping sat on the only carpet to be awarded space on the old, highly polished wood floor. The one wall without windows was floor-to-ceiling storage. Hannah guessed it must hold everything from shoes to books to stereo systems. It appeared there was nothing in the room he didn't need. The place was as empty of things as Kenninghall was full of them—and clean enough to perform surgery.

Yates went directly to his desk and flipped open a laptop computer. While he checked his e-mail, Hannah wandered the room, listened to the rain beat against the high windows.

Out of the corner of her eye, she saw him scan the computer screen, the lines of e-mail, but from what she could see, he neither opened nor replied to any of them. When he picked up the phone to check his voice mail, his attention swung to her, and his eyes followed her restless movements around his apartment. Then one message caught his full attention and his expression hardened; he turned his back on her. He replayed the message, and she saw him lower his head and run a hand through his hair. Whatever the content of the message, she sensed it wasn't good.

He hung up the phone, his gaze again fixed on her, now predatory, gleaming with speculation and purpose.

The sound of his footsteps came and went as he moved from hardwood to carpet to where Hannah stood by the window.

He stopped in front of her, cradled her face between his hands. "You know, I made a big mistake this morning." He moved his thumbs along her jaw. "I should never have kissed you." His eyes went as darkly gray-green as the rain-splattered windows. "I've wanted more ever since."

He didn't ask, he took, his mouth lowering to hers as if in homecoming, infinitely gentle, skillfully demanding.

Hannah softened into the kiss, her knees weakening when he deepened it and enfolded her in his arms. He pulled back; his gaze was smoky, intense. "Last night was a mistake, but damned if I can't wait to repeat it."

He held her hands, looked her in the eyes, and said, "Make love with me, Hannah. Now. In my bed." He brushed his lips over hers. "Give me something to remember when I'm rattling around in here."

Hannah left her hands to rest in his, but found herself hesitating. She hadn't hesitated to be the aggressor last night, but now, with the tables turned, she was oddly fearful. Not of Yates, but of something opening up inside herself. Last night she'd given herself to the sex, used it—and Yates—as tools to bring her body to life. She hadn't counted on resurrecting her withered soul, didn't know if she could risk it again.

"I need you, need to be inside you," he said against her ear, his breath a brand, his big hands moving silkily down her body.

"It won't be the same . . . today." She wasn't sure why, but knew it to be true.

"No. It will be better." He tugged her toward his bed, his kisses soft and easy on her lips, her chin, her throat. "And after that? Better yet."

In the face of his urgency, Hannah's resistance slipped from her brain to the soles of her shoes. She shucked them off to set it completely free. "What woman can resist a promise like that."

He smiled, unbuttoned the coat she'd not planned on taking off, the six buttons running down the front of her white blouse, and the two buttons on the waistband of her black slacks. The whir of her zipper was the last real-world sound she heard. From then on her heart beat against her eardrums with the incessant pound of a jungle drum. Beyond that the world was silent; gone was the rasp of breath, the lashing of rain against the windows.

There was only Yates.

When she was naked, and he was not, he tossed back the covers and pressed her down onto his bed. Standing back, keeping his unwavering gaze on her, he removed his clothes.

In the cool room, dimmed by the dark afternoon downpour, she watched him with fascination and a growing impatience. The few seconds he took to get to her side were an eternity.

He straddled her, and without a word took her hands in his, lifted and stretched them over her head. Grasping her wrists, he imprisoned them there with one hand, spread her before him as if she were a feast. Hannah sighed, shifted to raise her breasts. Memories of this moment, blending with those of last night, flooded her senses.

Yates kissed each breast softly, and when he lifted his dark head, cool air rushed to chill the moisture left by his mouth. He bent to caress each breast in turn, their soft undersides, then watched her nipples harden and peak, as though mesmerized. He tasted each pointed tip, then took one deeply into his mouth, drawing on her so luxuriously, so slowly, she moaned as though in pain.

Her body, newly awakened last night, ripened quickly to a deep and glorious bloom. The rainy afternoon, the faint light, the muted roar of traffic in the street below, and the tangle of his sheets brought an unreal sense of time being disconnected from its forward movement, of it stopping solely for her, for Yates. She was breathing, but barely, thinking, but not clearly, and reaching, but not grasping for what she hadn't even known existed until last night.

Still Yates held her hands above her head, taking his time, relishing her quivering, heated body. "You're so beautiful. I love the way you feel under me. The way I feel inside you."

His erection was hard and heavy against her, and as skin chafed skin, he shuddered. Hannah was buffeted by his need, sexually confused by it—holding back but aching to give, yet loathe to give up his magical taking. His hands, his lips, his dark whispers took her to a new edge, an edge sharp with promise, lush with longing. She hung suspended, and Yates kept her there, his every touch seductive, masculine perfection.

He moved his hand down, stroked the inside of her thigh, coaxed her to open her legs for him. She did, and he released her hands. She brought them down, buried them in his glossy hair, held them there as he kissed her belly before shifting his attention, and his lips, lower.

He looked up at her then, stroked her exquisitely. His eyes lust-black in the diffused light, he watched her, his mouth hovering so close his breath riffled between her thighs.

Hannah constricted her body, desperate to hold back, but more desperate for what she knew Yates was about to do. Thoughts flew in and out of her head. Agitated thoughts. Agitated body. She was needing again, too much need . . . mistake . . . dangerous to trust . . . hot, too hot.

Her hands slipped from his hair to grasp the sheets. She bunched them, held tight, opened and closed her fingers, tore at the clean gray cotton. Her breath was hostage, deep in her throat, her senses sharp and bright with expectation, fully and painfully focused.

Waiting.

His hot breath blew gently over the spiking nerves of her exposed, achingly sensitive folds. He licked, long and slow, breathed lower yet, murmured hoarsely before his mouth closed over her and his tongue found and caressed the center of her burning.

It was almost five o'clock; Hannah hadn't stirred yet. She'd been sleeping for close to two hours while he prowled the large loft like a wounded animal.

The wound?

The woman in his bed.

He glanced at her sleeping form and quickly looked away again. How the hell Hannah had managed to slip into his psyche, he didn't know. Until now the only women he'd ever given a damn about were Stella and his mother. He hadn't planned on another, and he wasn't going to start now.

Wouldn't do him any good anyway, because in the end, she'd hate him.

He'd known what he had to do from the second he'd heard Stella's message on his voice mail. She'd called to tell him how, after all these years, she'd heard from Greff, how strange the call was, and how in the end she'd hung up on him, because he gave her the creeps, "sounding threatening." Yates knew Greff had called Stella to make his point, remind Yates how easily he could get to her. So he'd made a decision. He'd take his good old dad's advice, screw Hannah's brains out, get the letters, then get lost.

The apple didn't fall too far from the tree, no matter how rotten the fruit.

He'd screwed her brains out, all right; his body hardened again when he thought of what they'd done, and what he'd done to her in the past few hours, he'd worked her with everything he knew, but in the end he'd worked himself, but good.

Yates closed his eyes against the surge of guilt and regret about to blow off the top of his head. He pressed his palms against the rain-washed window, lowered his head to the cool glass, told himself again what he had to do.

Stay focused. Get the letters.

Then he'd be able to forget about Hannah Stuart and move on. Simple. This . . . feeling for her was conscience, or his brain on overdrive, or maybe he was thinking with his dick. The woman was a living miracle in bed. Any guy in his not-so-right mind was bound to get confused.

He felt a warm breath on his back.

"You're cold." Hannah stepped up behind him and wrapped her arms around his waist. He'd pulled on some sweats, hadn't bothered with a shirt. She rested her head against his back, and her hair was like rose petals against his skin.

Rose petals? Fuck! Now he was a goddamn poet!

"We should get going. It's getting late," she said, her voice, like the rest of her, not quite awake. She ran her hand down to the hard length under the soft sweats, rubbed him softly. "Hmm, this is nice."

He sucked up some air.

Do the job, Yates. Focus. The first screwing went well, now move on to the second one.

He pulled his hands from the window and took her hands in his, held them to his naked middle.

"I was thinking." It was now or never.

"A habit of yours, I think. Want to tell me about it, or do I need a penny." She kissed his back, nestled into him. "Not that I have one—never seem to have a place to keep my money when I'm around you."

Yates knew she was naked, which meant she must be cold. He was anything but. He turned and drew her close. "Why not stay here tonight? Drive home in the morning?" He told himself he wasn't weakening, that it was easier to work on her here, in his bed—he winced inwardly at his choice of words—than in her own.

She looked up at him, thoughtful. "You know, I haven't spent a night away from Kenninghall since I moved in. Five years," she added, as if she couldn't believe it.

"Then make this your first."

She kissed his neck, played with the hair on his chest. "I've had a few firsts with you, Yates, but I think I'll pass on this one. I don't feel right being away from Kenninghall right now."

"The letters?"

"Uh-huh. I want to put . . . stay close to them until this Greff thing is over."

"He's not going to be skulking around Kenninghall. It's too dangerous."

"You can't be sure of that, can you?"

"No." Another truth. Sure, he'd told Greff to leave Hannah alone while he located the letters, but it didn't mean he'd oblige.

"Then it's best we go back to La Conner tonight," she said.

"What's best is for you to give the letters to me, let me put them in a safety deposit box, so you can forget about them."

"I'll never forget about them, whether they're across the hall or across the continent. There's nothing I'd like better than to be free of them, but they're my responsibility. Right now they're in a safe and convenient place, where I can keep my eye on them. That's where they'll stay until this thing is over."

Yates processed what she'd said: safe, convenient. *Across the hall.* "It's your call."

"Yes, it is." She went on her tiptoes and kissed his chin, then stepped away from him and gathered up her clothes. "Can I use your shower before we go?"

"Through there."

Across the hall . . . Bingo! *Milo's room.* If sex wouldn't do it, burglary would have to. He was running out of time.

* * *

Hannah checked the letters, put them carefully into their drawer, and returned to her room. She didn't like lying, but she had to do something.

Her instincts were to trust Yates. When he'd offered to take care of the letters, she was tempted—but then everything about Yates tempted her. But his job was to get the information on Greff's other sordid business, not take on her problems. Still, she was glad they'd agreed he'd stay at Kenninghall for the short term, go into Seattle during the day when he had to, and return to La Conner at night.

Yates didn't think Greff would "skulk around," but Hannah wasn't so sure, and she didn't intend to wait complacently to see which of them was right.

She took the revolver from her tote bag; it felt like a cannon. When she looked at it in her hand, she said a quick prayer she'd never have to use it. She opened the drawer on her bedside table and put it in. She dug into her tote again and pulled out the pepper spray, read the label again. *Very fine spray . . . useful up to ten feet, causes extreme pain . . . swelling of mucous membrane . . . incapacitation: thirty minutes . . . no permanent damage.* She added it to her arsenal.

She picked up the phone, ran her finger down a page in the telephone directory, found the number she wanted, and dialed.

A brisk voice answered. "La Conner Police."

"Hello, my name is Hannah Stuart, and I live at—"

"I know where you live, Miss Stuart. Everyone within twenty miles knows Kenninghall. What can I do for you?" He was pleasant; Hannah relaxed.

"It's probably nothing, but I, uh, heard someone on the property last night. It's the second time now, and I thought I should mention it." Surprising how easy the lies came once the first one was out.

"We didn't get a call from your security service."

"No, you wouldn't have. The alarm didn't go off. And I may be just hearing things, but there are so many valuable things in the house, I thought—"

"Better safe than sorry?"

"Something like that," she said.

"How about we keep a tighter watch on the Hall for the next while. Run an extra patrol or two. Would that help?"

"Yes, if it's not too much trouble."

"No trouble at all. La Conner's not exactly crime central. We have a little time on our hands. And next time you hear something suspicious, call immediately, hear?"

"I will. Thanks." Hannah felt better. She knew it wasn't much, but having the local police on alert couldn't hurt if there was any trouble.

"What was that all about?"

Hannah swung around so quickly, she knocked the telephone book to the floor. She bent to pick it up. "I didn't hear you come in." Damn, she was more uptight than she thought.

"I'm not in." Libby lounged against the doorjamb. "You forgot to close the door."

"What do you want?"

Libby ignored her question, eyed her carefully. "Who was on the phone?"

"The police."

"Why the lies? Last night was like any other night around here. Quiet as a tomb."

Hannah moved from the front of her bedroom desk to behind it. "It's not your business."

"You still don't trust me, do you?" she said. "And I'd thought after dinner the other night—"

"A dinner from which you disappeared," Hannah finished for her. "Leaving me in an uncomfortable situation, I might add." She thought of Greff's hands on her breasts, felt a chill, and hugged herself.

"I had a phone call. I took it in my room. I didn't realize—"

"You never 'realize,' you just do what's best for Libby."

"That's not true. Not anymore."

"Forget it. It's not important." Hannah didn't want to argue with her. It was a waste of time and words. Libby would do whatever she wanted as she always had. Wednesday night was no exception.

"I won't forget it. I want to help." Libby stepped deeper into the room. "Honestly. It's why I came here. Why your friend, Milo, asked me to come, but you keep shutting me out."

Hearing the words "Milo" and "friend" together was strange to Hannah's ear. An ancient notion now, in light of what she knew. "I don't need your help. Milo was wrong to have you come here." She squared the telephone book on her desk and met her stepdaughter's gaze. "It would be better for both of us if you'd leave, Libby."

Her eyes widened. "Why? Tell me why, at least."

Hannah knew her *why* encompassed much more than the reason she'd asked Libby to leave, and decided it was a question needing an honest answer. This dance with Libby had gone on long enough. "I don't trust you. I don't think I can say it plainer."

Libby shook her head, but surprisingly there

were no tears. Her look was dark. "This isn't about trust."

"No? Then what is it about?"

"Forgiveness. What you can never do is forgive me," she said. "For what I was. What I did to you. My dad. Little Chris." The breath she drew in was audible, and when she let it out, she sagged. "I'll go. There's a bus tomorrow morning. I'll be on it." She turned to leave, stopped at the door. "You know, Hannah, for me to get straight, I had to learn how to forgive myself, let a lot of . . . bad stuff go. It wasn't easy, but it gave me the strength to go on living. It's a cool thing, forgiveness. You should try it sometime."

Chapter 21

Yates stretched out on his bed and put his forearm over his eyes to block the soft light coming from the bedside lamp.

He lay there a moment, then pulled his arm down and stared at the ceiling. It was close to one A.M. He'd wait until at least three. Hannah was a light sleeper, and the floors creaked like hell in this old place. Getting into Milo's room without being heard would be a challenge, and there was always the chance it would be locked. The smart thing to do was wait until he was sure Hannah and Libby were out cold.

His cell phone vibrated against his hip; he flipped it on. "Yates here."

"Judging from how quickly you answered, I didn't wake you," Crayne said.

Yates heard music. Seeping through the phone, it was oddly out of place in the unending silence of Kenninghall. "No, I wasn't sleeping. What is it?"

"Tenassi's on her way back. Arriving tomorrow at Sea Tac. Want me to watch her?"

"No. Leave her to me." Crayne watching Tenassi might mean his picking up on Greff. Not a good idea. "I'll take her from here."

"Good enough. See ya."

Tenassi had dropped to the bottom of Yates's priority list. She held ten percent of Zanez, spent most of her time in Europe or her place in Aspen. There was nothing he could learn from her he didn't know already. And there was a good chance she knew nothing at all. She'd been a shareholder in Zanez for six years before Greff bought controlling interest, had inherited from her father. And the kicker was, even if she were involved, there wasn't a damn thing he could do about it. Because when Greff walked, everyone involved walked.

It was the safest way to play it.

Yates swung his feet to the side of the bed, sat up, and took a long pull on the glass of water he'd put there. He felt like a chained dog in a collar so tight it choked off the oxygen to his brain.

He needed air, but he couldn't risk leaving the house and waking anyone up. He'd stay where he was.

He looked at the clock again. 1:10. Shit! It was going to be a long night.

Hannah came awake slowly. Months of sleeping with an ear sensitive to every whisper coming from Milo's room made her a restive sleeper, stirred by the slightest sound. In the months before his death, she'd lie awake, anticipating the cough or painful wheeze that would send her rushing from her bed to Milo's.

She knew every creak and shudder of Kenninghall, which part of each step to use in order to avoid the worst groans from the stairs, which oak plank in the long hall squeaked as if in pain if you stepped on it just so, and all the clicks and mutters of the old pipes hidden behind the walls; like bats, they came in the hours of darkness, determined to be heard. The night sounds of Kenninghall were as much a part of her as the beating of her heart—even to the swish and scratch of the cedar branch against her window when the wind came in from the east.

She sat up in bed now, listened, hearing nothing but sensing the unfamiliar. She waited, ear cocked. Still nothing. Perhaps she was wrong.

No! There it was . . . a soft slapping sound—a bare foot against wood? She crept from her bed, crossed the carpet with the silence of a ghost, and pressed her ear against her door, every nerve in her body tingling.

Then . . . the slightest of rasps, metal grinding metal, an old hinge too long without oil.

Milo's room.

Hannah covered her mouth with her hand, convinced the sound of her short, uneven breaths would alert the person on the other side of the door.

Her first thought was Greff—or someone he'd hired. Somehow they'd bypassed the alarm.

Her second thought was her bedside table drawer, the gun, the pepper spray. She wished she'd never bought them, then she wouldn't have to face the

idea of using the awful things. She could hide.
Whoever it was would never find the letters; she
was sure of it.

Was she?

She heard another slight rasp as Milo's bedroom door closed. Then an unearthly silence.

She crossed back to her bed, put on her robe,
and stared at the drawer in her night table. Inhaling
some courage, she took out the gun. It was small;
made for a woman, the gunsmith had said. And
safe—if she aimed low. From the groin down, he'd
said.

She forced herself to hurry.

Hannah held on to the gun and put the can of
pepper spray in her robe pocket, and silent as a
wraith, made her way downstairs to the library. She
was the only one other than Milo who knew the library connected to his bedroom.

Clutching the gun in her right hand, she pulled
out two books with her left, *Tom Sawyer* and *War
and Peace*. Behind them, at the back of the bookcase, was a three-inch brass lever. She flipped it up.
She pushed on one side of the bookcase and it
rolled open, wide enough for her to pass behind
it. The narrow stairs leading to the bedroom were
in total blackness, so Hannah moved slowly, careful not to make a sound.

On the top step, she stopped in front of the
plain plank door leading to Milo's room and put
her ear to it. At first she heard nothing and her
breathing came easier. She'd been wrong, she told
herself, suffering from a hyperactive imagination.

Then she heard a drawer open and close.

She opened the door a sliver at a time, knew

when she stepped fully into the room she'd be hidden by the heavy draperies behind Milo's large bed. She took that step.

Once in, there was no mistaking the furtive sounds of someone rifling through the bureau.

Hannah knew if she hesitated she'd lose whatever courage she had, so she slipped through the drapes and switched on Milo's bedside lamp. The light wasn't bright, but it was unexpected enough to make the person going through the bureau swivel to face her.

Using both hands, Hannah held the gun steady. "You!" She should have guessed.

Libby stared at her, her eyes wide in shock. "Hannah, this isn't what you think."

The door opened and Yates walked in. His gaze swept the room; he immediately headed toward Hannah.

"Jesus, give me that." He took the gun from her now unsteady grasp. "What the hell is going on here?"

"I was—" Libby started.

"She was going through Milo's things. She was looking for—" Hannah stopped, not sure what Libby was looking for. It couldn't be the letters; she'd never once mentioned them to her. No. It was the old Libby, looking for a quick score. Hannah's heart hardened. "She was looking for something to steal, because I asked her to leave."

"I wasn't! I was—"Her gaze flew to Yates, back to Hannah. "Oh, what's the point, you won't believe me anyway."

"No. I won't," Hannah glared at Libby.

Libby glared back, her face sullen. "You think I—"

"Look, it's late," Yates interrupted, perhaps sensing he was in for a catfight. "Why don't you hash this out in the morning." He turned Hannah's revolver over in his hand, examined it more closely. "What is this thing?"

"It's exactly what it looks like, a gun."

"It's been modified."

Hannah nodded. "To take rubber bullets."

He shot her a cold look. "Did you consider the person you pointed it at wouldn't know that? If they had a real gun . . ."

"And did you know that ninety-eight percent of the time, when a gun is pointed for self-defense, you don't have to fire it?"

"You took a hell of a risk." He looked angry. He glanced toward Libby, who stood barefoot by an old bureau. She hadn't moved. "Get out of here, Libby. We can talk about this in the morning."

Hannah's voice was steel when she said, "There isn't going to be any talk, because Libby will be leaving on the first bus."

Libby took a few steps toward the door. "I'll leave, but as God is my witness, I was *not* trying to steal from you." She turned her now cool gaze toward Yates. "By the way, maybe someone should notice how quickly you arrived to save the day, Lang." With that, she opened the door and disappeared down the hall.

Hannah stared at the door, then looked at a frowning Yates. She'd told herself not to trust anyone, but despite that she trusted Yates. She hated the idea she may have been suckered again. "She's right. You were here awfully fast. And you couldn't have heard anything from the third floor." She gave him a wary, guarded look.

He seemed to turn her accusing words over in his mind. "I wasn't on the third floor," he said, his voice level. "I was on the second."

"Why? What were you doing prowling around here at three in the morning?"

"I was *prowling around* because I couldn't sleep." His eyes lingered on her. "After two nights of the best sex I've ever had, I was . . . edgy. I was thinking about knocking on your door."

He stepped toward her and his gaze heated. "I wanted you. Again." He exhaled heavily. "But, that admission made"—he kissed her forehead as if she were a child—"I suggest we go to our separate beds, uninviting as they are, and get a good night's sleep."

He was right, of course; it was exactly what they should do. Exactly what she'd told him she wanted when they'd arrived at Kenninghall last night. But when she saw the regret in his eyes, felt the sea of need in her body, she did what every smart woman had the god-given right to do. She changed her mind.

"We could go to your room and forget about sleep." Hannah knew what Yates could do, where he would take her. She wanted that. She wanted him.

He looked at her, craving mixed with curiosity. "And that would be your way of forgetting about Libby? What happened here tonight?"

"Partly."

"Sex won't work forever, you know."

She thought about that, the "forever" part. "I know," she said, not knowing at all. What she knew was that among the morass of confusions dredged up since Milo's death, her feelings for Yates were at the top of her terrifying list. She'd gone past the attraction phase with him, past the "cold-hearted sex" phase. Where she was now didn't bear thinking about.

In his arms she found a savage calm; her mind stopped, her memories stopped. There were hours—actual hours—when she didn't think about Milo's deception . . . or Will and Chris. And when the memories returned, she wanted him again. But he was right; sex wouldn't work for forever.

Only justice would. And the only justice she could find was secondhand at best: Milo's letters.

Yates studied her face, his own expression shuttered. "Don't count on me for anything. It wouldn't be smart. Don't . . . plan on anything."

Hannah knew what he'd seen in her eyes disturbed him. This was a man who didn't want company on his life's journey. Not things, not people. For the first time she realized how little she knew about him.

He had a sister, a father somewhere, and a sharp mind fed by eyes and ears that preyed on the smallest piece of information. He was cautious, deliberate, and knew more about pleasing a woman in bed than a man had a right to know. And unless her senses were wrong, he was as much afraid of her as she was of him.

"I'm not planning anything." She used a light, more cajoling tone, as if she were talking to a nervous, wild panther who'd bolt at the first sign of entrapment. "Other than relieving that edginess you mentioned."

"I'll handle it," he said, his voice husky.

She touched his face, felt the want of him grow deep in her belly. "I have some edginess of my own, you know."

He stared at her for a time, shook his head. "Not tonight. We'd be smart to leave each other alone until"—he glanced away, then back—"our business is done."

"You don't want to make lo—have sex?"

"I didn't say that."

"It's what I heard."

"You heard wrong. And Hannah, think about this—a smart woman never sleeps with a man she doesn't trust." He gave her back her gun. "And get rid of this thing. Even a rubber bullet can kill if it finds the right spot. I'll see you in the morning." He walked out the door, the pace of his footsteps picking up as he reached the staircase.

Hannah stared after him, his words echoing in her mind. *Never sleep with a man you don't trust.*

Hannah, had she found some in her tired soul, would have laughed. If she followed that rule, she'd never have sex again.

Except maybe with Yates. But he thought, because of what Libby said, she didn't trust him!

She did trust him. Didn't she?

She looked at the gun in her hand, remembered the stark fear in her heart at even the thought she'd have to use it, and she made a decision.

Chapter 22

The next morning, Hannah walked into the kitchen and was met with the rich aroma of baking bread, and Meara busy at the long table.

"Mornin', Hannah," she said, continuing to scramble the eggs in the cream-colored bowl she favored for the purpose. "Do you know if Libby will be joining us for breakfast this morning?"

"Libby's gone, Meara. She left half an hour ago." Hannah had watched the cab pull up out front, seen Libby toss her bags in, get in the back seat, and look up at the house. The look troubled Hannah, brought a flood of guilt. Will would hate to see his daughter so unhappy, and he'd be disappointed in Hannah for causing it. Still, she was grateful Libby hadn't sought her out to talk about last night—and even more grateful she was gone.

"Lunch, then. She'll be back for it?"

"No, she's gone for good."

Meara glanced up from her task with the eggs.

"Ah, but that's too bad. I liked having the girl around. Very funny, she is."

Libby, funny? News to Hannah. But when she touched the letters in her pocket, she forgot about Libby, forgot about everything except her plan. She'd thought about it all night, but hadn't changed her mind. If she were to stand a chance of living a life remotely normal, she had to do this.

Yates walked in and acknowledged Meara with a smile and a quick kiss on the cheek, which made her egg-beating activity grow in fervor.

He stayed her whirling hand. "Hey there, what'd they ever do to you?"

"Oh, you . . ." she said, putting down the bowl. "Breakfast will be a few minutes yet. May as well wait for the bread."

When Yates went to sit down, Hannah took his hand. "Let's take a walk."

"You sure?" He gestured outside. It was raining, but lightly.

"Come on."

"I said breakfast in a few minutes, now—not half an hour," Meara stated firmly.

"We'll be right back."

Outside, Yates waited to see which direction she chose. She took his hand and they walked through to the garage.

"What's the deal?" Yates surveyed the gloomy interior of the garage. "What are we doing here?"

Hannah stopped at the '37 Cord, opened the door. "Get in. This won't take long."

Yates gave her a quizzical look, but got in the car.

She faced him across the wide front seat. "I want you to have these." She took the letters out of her pocket and held them out to him. He looked at them but made no move to take them from her hand.

"What brought this on?"

"Last night. Two things. First, I realized if it came down to it, I couldn't do what needed to be done to protect them—"

"Looked to me like you were armed and dangerous."

"Armed with a gun suitable to repel squirrels and chipmunks." She scoffed at herself. "And I was shaking like an aspen in a twister." He still hadn't made a move to take the letters from her hand, so she dropped them back in her lap. "I wasn't thinking. These"—she nodded at the papers on her knees—"need to be put somewhere safe, somewhere away from Kenninghall."

"And second?" He tilted his dark head, his tone, his expression sharply inquisitive.

She looked him straight in the eyes, her heart a noisy drum. "Because you were right. A woman should never sleep with a man she doesn't trust." Again she handed him the letters. "Take them, Yates. Put them somewhere safe. When you've finished your business with Greff, bring them back to me, and I'll . . . do what I have to do." She shoved the letters onto his lap. "It will be a relief to be free of them."

He picked them up—reluctantly, she thought. "You're sure about this?"

She nodded. As sure as she'd been about anything since being forced to live again. As sure as she'd ever be again.

"Okay. I'll drive into Seattle, put them in a safety deposit box."

"There's something else you should know."

"Uh-huh?" He looked preoccupied, kept turning the letters over in his hand.

"I think I'm falling in love with you." Surprisingly, she didn't stammer, didn't stumble, and didn't freeze up. The words, however tenuous, were glory on her tongue. She'd never thought she'd say them again, that she'd feel this way again. Of all the decisions, all the actions she'd taken in the past few weeks, this one felt the most right.

She *would not* be wrong about Yates or her feelings for him.

Yates looked as if he'd been hit from behind. Then it was as if he did some kind of mental countdown. It was a while before he spoke. "We had sex, Hannah. Spectacular sex, but the operative words in your statement are 'I think.' This has been a tough time for you, and—"

"Stop." She leaned over, kissed him to silence. "Don't say any more and don't tell me what I feel. I'm beginning to think I can figure it out for myself. And it's a pretty good feeling." She moved away from him, put her hand on the door handle. "Meara's waiting breakfast for us. You can tell me why I can't love you when this ugly mess with Morgan Greff is behind us."

When Yates left immediately after breakfast, the rain gave way to a warm autumn sun. He didn't say good-bye, and Hannah hadn't seen him leave, but she didn't mind, knowing he'd be back later tonight. She wouldn't think past tonight, refused to let doubts mar the clear surface of her mind. Somehow, by saying three simple words, she'd gained a lighter heart. Knowing she was capable of love was a miracle. For the first time in years, she felt whole, as if in a state of grace. Maybe she didn't deserve it, but she couldn't will it away.

She spent the morning in her office, the work solid and satisfying. Meara came in to dust, using a lemon polish that filled the room with a clean, bright scent. It lingered still.

As did thoughts of Yates Lang.

It was nearly one o'clock when Hannah pushed herself away from her desk and went to the kitchen to fix herself a light lunch.

She stopped in the doorway. "What are you doing here? I thought you'd left." Libby sat on one of the stools at Meara's island, her bags on the floor at her feet.

"I came back. Meara let me in before she left."

"I see that. The question is why." Hannah walked around her to the fridge and opened the door to peer in. Meara had left a salad, bless her. Salad in hand, she said, "I meant what I said last night, Libby. Nothing's changed."

Libby got up from her stool. "I think it has—or will when you look at this." She handed Hannah a faxed copy of a newspaper clipping with a few lines of text and a grainy picture.

Hannah scanned it but nothing registered. She raised blank eyes to Libby. "I don't see what—"

Libby took the salad bowl from her hand. "Look harder. The caption."

Hannah took the paper to the island where the light was stronger, saw what Libby intended her to see—and felt her brave new world collapse under

her feet. Her knees threatened to buckle, and she
sat heavily on the stool Libby had vacated. "Where
did you get this?" She couldn't tear her gaze away.

A family stared out from a grainy newspaper
photograph: Morgan Greff, his wife Eleanor, daughter Stella—and his seventeen-year-old son Morgan
Greff, Jr. There was no doubt who the son was—
Yates Lang. The picture was taken at the launch of
a new freighter being "put into service by Lang
Shipping."

"Tom Colwood got it for me. Before he started
working in addiction, he was a reporter for the
Chicago Tribune. He knows how to . . . find out
things." She set the salad bowl on the island. "That
night—when Greff was here?—when I went to my
room to take that phone call, I decided to have a
cigarette. I'd opened my window and was sitting
there finishing it when Greff and Yates came outside. They started talking. I heard Greff telling
Yates to . . . I hate this part." She grimaced and
looked at the ceiling, then back to Hannah. "Greff
told Yates to 'bed the bitch' and 'get the effing letters.'" She stopped. "When I didn't hear Yates say
no, or tell Greff to go fu—screw himself, I got curious. I called Tom, gave him both names and asked
him to do some checking." She gestured to the
paper in Hannah's hand. "I had him fax it to the
mail and packing service in La Conner. Apparently
Yates took his mother's name when he was in his
mid-twenties."

Hannah didn't speak, didn't know what to say.
Her interior was cold, her mind empty of thought.
It was if she'd stepped back into the void she'd
been in when Milo came for her five years before.
Milo, her friend . . . the sudden sense of missing him

shocked her. She steeled her softening thoughts; Milo had been a creation of wishful thinking—as was Yates.

Libby went on. "I was afraid I wouldn't have the chance to make things right with you, but when I checked for the fax this morning, it was there. I've been trying to drum up the courage to show you ever since." She gave Hannah a direct look. "And Hannah, I was *not* trying to steal from you; I was looking for the letters. I'd spent the entire day going through the house. The only room I hadn't checked was Milo's." She sat down, took the stool beside Hannah. "What the hell they were about, or what I'd do with them if I'd found them, I had no idea. I was just tired of being on the outside looking in."

Hannah got up, walked to the cutlery drawer, and pulled out a fork. She picked out a cloth napkin from the kitchen linen cupboard beside the fridge. She took both items back to the island, then pulled the abandoned salad toward her and centered it. She began eating. One forkful after another. She tasted nothing.

Libby gave her a worried look. "Are you okay? What are you going to do?"

"I'm going to eat my lunch."

"Hannah, you don't look right. I should call someone. The police would be good!"

"No police." She turned to face Libby. "And I'd like you to go, please. What you discovered . . . I'm grateful, but right now, I need to be alone." Alone in the safe shadows of Kenninghall, because the shadows were all she could trust.

"This is crazy. You can't stay here all by yourself. What if he comes back?"

"He has what he wants. He won't come back." Hannah put down her fork, rubbed at her temples. "I appreciate what you've done, but all I want now is . . . Kenninghall. So, go. Please. Just go."

Yates stood outside Connery's, a third-rate tavern not far from the Zanez Shipping office. He turned up the collar of his windbreaker against the cool waterfront air. He'd been standing outside for ten minutes, telling his legs and feet to carry him in. But his brain blocked the signals.

It wasn't every day a man seduced and conned a woman so he could become an accessory to murder. But that's what he'd done, and that's what he'd be, the second he cut his deal with Greff. But there was no turning back now. And thinking about Hannah didn't make things any easier.

The letters were in his pocket.

And Greff was in there waiting for him.

The smart thing to do was get it over with.

Yates pushed open the door. The bar was dark, dirty, and smelled as if it had been marinated in cigarette smoke.

He spotted Greff in a booth at the back. Greff saw him at the same time and, unsmiling, lifted his glass. Yates's gut cramped. *Do it,* he told himself. *Think of Stella and do it.*

He slid into the scarred booth opposite Greff. The bartender yelled from behind the bar. "What'll it be?"

"Nothing, thanks." No way was he going to drink with him.

Greff tipped back his beer, eyed Yates with the stare of a cobra. "Do you have them?"

"Yes."

He smiled. "You must be as good in the sack as your old man. I always said the way to a woman's heart is through her c—"

"Shut the fuck up!" It was all Yates could do not to reach over and tear the skin from his skull.

"How about that?" The smile curled into a sneer. "The wiseass has taken a dive. Fallen for the mouse." He finished the last of his beer, signaled the barkeep for another.

"We're not going to be here long enough for you to finish that." Yates nodded toward the fresh beer. "You know what I want, give it to me. And don't even think of trying to screw me over."

Greff's cold eyes met his. "Zanez is history—or soon will be. And it's all nice and legal. Nationeer Shipping bought all five vessels. The deal's set to close within the week." Bastard looked like a cream-filled alley cat.

Yates knew Nationeer, one of the biggest, most reputable shipping companies working out of Seattle. But this kind of deal took months. "You were planning on getting out all along."

"Joke's on you, boy. You got me once, when you forced me out of Lang Shipping. I don't let any-body—I mean anybody—get me twice."

"Let me see the papers." The expensive stink of Greff's musky aftershave made Yates's stomach turn. Not to mention the man himself. A man about to head off into the sunset rich as Midas and free as a damn bird.

Greff shoved a file folder across the desk. "Sure you don't want a drink?"

"No." Yates scanned the documents. A completed purchase agreement, clauses initialed by both parties, no subjects to, witnessed signatures, and the company seal. Totally legitimate. He should be relieved, not disgusted. The date of closing and the transfer of funds was set for next week. In a few days, Nationeer would put millions in Greff's filthy hands.

"Nice, huh?" Greff looked at the documents as Yates stuffed them back in the folder, then at Yates, obviously enjoying himself.

"I'll keep these a few days."

"Keep them as long as you like. The originals are at the office." Greff had fulfilled his part of the bargain, but surprisingly didn't immediately demand Yates fulfill his.

Instead, he shoved his beer toward the table's center, cradled the glass in both hands. "You know, I didn't mean to kill that family. But the dumb-ass behind the counter refused to take us seriously, looked at Milo and me and told us to get the hell out of his store." He looked angry, as if the event were yesterday instead of years before. "Mean little bastard. Milo froze up, wanted to run." Greff snorted. "People can smell fear, you know—especially when it's running down a kid's leg. But I'd come for the money, and I meant to get it."

He sat farther back in the booth. "But this guy? He wanted to play hero. When he reached under the counter, I fired. Him or me. No contest. Then damned if his wife didn't show up with the kid." He shrugged. "Leaving witnesses isn't smart. Bloody mess, the whole thing. I had to drag Milo out of the fuckin' store. The idiot wanted to call an ambulance." He shook his head. "Can you believe it?"

"What the hell are you telling me this for?"

Greff looked unperturbed. "I don't know. Maybe I want you to understand?"

It was Yates's turn to shake his head. "I understand you killed a family in cold blood. I understand you ruined my mother's life. I understand you're a scumbag willing to sacrifice his own daughter to protect his lousy, worthless life. What more is there?" Yates stared at him, his jaw locked so hard it felt like cement.

Greff's expression turned feral. "You don't understand a damn thing, because you can't see through your high and mighty attitude. Hell, you're a fucking millionaire, and you live in a damn slum. Probably afraid some of the Lang money is still dirty." He laughed. "So I guess you'll be glad to know you got roughly half of what Lang Shipping was worth. You might have shut me down, but you didn't get a dime of mine."

Yates looked at the man who was his father. He might as well have been an alien life-form. "It's all about money, isn't it? Always has been. You kill a shopkeeper for a few bucks, you turn your wife into an addict to get control of her family company, you profit by preying on kids—selling innocence to the highest bidder. Shit! You're worse than scum, should have been locked up years ago."

Greff drank some beer. "And to think when I was a kid, I wanted to be a cop." He grinned before hardening his expression. "You've said your piece, and you've got what you came for. Hand over the letters. The sooner we see each other's asses walking in different directions the happier we'll be."

"That'll suit me fine, but first you and I are going to take a walk. To the Zanez Shipping office."

"What the hell for?"

"You're going to show me the originals of these"— Yates tapped the file—"and you're going to call the captain of the good ship *Naarmu* and tell him to turn the ship around."

Greff stilled; tension emanated from his body and invaded the confines of the booth. "Now why would I do that?"

"Because you don't have a choice."

"I always have a choice."

"Not this time. You want those golden years you're so set on, you'll do what I say, and you'll do it now."

Greff's eyes flicked across Yates's face. "I don't do ultimatums."

"You'll *do* this one."

"And why's that?"

"Because if you don't, when the *Naarmu* comes in, the cops will be all over it. And when they discover your sick idea of cargo, they'll be all over you."

"A few questions. Nothing I can't handle." He lifted a shoulder. "There's nothing to tie me to the ship's load. Captains out to make a buck bring illegal stuff in all the time. Awkward, not life-threatening. You're going to have to do better than that."

To Yates, hearing the sad-eyed girls called *stuff* was a poker in the eye. He worked to stem his revulsion, stick to business. "Okay, how about this? An investigation ugly enough to dock your ships and make Nationeer back off. You'd lose your deal."

Yates could see the slither of Greff's reptilian brain as it reacted to a new threat, and he took a grim satisfaction in watching the bastard boil in his own oil for bit. "How did you find out about the *Naarmu*?"

Yates wasn't inclined to be helpful.

"Vonecker," Greff said at last, nodding to himself. "Had to be." One finger drummed on the tabletop. "I knew I didn't do him soon enough."

"You killed Vonecker." Yates's lungs imploded, and for what seemed an hour, but was barely a second, his mind went black. Adding a fresh murder to the list of Greff's crimes wasn't a straw, it was a two-by-four to the head.

Greff looked briefly uneasy. "I retired him."

"With a crowbar."

"I killed him. So what?"

The question clanged in Yates's mind with the eerie clarity of a Sunday bell.

"Yeah, so what? What's another murder or two." A hard calm settled over Yates's mind. He let out a long breath, released the rigidity in his chest. Mind hard, body relaxed, he tossed some cash on the table. "Let's go."

"I'm not going anywhere, because you're not going to call anybody about the *Naarmu*, least of all the cops." Greff appeared totally relaxed. "Nothing's changed. Stella's still your darling sister. Am I right?"

Yates stood, looked down on him. "You're right about two things. Stella's still my sister, and I'm not going to make the call."

Greff didn't move.

"Anne Chapman is." Yates looked at his watch. "In less than an hour. And there's not a goddamned thing either you or I can do about it. So you either make the call, or you, me, and Stella go down together."

* * *

Bone loaded the last of his supplies into the van. He'd gone over the whole job in his mind close to a dozen times and done at least three drive-bys. Last night he'd walked the property; the house was ripe for burnin' and would be an easy set.

He was past ready and prickling with anticipation.

He'd hated doing those last couple of drive-bys. Hell, this damn place was flat! Might be good for the damn tulips or whatever the hell they grew around here, but it made a white van crawling around country roads stick out like a beacon in a dark park.

The bitch who hired him was getting to be a real pain in the butt, too, always checking up on him. Last time he'd work for a woman—for sure. He itched to get the job done, get the hell out of here, but damned if it would stop rainin' long enough for a man to light a match. This place should be a swamp, all the water coming down. He couldn't wait to get back to San Diego.

Bone hadn't counted on so much rain. For a minute or two there, a couple of days back, he'd even thought of scrapping the fire idea altogether, but the vision of that big house going up like a torch in the night was too seductive. A man didn't get a chance like this every day.

And this morning—finally—the damn rain had let up. He'd have preferred more dry time, but he wasn't about to push his luck and wait it out.

Tonight. He'd do the job tonight.

She'd be dead as crisp toast, and the police would be suckin' up his exhaust all the way south on I5.

He went into the motel room, glanced at the bedside clock. Time for a beer and a short nap.

Then he was out of here.

Chapter 23

As the day went dark, Hannah set about checking and securing every door and window in Kenninghall—no small feat given three floors and too many rooms to count. She also double-checked the alarm.

She knew it was all a waste of time; there would be no one coming for her—not tonight anyway. Greff had what he wanted thanks to his son, Yates. No doubt the letters she'd given him were a heap of ash by now. And Greff and Yates were comparing notes on how stupid she'd been. She pulled her sweater around her to fight the chill.

When she thought of herself shoving the letters into his hand—his feigned reluctance, her foolish hope—she went weak. Her mouth went dry, and she sat heavily on her bed. Yates deceived her, *used* and deceived her, and she'd let him.

In her search for oblivion, she'd used him, too. To forget. For five years she'd tried to forget.

She'd used Milo.

She'd used his sleeping pills.

She'd tried work.

Then sex—hot, mindless sex.

And when that didn't work, she aimed higher, moved on to love, the most powerful narcotic of all.

But all of it was behind her now.

Yates walking out on her, taking the letters to Greff, was the best thing that could have happened. And whether he intended it or not, under his hand, in the shadow of his deception, she'd grown stronger. She wasn't afraid anymore. He'd given her much more than he'd taken.

Tired of her thoughts, restless, she stood.

The decision now was what to do about Milo's confession, how to deal with it quickly and effectively. How to tell Miranda. But not tonight.

She walked to the window of her bedroom, pulled the curtain back, and looked across the fields to Miranda's sprawling cedar-shingled house. All the lights were on. It was Scrabble night again, and Hannah knew Miranda, Claire, and Meara would be fighting it out for hours yet.

Glad to have another reason for procrastination, she let the curtain fall. At the same moment, the doorbell rang.

Hannah started, but quickly quashed the tremor of fright, a fright rooted in reflex not reality.

The bad guys aren't interested in me anymore. They have what they want. Kenninghall is safe.

The bell rang again, a few seconds before Hannah reached the door.

Hannah peered through the stained glass on the door.

"Libby," she said, opening the door wide. "I thought you'd gone."

"I've been wandering around downtown La Conner and just couldn't get on the bus. I kept thinking of you alone here, and—"

"Come in, then. The night's clear enough, but it's still cold." She reached for her bag. "Have you eaten?"

"No."

"Neither have I."

Libby stepped in, stared at her. "You're not . . . angry? That I came back."

"No. I'm not even sure why I asked you to leave. The old shoot-the-messenger reaction, I suppose. If you hadn't come back, I was going to call you." And that was the truth. Libby had brought her the truth, and she'd gone on auto pilot, the disappointment over Yates's deceit triggering her old impulse to hide when things went bad. Since then, she'd thought things through. And the new Hannah didn't do the run and hide thing. "I'm sorry, Libby. For not giving you a chance . . . and for doubting you." Hannah offered her a hand.

Libby ignored the hand and pulled Hannah into a soppy hug. "I'm sorry, too. You can't know how much. I'm sorry about Dad and Chris's funeral. Sorry about stealing your Mom's ring. Just sorry, sorry, sorry."

Hannah hugged her back, and it felt good. Warm. She remembered the young Libby, the miserably unhappy teenager she'd struggled to befriend, an adolescent who thought the streets and drugs would burn away the pain of losing a mother. Hannah should have known. The dark shadow of unresolved grief was her evil twin, after all. They were a pair, Libby and her, women with a tangled past and uncertain futures. Women who'd survived.

They stepped back in unison, Libby rubbing the dampness from her eyes, Hannah blinking away the moisture from her own. "Soup?" she asked, bringing a tissue from her sweater pocket to her nose.

Libby sniffed. "Pardon?"

"Meara made soup. There's plenty for two. Will it be okay for dinner?"

Libby gave her a shaky nod. "Let's do it." Then she put her hand on Hannah's arm, stopped her from moving away. "I'm sorry about Yates, too, Hannah. It can't be nice to find out you've been sleeping with the enemy."

"You knew?"

"You had that . . . glow. Anyone could see it." She held Hannah's hand, tight. "What you're feeling—that awful hurt?—it'll pass. Time, the great healer, and all that."

Hannah's throat tightened, and she squeezed Libby's hand before pulling it free. "I'm counting on it. Now, let's eat."

On the way to the kitchen, for the first time in weeks, Hannah felt . . . centered. She hadn't closed the hole in her heart left by Yates, but she'd work on it. He'd been a terrible error in judgment, but he'd brought her body to life—the rest was up to her.

She'd loved and lost—badly—but Libby was right; in time the hurt would be nothing but a bad memory, a memory she would *not* harbor.

A love lost, a lesson learned.

There were worse things that could happen.

*   *   *

Greff withdrew his key from the lock, walked in, and disarmed the Zanez Shipping security system.

Yates followed him in. What the hell they needed security around here for was a mystery to him. The Zanez Shipping office was a mess, paper everywhere, some tall gray filing cabinets with so many dents they looked as if they'd been dropped from the Space Needle. There were more file storage boxes packed tight in the corner, three grubby computers, the traditional office coffee pot left half full sitting on a metal table, and the dirtiest windows Yates had ever seen.

He looked at the immaculately clad Greff, whose penchant for order and hygiene used to rival the legendary Howard Hughes. He was also a borderline hypochondriac back then. Hell, he was probably showering in disinfectant by now. This place didn't fit his image. He guessed Greff didn't spend any more time here than he absolutely had to.

There were two glass-fronted offices toward the back of the room. Greff went into one of them and Yates followed.

Greff looked at him, then around the office. His face showed his distaste. "We could have done this at a telephone booth."

"We could have. But I'd like to be in on both ends of the conversation."

Amused, Greff picked up the phone and dialed. Yates picked up on another line, first hearing nothing but static, then a ring. "Jom?" Greff said. "This is Don Hallam. We've got trouble. I want you to turn the ship around. And I want you to do it now."

What followed was a hybrid of what Yates assumed to be Thai and very bad English. Turns out

Jom was more afraid of the gangs in Bangkok than he was of U.S. Immigration, and it took Greff ten minutes to make his point—something about dumping him overboard encased in concrete if he brought the *Naarmu* into the Port of Seattle.

Listening intently, Yates snagged the piece of information he needed. The port the *Naarmu* was headed back to was Songkhla in the Gulf of Thailand.

When he hung up, Greff said, "That bastard is shark meat wherever he lands." He looked at Yates, still angry from the call. "But if you're thinking this will do anything for the *cargo,* think again. The Triad boys will just hold them until they find another ship. So if you had visions of loving parents meeting them at the dock, forget it. Over half of them were sold by their parents, and the other half probably don't even know who their parents are."

"How the hell do you sleep nights, anyway?"

"Hot sex and a single-malt scotch. Works every time." He came from behind the desk, brushing dust from his hands. "Okay, I've done my part. It's your turn." He put out his hand, palm up, and flicked his fingers in a come-to motion. "The letters."

Yates gave him a dead-level stare. "I don't think so."

There was no surprise on Greff's face, but his features set to stone, and a muscle ticked in his jaw.

"You never intended to give them to me, did you?"

Now there was a question Yates couldn't answer, because the minute Hannah shoved those letters onto his knees, her eyes bright with trust, he'd been unsure. "They were never mine to give."

"I'll make you sorry. You and Stella."

"You made us sorry from the day we were born."
He refused to think about Stella, what this would
mean to her. He'd figure something out. Right
now he had one goal, to return the letters.

He looked at his watch, after ten. Traffic would
be light; he'd be at Hannah's before midnight easily. He turned to go.

He was at the door when he heard Greff say.
"This isn't over, Yates."

Yates strode to where Greff stood in front of the
battered desk, grabbed him by his raw silk shirt,
and pulled his face to within an inch of his. "It is
over. So forget the letters, take your goddamned
money, and run as far and fast as you can. Leave
me, Stella, and Hannah Stuart alone. You got that?"

Silence, sharp and deadly.

Greff's eyes, chips of blue ice, ticked slowly over
Yates's face. Not a trace of fear or resistance. "You're
more of a fool than I thought, boy."

Yates hauled Greff's face so close to his, father
and son's breath mingled. "Better a fool than a
fucking psychopath."

Gazes locked hard; neither man flinched, neither man spoke. Yates let go of Greff's collar and
shoved him back, dimly aware of a button falling,
clicking as it bounced on the stained tile floor.

He headed for the door and didn't look back.

Greff watched his son leave, heard the whoosh
of air as the Zanez door slammed behind him, and
immediately went to one of the file cabinets. He
pulled the top drawer all the way out, dug in the
back, and withdrew a Ruger automatic.

He turned it over in his hand, hesitated.

Him or me. No contest.

The revolver disappeared into his jacket pocket. He waited long enough for Yates to have a short lead, got in his car, and followed him. It didn't take long before it was obvious his destination was La Conner.

Greff eased his foot off the gas. If Yates was headed to Kenninghall, it meant he had the letters on him, and he was taking them back to the mouse.

He was thinking with the brain in his pants.

His bright kid wasn't so bright after all.

Hannah stepped out of the shower, toweled her hair, and wrapped herself in her terry robe. There was a chill in the air tonight and—when she thought about Yates—a deeper chill in her heart. She walked out of her bathroom and looked at her bed. Pristine. Cold.

It was after midnight, she was exhausted, but she still couldn't face her waiting, unruffled bed. She caught her hair up turban-style in the towel, decided she'd go downstairs for a glass of milk. She needed to think about tomorrow, what she was going to say to Miranda. She'd put it off long enough. It couldn't wait any longer.

She was in the hall when she heard an insistent rapping on the front door. She looked over the balcony; the porch light etched a formless shape on the stained glass in the door. She backtracked into her room, retrieved her gun, and slipped it into her robe pocket.

When she reached the foyer, the rapping stopped. The shape on the glass was gone. Cautiously, clutching the gun in her pocket, she opened the door and looked out.

Yates stepped from the gloom beyond the light. Hannah's heart leaped in fright.

"Jesus, either use that damn thing or get rid of it."

Hannah hadn't realized she'd pulled the gun. A gun Yates took and stuffed in his jacket pocket. Hannah's shock subsided, replaced by anger. "What are you doing here—no, don't answer that. Just leave." She stepped back, planning to slam the door shut.

Yates put a hand on it, looked into her eyes. He dropped his head a second and exhaled. The sound was rueful and weary. "You know."

"I know you're a liar and a thief." She pushed on the door.

He held it in place. "That's a start. But if you'll listen, I have a few things to say."

"I don't want to hear them."

"But you will." He shoved the door open and stepped into the hall a few steps past her.

She didn't close the door, spun to face him. "Go, Yates. Now!"

"I'll go, but first I want to give you these." He held out the letters.

Hannah stared at them but made no move to take them from his hand. "I know who you are." She lifted her eyes to his. "Morgan Greff, *Junior.*" She ground the words out, pronounced each clearly, relished the surprise and irritation on his face.

"How the hell do you know that?"

"You're not the only one with sources," she snapped. "Are you going to deny it?"

"No, I'm not going to deny it. Greff is my father."

"And you were out to get the letters all along, weren't you? That's why you came to Kenninghall. You wanted to keep them in the family?" She faced him, fury a flame in her heart. "And are you in the slave trade, too, *Morgan Greff, Junior,* or was that one of your more creative embellishments to stop me from going to the police?" Hannah's voice rose; she couldn't stop it. She forced herself to be calm, reminded herself she had the upper hand. Or thought she did.

He grabbed her wrist. "Don't ever call me Morgan."

She yanked free of him. "I'll call you worse than that if you don't get out of my house."

He ignored her. "I'll admit when I found out about the letters, my first thought was to get control of them—although not for the purpose you think. I don't give a damn about Greff. As a father, I wrote him off years ago." He walked up to her, grasped her shoulders. "And I am not—repeat *not*—remotely connected to his filthy business. You got that?"

She gave him a chilling look, crossed her arms. "What I've got is a man standing in front of me who slept with me, lied to me, and stole from me."

His face flushed, and he ran a hand roughly through his hair, his frustration as obvious as his lack of reply. Hannah had him. He had no defense. None. He stopped abruptly, looked at the letters in his hand, then at her. "You gave me copies. You were testing me." He looked momentarily stunned.

"Of course they're copies. Do you think I'm a complete idiot? I had them done the day we were in Seattle." She lifted her chin.

Yates's head snapped up, and he leveled his dark eyes on her. He studied her for a long moment, surprise turning to admiration. He laughed softly. "Hell."

"Yes. Hell. Which is exactly where you can go. You and your father."

"He's not my father, he's an accident of birth. Before a couple of weeks ago, I hadn't seen him in sixteen years. And I don't plan on seeing him in the next fifty—if he lives that long." He glanced away. "There are things you don't know about me, my family—"

Hannah snorted. It was far too late for a family history. She adopted a bored stance and looked pointedly at the still open front door.

He ignored her, carried on, "Things you should know if we—"

"I *cannot* believe this! There is no 'we.'" Hannah walked to the door. "Now will you just go."

"I'm not go—"

"Hannah!" Libby came racing down the stairs. "There's a fire!"

Yates and Hannah looked at Libby in unison, both uncomprehending.

"It's Miranda's house."

Greff saw the spires of flame well before he got to Miranda's property. When he reached her front yard, the house was already enveloped in fire. He stared in amazement at the symmetry of it, saw it had been set around the base of the house and planned carefully. A fire designed to fry anyone inside by blocking all exits.

And inside was his bloody lifeline. Miranda.

If she died, he fried.

He threw the car into park and leaped out, grabbed his suede jacket from the backseat. He either got into the house and got Miranda out or he was a dead man. And all the shit he'd gone through would be worth nothing.

He ran the perimeter of the house, looked desperately for a way in—a back door, a window, anything—but whoever set the blaze made sure they were covered. The smell of gas was everywhere.

He spotted a narrow ground-level window on the side wall of the house; it offered a chance and he took it. Pulling his jacket over his head, he sucked in as much fresh air as his lungs could take, and punched through the glass with his shoulder.

Inside was thick with smoke, black and stinging. He called out. "Miranda! Are you here? Miranda!" He stumbled down a long hallway. No lights. He heard a dog bark and he headed toward it.

The living room. No.

He was having trouble breathing, eyes running like rivers, the air blast-furnace temperature.

"Miranda . . ." He tripped over a table, hit the wall, and stumbled to his knees. The dog barked again. Too far. He couldn't get up.

He couldn't breathe, was terrified to open his eyes to the searing heat and smoke.

Christ, the fluid in his lungs was boiling. He shoved his face close to the floor and pulled himself around a corner. The dog again. He thumped on what he thought was the door.

"Miranda!" To yell he had to breathe. He gasped, inhaled air like hot ammonia. "Anybody . . . you there?"

A dull roar came from behind, and he raised burning eyes in time to see a surge of flame moving toward him from down the hall.

Frantic, he drew in another lung-blistering breath. Flames tore at his feet, his ankles, licked up his thighs. His scream joined the roar of the flames before he put his nose into the join of floor to wall and entered blackness.

The last thing he heard was the dog.

Chapter 24

Yates braked his car to a screeching stop outside of Miranda's house, and Hannah and Libby leaped from the car. He registered the Ferrari in the driveway, had a moment of confusion, but no time to think about it.

The fire was bad. Really bad. "Where's her room?" he shouted to a stunned Hannah.

"There." She pointed to the left side of the house. Ground floor, thank God.

He started to run and Hannah ran after him, grabbed him by the jacket, and stopped him near the garden shed. "Stop. Wait!"

When he spun around to yell at her, tell her to let him go, she turned a garden hose full on him, drenched him completely. Then she pointed at the window again. "Go," she screamed, turning the hose toward the window.

He was aware of sirens in the distance, but he couldn't wait. There was no time.

Yates pulled his sodden leather jacket over his head and plunged into the room. It was filled with smoke, but not half as bad as he'd expected. Someone had been smart enough to put a towel under the door. But there was heat and smoke, enough to burn the eyes and disorient. "There." The word came from the smoke beside him. "The bathroom!"

Jesus! It was Hannah. She pointed toward a door. She was as wet as he was; her robe was soaked, as was the towel draped over her dark hair. She held one end of it tight to her mouth.

He heard a dog bark.

He butted the door with his shoulder. It opened to reveal two women huddled in a bathtub full of water—and a small dog, in terminal bark mode. The air was cleaner here, until the smoke from the bedroom took hold in the confined space. The younger of the two women shouted, "You'll have to carry her, I'm all right." She stepped quickly out of the tub. "I'll follow."

The old woman protested, something about Shasta, but he couldn't make out her words. "Take a deep breath," he instructed. He scooped her up easily, held her face to his shoulder, and ran out of the bathroom.

Hannah grabbed the yapping dog and took the other woman's hand. "Hang on, Claire."

"Stay right behind me. I'll move fast," Yates yelled back. The roar of the fire filled his ears as viciously as the smoke searing his lungs.

He vaulted through the bedroom and clambered out the window, keeping Miranda as close to his body as possible. Hannah and Claire followed. When they'd cleared the house, both women dropped to their knees, gasped for clean air. Hannah still clutched the dog to her breast. It still barked.

The frail woman in his arms said something, pointed a shaking hand toward the house. "There's someone in there. I heard him . . . outside my bedroom door."

Yates remembered the car, cursed. It had to be Greff. The fire was eating the wood house raw, tearing into it, the flames high and stubborn against the steady stream of water now being directed at it by the firefighters.

If he went back in there now . . . if he opened the bedroom door, he'd be roasted.

He placed Miranda on the ground as carefully as he could. "Take care of her," he said to Hannah, his voice hoarse and choppy. He sprinted back to the house.

He heard Hannah call his name, but he didn't stop. He had seconds and he needed every one.

He tumbled through the window of Miranda's bedroom. The smoke overwhelmed, hot ash burrowing deep into his lungs. He felt the bedroom's entry door. Hot, but tolerable. Maybe.

To give himself an edge against the rush of flame he expected from behind the door, he stood as far back as he could, yanked open the door.

It wasn't fire that nailed him, it was smoke. So intense, so harsh, it forced him back and dropped him to his knees. He put his mouth to the floor, sucked up the last of the useable air from the bedroom, and crawled toward the hall.

He didn't have to crawl far.

A body was tucked into the doorway, curled into a tight ball. Dead? Had to be. No one could survive this. Yates tugged at Greff's shoulders, hauled him back into the room, started dragging him toward the open window. At least where he thought there was an open window. The smoke, acrid with the chemicals in the paint and carpets, scorched his eyeballs.

He groped his way along the floor, hoped to hell he was headed in the right direction. The body he pulled behind him was a dead weight.

A weight that moaned. Greff was alive.

Fire poured in from the hallway, started to chew on the wallpaper and drapes in the bedroom; it surged to greater power when it caught the breeze coming from the broken window.

Yates saw the opening, but Greff had gone silent again. Inert, stone heavy, no movement at all. At the window, Yates struggled for a better grip, managed to lever his arms under Greff's shoulders, strained to sit him up.

Christ! Greff's fucking feet were on fire.

Out of here. They had to get out of here. Now!

He lurched to a standing position, used every aching, burning muscle he had to maneuver Greff to the windowsill. He tumbled him through and followed in a blind roll. Gasping, unable to breathe, he landed face down in the soaking grass. He tried to get to his hands and knees. Impossible.

Someone rolled him over and covered his legs.

"Get the ambulance!" someone yelled.

"His feet," Yates mumbled. "Fix his feet."

He heard Hannah scream his name before his head rolled to the side and he passed out.

Hannah worked to ignore the sharp signature smell all hospitals shared, a by-product of the gallons of cleaners and antiseptics they sloshed around in their war on germs.

They were letting Yates out today, and she hadn't seen him since he'd been brought in unconscious three days ago.

She stared at his hospital room door, reluctant to go in, unable to leave. She was dithering, and knew it, but she couldn't help herself. Nothing had changed between her and Yates; the fire hadn't burned away his betrayal, but she had a debt of gratitude. As did Miranda.

If it hadn't been for his courage, Miranda and Claire would have died in the fire. Of course, if that had happened, Greff would have gone to jail. Unselfish act, selfish root.

She sat heavily in a chair a few steps from his door.

"Are you here to see Yates?" a short, fair-haired woman asked, giving her a curious look. "I'll bet you're Hannah Stuart."

Hannah got to her feet. "Yes."

"I'm Yates's sister, Stella Lang. I think we spoke on the phone once or twice. A couple of years ago? I bought some pieces from Milo."

Hannah shook her outstretched hand and checked her memory. "Sorry, I don't remember."

"No matter." She smiled, gestured toward the door. "Have you been in?"

"Not yet." Short, round, and brown-eyed, Yates's sister looked nothing like her tall, green-eyed brother. Hannah wasn't sure how she felt about meeting another of Greff's offspring, and she couldn't think of a thing to say other than, "How is he?"

The smile left Stella's face. "He's good. The burn

to his leg is a bit vicious, but the doctors were really worried smoke inhalation had damaged his lungs. Everything looks clear, thank God. They're letting him go home today." She smiled affectionately. "Although I suspect he'd walk out anyway. He's having the typical male reaction to being told to lie still and take his medicine."

Hannah met Stella's eyes. "And your father. How is he?"

Stella raised a brow. "You must know Yates better than I thought, if he's told you about Greff."

"He didn't exactly tell me."

"Ah . . ." She looked interested, but let it go, lifting a shoulder in the trace of a shrug. "Greff wasn't so lucky. Both feet have fourth-degree burns. He'll be in here a long time."

"Have you seen him?"

Stella hesitated. "Not yet. I'll probably wait to do it with Yates."

"Then you'll wait a hell of a long time, Stel." Yates, wearing jeans and a black T-shirt, stood in the open doorway of his room. His eyes shot to Hannah. "How's Miranda?"

"Miraculously, she's fine. She's staying at Kenninghall and being fussed over by Meara, Libby, and Claire. She's hating it, but she's all right."

"I'm glad to hear it."

Hannah couldn't stop the "I'll bet you are" response that jumped into her head, but she kept the thought to herself, saying instead. "She owes you her life."

Yates ignored her comment, and asked, "Any word on what started the fire—or who?"

"Nothing definite. An officer from the La Conner police came by the following morning. He said there was no doubt it was arson, and they were looking for a van seen cruising our area late at night. Meara reported it once along with a couple of other people on neighborhood watch."

"Who would do such a thing. And why?" Stella asked, looking shocked.

"Good question," Yates said.

"There's always a chance they got the wrong Biehle house," Hannah said, her voice level. "Mistook Miranda's house for Milo's."

Yates's gaze swung to Hannah, bored into her. "Why would you think that?"

"Maybe someone thought if Kenninghall was gone, a few other things would be gone, too."

Stella looked confused.

Yates looked furious. "You can't possibly think—"

"I don't know what I think, and it doesn't matter." Hannah straightened her shoulders. "I'm here because Miranda insisted I come. She wants you to come to the house so she can thank you in person for saving her life."

Yates looked at her a long time. Stella looked at each of them in turn. Finally, Yates said, "Tell her thanks, but it's not necessary."

Hannah didn't know if she was relieved or disappointed. Seeing Yates again was both confusing and exhilarating—but neither reaction mattered. "I'll tell her." She turned to Stella. "Nice meeting you."

She walked away.

Stella looked at Yates. "What was that all about?"

Yates watched Hannah practically run down the hall. When she stepped into the elevator and didn't look back, he turned to his sister. "Stella, you and I have some talking to do. And it might as well be right now and right here."

When Yates finished laying it out for his sister, she sat for a long time in silence, as if trying to digest it. Yates, who'd been pacing as he talked, sat on the edge of his bed, his burned leg aching. When he sat, she rose.

"All these years," she said, her face solemn. "And he hasn't changed one bit. But God, the sex trade. Kids! I never thought he'd go that far."

"I can't do it, you know. I can't let him get away with it—any of it."

"Of course you can't! Why would you think for a minute I'd expect you to?" She glared at him. "Okay, so I'm ambitious, I want a political career, but I don't want it built over young girls' souls and the skeletons of Greff's murder victims. Actually, the more I think of it, the more you're pissing me off."

"I didn't intend you to know."

"He's my father, too, Yates—more's the pity."

"Yeah."

"And as for that trumped-up idea of his for a murder charge—let him do his damnedest."

"It'll be dirty."

Stella walked over and hugged him. "We've been smeared by our father's selfishness and dirt all our lives. It's past time to do a cleanup."

He kissed her forehead. "Yeah. Past time."

"But you know what?"

"What?"

"The fire. After all you've told me. It bothers me." Stella sat beside Yates on the edge of his rumpled bed, her brows knit in thought. "What if there's someone else out there who wants to get Greff—

he's not exactly Mr. Popularity—and they intend to use Milo's letters to do it. Maybe they didn't burn down the wrong house. Maybe they meant to kill Miranda Biehle."

And now Miranda was at Kenninghall.

Blood rushed to Yates's head. *Damn it to hell!* He should have seen it right away. He was either losing his touch, or they'd pumped one too many drugs into him since the fire. Either way, Hannah was in danger.

Stella was right; someone else knew about the letters, and that someone was out to get Greff.

Hannah and Kenninghall sat square in the middle.

"You're brilliant." Yates tugged his sister's arm, pulled her to her feet, and kissed her soundly. "Let's go."

Stella grabbed her coat and handbag. "Where to?"

"Kenninghall. I've changed my mind. I'm going to let Miranda Biehle thank me after all."

Chapter 25

Greff hovered between light and dark, consciousness and unconsciousness. He'd screwed up. And in his painful sleep came a nameless dread. He wasn't going to make it. They were going to get him. Miranda was dead. His luck had run out. He was going to live and they were going to put him away.

"Lena," he murmured. Beautiful Lena. She'd take care of him. He drifted on cool silk water to a warm beach. White beach. Hot sun. Lena . . . Everything he'd earned. Money. Money. The Zanez deal. He had to be there to sign.

"Mr. Greff?" A voice close to his ear. "Here now, drink some of this." Someone lifted his head. Water on his lips, in his mouth, seeping over his chin.

Hot sex and a single-malt scotch . . .

He was drooling.

Lena. The deal. It had to close. She'd have to take care of it. He needed to call. Get up.

"Easy now. You'll be fine. Lie back now." The

voice again, pressure against his shoulder. "I'll give you something to help you sleep."

He felt the needle. Wanted it. Didn't want it. Luck running out like sand . . . the beach.

Scrambled voices. "IV morphine . . . not enough. Feet . . . fourth degree, muscle, bone, and tendons. Critical."

A tear oozed from the corner of his eye.

Lena, I need you. "Lena."

A cool hand touched his forehead, stroked softly. "I'm here, baby. Go to sleep now. Rest. And you hang on. Hear?"

She'd come! He wanted to tell her what to do, but he couldn't remember. "The jet, then . . . the letters . . ." He grabbed her hand. "Get the le—"

"Shush, now. Relax. And don't worry. I'll take care of everything."

Hannah opened the door to the last people she expected to see on Kenninghall's doorstep, Yates and his sister. When she only stood there and stared, Yates said, "I changed my mind."

Stella added with a half smile of apology, "He does that."

"Fine." Hannah stepped back, and reined in the traitorous leap of god-knew-what that made her heart pound against her rib cage. "Come in. Miranda's upstairs, but she's sleeping right now." She gestured toward the library, nodded brusquely. "You can wait in there. I'll get you a drink."

"Get Stella a drink. We need to talk."

Hannah rolled her eyes. "We've been through this, Yates. You and I have nothing to say to each other."

Libby walked in. When she saw Yates, a look of bafflement and irritation crossed her face. "I can't believe you've got the balls to show your face here."

Stella looked at Hannah, Libby, and then Yates. "I seem to be out of the loop around here." Her eyes on him, she said, "I hope you'll tell me what you've done to earn all this female adulation."

"Later," Yates said, and turned to Libby. "Would you take my sister into the library? Hannah and I are going to take a walk."

By his tone, Hannah expected his next tack would be to drag her by the hair to the nearest cave. Instead, he took her hand, tugged it gently. "Please."

She drew her hand back. "I'll get a sweater."

"Hannah, you can't trust him." Libby looked alarmed.

"It's okay, Libby."

Outside, they walked side by side to the garage, Yates's burned leg ensuring they took it slow. He opened the passenger door of the old Cord, and Hannah got in. By the time Yates got settled in the driver's side, she'd plastered herself against the door, as far away from him as she could get.

It maddened her when he did the same.

Yates shifted, eased his leg as straight as possible under the steering wheel, then gave her a direct gaze. "You're in danger, Hannah."

"I've heard that one before." She clasped her hands over a knee. "But it seems to me, I'm in a lot less danger now I know who my enemies are." She gave him a pointed look.

"I'm not your enemy—not anymore."

She tried for a long-suffering look, but the bleak expression on his face made her heart twist painfully.

She ignored it. Her heart had taken more than its share of abuse in the past few days; she didn't intend for it to take any more. "Okay, I'll bite. Who is my enemy?"

"I don't know."

She rolled her eyes. "That's helpful." She reached for the door handle. "If we're done here—"

Yates was across the seat so fast, she didn't have time to draw a breath. His face inches from hers, he said, "If words don't work, why don't I try something more physical?"

"Yates, don't—"

Too late. He kissed her. Hard. And for the briefest of moments, she pushed against his leather-jacketed chest. But when his mouth softened against hers, when she heard the low, harsh moan coming from somewhere deep in his throat, she clutched at the leather, used it as a leash to bring him closer. She took his tongue, played with it, slowly losing her mind.

Clarity!

He'd lied to her, cheated her, taken the letters.

She shoved hard against the wall of man now almost on top of her, pulled her head back so forcefully she bumped it against the window.

"This is crazy," she said.

"You are one hundred percent right. It is crazy." He slumped back against the door, draped an arm over the steering wheel. He looked as if he had a mouthful of tacks. "And if you want to know what's even crazier . . ." He looked baffled. "I'm in love with you. I don't know what the hell else this chewed-up feeling can be. Christ, it's like I'm half a man when I'm not around you. I think of you . . . all the time. Shit! What else could it be?"

Hannah blinked, stared. "I don't believe this."

"Neither do I."

She met his gaze. "And now, based on your . . . *poetic* declaration, you expect me to do what? Fall into your arms? Swoon?"

He cocked his head, raised a brow. "You did a good imitation of the swoon thing a couple of minutes ago."

She was about to protest when he reached over and closed her lips with a touch of his index finger. "How about you being quiet. Hearing me out. Because before we get to *us,* we need to talk about *them.*"

Hannah shuffled her thoughts as though they were papers on her desk, tried to stack them in orderly piles; they resisted. She couldn't get past the "I'm in love with you."

Her brain was alive with it, turned it over and over, unable to think in the process. She wasn't dumb enough to believe the old saw about love conquering all, but damned if his words hadn't snuck in to rest like a crown on her worn-out spirit.

She made fists in her lap, sealed her lips into a straight tight seam. All the I-love-yous in the world didn't change a thing. "There is no us, Yates," she said, her tone measured and cool. "And while Greff's in the hospital, there's no *them* to worry about. The only one who's suspect around here is you. And the mythical 'danger' you've cooked up."

"You think I'm lying?"

"Wouldn't be the first time. You're as good at lying as you are in bed, Yates, but neither will work anymore. You took the letters to protect your father. I'm not letting that happen again." A part of her still wanted him to deny it, prayed for a miracle.

"You're right." He put his head back against the window, massaged his brow as if to loosen his thoughts. "I took them because I didn't want him to go to jail. I'd have done anything to prevent it."

The walls of Hannah's lungs collapsed. She knew this, but hearing it said flat out had the emotional blast of gunfire. Her response was lame. "I see." And in an odd way she did. Maybe if it were her father, she'd do the same. Maybe a person automatically protected his or her family no matter how heinous the crime. Maybe it was a genetic compulsion. How would you know until you were tested?

"No, you don't see. And you never will if you don't hear me out. I was wrong. Dead wrong to do what I did." He glanced away. "Greff is my father, you know that, but I haven't laid eyes on the bastard for years. Whatever feelings I had for him—and I suppose I did have them as a kid—died years ago." He lapsed into silence, and she left him to it.

"Look, I'm going to give you the *Reader's Digest* version, okay?" He glared at her. "I hate talking about it, hate thinking about it. But the truth is I feel nothing for my father. He's a career criminal, a man so selfish and sick with greed, he's never given a thought to anyone but himself for as long as I can remember. A narcissist? Or a psychopath? I don't know . . ."

He massaged his forehead so hard it reddened. "He introduced my mother to drugs, then fed her addiction to get control of her business. When I was old enough to do something about it, I did. Took my mother and Stel away. I managed to get

315

some of Mother's family money back for her to live on. She went into rehab, but"—his face softened into regret—"it never took for long. The last was the best. Three years. Stel and I thought she'd made it. She hadn't. She overdosed two years ago. Stel was with her when she died."

Hannah didn't know what to say, didn't know what to feel. The urge was strong to reach across the car seat and touch him. Soothe him. But distrust paralyzed her.

His tone turned brisk, the kind of pace you used to gain speed, jump over things. "The upshot of it is, when Greff found out I knew about the letters, his first instinct was to use me to get them. He threatened Stella."

"Threatened? As in bodily harm?"

"No, Greff's more creative than that. He prefers to ruin people's lives." He rubbed his jaw. "I wanted to protect her from scandal—she's a political animal, my sister. Recently got some high-level backing. Having Greff's dirty history, the ships, the girls, the old murder made public would destroy any chance she had. I didn't want that to happen."

She kept her eyes on his face, heard his breathing shallow out.

"He said either I get the letters or he'd see that Stella was charged with giving our mother a fatal overdose. Murder."

"My God! The man is a monster."

"Yes. He is."

Fearful of her softening reactions, she kept her responses tight, short. "But you brought the letters back."

He nodded.

"Why?"

"I had to."

She wanted to ask if he'd done it for her, but she couldn't, because she was too afraid of his answer.

He went on, "Because of a lot of things. You, Hannah Stuart"—he reached over, tucked a length of hair behind her ear—"were the big reason. I know what those letters mean to you, and when it came down to it, I couldn't let him walk. I couldn't do it to you, and I couldn't do it to me. I figured Stella and I had been dealt Greff as a hand, and we'd have to play it out." He hesitated, looked confused, as if headed down an unknown road—or a rocky emotional one. "And I don't think I'll ever be free of the bastard . . . the mess he made of my family until—"

"Justice is served?" Her finish to his sentence sounded stilted, but it was all she could think to say.

"Yes." His gaze slid to hers, and with it a cheerless smile. "After all this, Hannah, we're on the same side."

A dangerous warmth gathered in Hannah's chest. She told herself to be careful, not to jump where there might not be a net to catch her, but God help her, she believed him—or thought she did. *Careful, Hannah!* "What now?"

"It's up to you. I have nothing on Greff strong enough for him to be picked up before leaving the country. It would be the classic my-word-against-his scenario."

"But his burns are horrendous, he'll be in the hospital a long time, surely by then . . ."

Yates shook his head. "As soon as they ease back on the painkillers, and his survival instincts kick in, he'll have himself airlifted out. With enough

PERFECT EVIL   317

money, you can do anything. There's no way he'll hang around the hospital."

"So that leaves?"

He looked across the car seat to where she sat, back to the passenger door. "It leaves you. And it leaves the letters. You have to turn them over to the police, and you have to do it now."

Hannah went weak. She was afraid of this. It had all come back to Milo's vile confession. Her voice was lower when she spoke. "I can't do it."

"I don't get it. I thought nailing Biehle and Greff was exactly what you wanted."

"It was . . . it is." She looked away.

For a time, Yates said nothing, then, "Miranda?"

"Yes." She looked at him. "When you took the letters—"

"What I thought were the letters," he corrected.

"Hmm . . . anyway, when you left I was determined to talk to Miranda, prepare her as best I could, then go to the police, but—"

"But?"

"I kept putting it off. I told myself I was procrastinating, afraid to face her. And that was true, but I was also afraid of hurting her." She fidgeted with her jacket collar. "Even killing her. Her heart's not strong . . ."

"If you didn't tell her? Would she have to find out?"

"I couldn't risk it. Miranda's a nonstop news hound. I think it's the only reason she has a television." Hannah paused, locked her hands together in her lap. "And then there was the fire and . . . after everything she's been through, it would be too cruel to tell her now."

"It may be cruel not to."

"What are you saying?"

"I'm saying the fire was no mistake. The target was never Kenninghall. I'm saying there's someone else out there who wants those letters exposed and is prepared to kill Miranda Biehle to do it."

Meara heard the phone ring, and when it appeared no one else was going to pick up, she pulled her hands from the bread dough, wiped them on her apron front, and answered.

"Yes?"

"May I speak to Hannah Stuart, please?"

"I'm sorry. She's not about right now. Can I give her a message?" Meara picked up a pen.

"Oh, darn! I'd so hoped to catch her. When will she be back?"

"Of that I'm not sure. Can I help you at all?"

"It's about a pair of candlesticks we talked about a while back. I've changed my mind, decided to buy them."

"You've talked to Hannah, then?"

"Yes, I told her I'd think about them." She laughed. "Even for me, fifty thousand dollars causes a second thought or two. But I've decided they're too perfect to pass up. I'd like to pick them up early this evening, if I can. I'm leaving for New York tomorrow morning."

Meara shook her head in wonder. She'd lived in Mr. Biehle's house, surrounded by such treasures, for years, but she never ceased to be amazed at what people were willing to pay for them. And this sum of money would surely interest Hannah. "Now, why don't you give me your number and I'll have Hannah call you."

"The problem is, I don't have a number. My cell isn't working, and I've already checked out of my hotel." She stopped. "Why don't I drop by later, bring a check, and pick them up. Say seven or so."

"Oh, I don't know now. I'm not for arranging appointments."

"Please, this is important."

"All right then. Who should I tell her to expect?"

"Erin Calder. Just tell her it's about the George III silver gilt figural candlesticks. Hannah will know the ones."

Meara wrote down the information the second she got off the phone. She knew the candlesticks. Hadn't she dusted and polished them often enough? The two of them sat on the mantel in the library.

Heavy as gravestones, they were.

Hannah and Yates stopped at the kitchen door. Since they'd left the garage, neither had spoken. Yates was lost in thought, while she struggled with all he'd told her and the inconceivable idea someone intended to kill Miranda. He probably could hear her mind jerk and whirl as it tried to make sense of a situation that went far beyond rubber bullets and pepper spray.

She so badly wanted to trust him, but . . .

Before opening the kitchen door, she said, "You're not lying to me, Yates. This threat to Miranda—it's real and serious." She watched his eyes, but that was a waste of time. Windows to the soul, maybe, but windows to the truth in Yates Lang? Not so far.

"Very real and dead serious."

"But who? Who would want to do such a thing?"

"I don't know, but I intend to hang around long enough to find out," Yates said.

"That sounds like a statement, not a question." She didn't know how she felt about his being here, her head, her hormones and her heart—heavily armored against being hurt again—all fighting for safe ground

"Take it as fact. I'm not leaving Kenninghall. Not until this mess is over, so you might as well get used to having me around again." His jaw set hard and his gaze didn't waver.

Hannah remembered how Yates raced into the flames to save Miranda—then his father. Like it or not, fate in its twisted way had conspired to put her, Greff, and Yates on the same team. "Okay," she said. "And I'll organize some extra security."

Yates stood close to her, looked down. "Do it, but keep it arm's length. Give whoever it is room to maneuver." He grasped her by the shoulders. She could feel the tension in his hands. "If we get this guy, there's a good chance we can get Greff."

The heat from his hands made her edgy. Afraid he'd start moving them, caress her, confuse her more than she already was. She stepped away. "What makes you so sure it's a man?"

"I'm not sure of anything." He dropped his hands to his sides. "But there's something else you should know."

She tilted her head, waited.

"Greff killed Vonecker, beat him to death with a crowbar."

Hannah put a hand to her mouth.

"For a while there, I told myself I could overlook murder—especially one over forty years old. As if murder has some kind of sell-by date." He shook his head. "Thought if I could stop Greff's rotten business, it would appease my conscience. It won't." He took her shoulders again. "But if you still think I'm that kind of man, I'll walk away right now."

Hannah looked through him, then past him into the darkness of the endless Pacific Northwest rain. She wanted to see his soul in all its shades of gray, but in the end all she could do was look into his eyes. "Can you appreciate that I'm wary—and damned scared?" Hannah wasn't sure she had the energy for another unequivocal leap of faith.

He touched her face. "So am I."

His touch was soft and brief, but it opened a tiny door close to her heart, a door labeled Hope. She wanted to close it again—be safe again—but it stuck, as surely as if Yates had put his boot in it. "Can we be tentative about this?" she said finally.

"You mean platonic, don't you?"

"Yes."

"Like I told you. Never sleep with a man you don't trust." He kissed her hair lightly. "That'll definitely give me something to shoot for."

Chapter 26

"Why don't you come with us, Yates?" Stella asked, donning her coat at the door. Beside her, Libby was doing the same. They were going to La Conner for shopping and lattes. And, Yates suspected, to get away from Kenninghall.

The old house didn't wear the rain well, turning gloomy and gray behind its heavily draped windows. In the last couple of hours, Yates had checked every inch of the place, familiarized himself with the security system and all possible points of entry. The big rooms with their dim light, lofty ceilings, and sheet-draped furniture were anything but cozy. Hell, he expected to see Igor pop out of the woodwork any minute.

"No thanks. I'll take a pass." He looked at Libby. "Besides, I doubt Libby would enjoy my company. She still thinks I'm the big bad wolf come to burn Kenninghall down."

Libby stopped zipping up her jacket midway. "I'm not sure what I believe, but it's Hannah's house. If she thinks it's okay you're here"—she finished her zipping job—"then it's okay." She took an umbrella from the stand. "And while you may be the bastard I figured you for, I like your sister. We've had some good talks . . . about your mom and all."

Yates didn't have any comeback to that, nor did he get the logic, so he let it be.

Stella kissed him on the cheek. "We won't be long. Why don't you take a painkiller and lie down. I don't think you've been off your feet for half an hour all day."

"I might just do that." He kissed her back. "Enjoy."

They ran out to Yates's car, heads bent, umbrellas pointed into the rain and wind.

Yates closed and locked the door and reset the alarm. He massaged his thigh. His barbecued leg was board stiff, and felt as if it was being blow-torched.

Hannah came up behind him. "Stella's right. You should rest."

He nodded. "And you?"

"I've got some paperwork, then a customer coming."

Yates's antenna went up. "Someone you know?"

"Yes. Her name's Calder. She came by quite a while ago to see some candlesticks. I didn't think she'd be back—they're very expensive. But she spoke to Meara today and said she'd be by around seven to pick them up."

Yates looked at his watch: 5:35. "I'll be down by then. And I'll check on Miranda before I stretch out." He'd spent the better part of an hour with Miranda Biehle today. She wore those eighty-eight

years of hers as if they were fifty and she was counting backward. He liked her.

"I just came from her room. Claire's with her.
She's fine."

"Okay, then I'll do another perimeter check
and see you in an hour."

She smiled.

"What?"

" 'Perimeter check.' It sounds like something
from a Bond movie."

"I guess it does sound melodramatic, but—"

"Better safe than sorry?" she finished, her expression going solemn.

"Yes." He could lean down and kiss her right now,
but if it went where he wanted it to go, it sure as
hell wouldn't fit her definition of platonic. "See
you in an hour, then."

She must have nodded, because he didn't hear
her answer as he limped toward the stairs to start
his painful ascent to the third floor.

*"Step away from the car, please," the patrolman said,
his hand resting on the revolver holstered at his hip.*

Shit! *"Hey, what's the problem, Officer?" Bone kept
his voice even and his hand on the trigger of the pump
nozzle disgorging gas into his van. Hell, he was losing
his touch; he hadn't even seen the cop car. He frowned,
looked around again, still didn't. Where the hell had the
fucker come from! He glanced past him. Saw no one other
than the jerk sitting in the station reading the paper.*

*"I said step away from the car. Now." The voice was
low, laced with authority.*

*Bone knew the cop wouldn't make a move until he
did, giving him precious seconds to think. With two un-*

*registered handguns under the fast-food wrappings in the
front of the van, and a dozen or so empty gas cans in the
back, he was in major shit here. He cased the guy, kept
his expression relaxed and unthreatening.*

*He was in luck. This asshole was not only alone; he
couldn't be more than a day out of the academy. Bone felt
better already. He pasted on a bland smile.*

*"What's your beef, Officer? I'm just fillin' up here."
Bone gripped the nozzle's trigger tighter, eased it to the lip
of the tank. "Just fillin' up and movin' on. Yes, sir."*

*"I don't think so." The cop pulled his gun and, using
both hands, aimed it at Bone. "Put your hands on your
head, and step away from the car. Real slow."*

"Okay, okay, buddy."

*Bone yanked the nozzle from his tank and spun.
Squeezing hard on the handle's trigger, he arced it high,
sent a rainbow of gasoline toward the young cop. Gas
ran down his face, the front of his uniform, made a
bitchin' pool of the stuff for him to stand in. Bone held
his fingers hard to the trigger, kept the gas flowing.*

*His heart raced. He could do it. He could blow this
place and the fire would dance for hours. Pleasure
clutched at his groin; his breathing came in short excited
gasps. He could do it, and he could watch it all in his
rearview mirror. It would be beautiful. Flames . . . high
as a skyscraper, lickin' the fuckin' stars.*

*While the cop sputtered, coughed, and rubbed at his
eyes, Bone dropped the nozzle, reached into his pocket,
and pulled out a fold of matches. He tore out a single
match.*

*He grinned at the stunned cop, who looked at the
match in Bone's hand then down at his gas-soaked uniform—the lake of shit he was all but floating in.*

*"Jesus, man!" he yelled, the fear and desperation on
his face warming Bone's excuse for a heart.*

He saluted the young cop, lifted the match toward him as if it were a toast. He was already seeing the flare, feeling the blast. Tasting the sex of it on his tongue.

"Don't even think about it, you no-good motherfucker."

Bone closed his eyes against the prod of a gun barrel at his nape. He squeezed the narrow inch of sulfur-tipped cardboard in his hand—just an inch from the striker strip on the match cover.

Just an inch . . .

The metal at his neck tilted up until it was lodged hard and deep at the base of his skull. "You hear me, asshole!"

The gun barrel forced Bone's head forward and down. The gas had snaked back, seeped under his boots and the cop shoes behind his. He breathed in its scent.

He could go out clean.

Less than an inch . . .

When the doorbell rang, Hannah looked up, briefly disoriented by the attention switch from the inventory list to the deep clang of Kenninghall's old door chimes.

The clock on her desk said ten after six. She thought about calling up for Yates but decided it was probably only Mrs. Calder coming early. She'd seem a spineless fool. Still . . . She reached into her desk drawer, pulled out the pepper spray, and dropped it into the pocket of her sweater pocket. No harm in being cautious.

It was Erin Calder. Hannah deactivated the alarm and let her in, looking past her into the black, winter night before closing the door. "It's awful out there, isn't it?"

"Yes. Makes me glad I don't winter here." She smiled, and brushed her dark hair back from her forehead. When Hannah took her coat, she shivered, rubbed her upper arms.

"You *are* cold. Come into the library. There's a fire in there." Hannah hung her damp coat on the stand near the door.

The woman's eyes followed her every move. "This is an amazing place. Even that"—she nodded toward the ornate coat stand—"is intriguing."

Hannah said by rote, "Regency mahogany, circa 1826."

"And this?" She ran a hand over a kneehole desk near the door.

"Queen Anne, 1710, I think." Hannah headed to the library and Erin Calder fell into step beside her. "Can I make you some coffee?" she asked.

"Something stronger if you have it."

"Of course."

In the library Erin Calder wandered about. "What an amazing place!" she said again, smiling. "But the heating bills must be hell."

Hannah smiled back, suddenly remembering how much Milo had enjoyed others' reactions to Kenninghall. As usual, when Milo came to his place there, her heart slowed and warmed—until she bade him and his ugly secret to go. "Yes, they are, Mrs. Calder, but your buying the candlesticks should keep us warm for a month or two."

She laughed. "Erin, please."

"All right." Hannah led her to the mantel. "Here they are." She touched one of the candlesticks. "They're wonderful, aren't they?"

"Oh yes." She took one down, reverently stroked its golden surface. "Incredible workmanship."

Hannah was pleased the candlesticks were going into appreciative hands. "Now, what would you like to drink?"

"Scotch, if you have it. Single malt?"

"I have Glenlivet. Will that do?"

"Perfect." Erin continued to study the gilt and silver candlesticks. "I'm *so* excited about these." She ran a scarlet-tipped finger along the gilded skirt of the female figure forming the stem of the stick. "Oh, and I've brought you a certified check."

"Thank you." Hannah went to the liquor cabinet, poured a short scotch for Erin and a glass of water for herself. Both glasses ready, she turned.

The scotch hit the floor and the glass shattered, shards skittering across the dark hardwood like diamond spiders. She stared dumbly into the muzzle of a gun, the water glass held by a death grip in her left hand.

Stupefaction more than fear glued her to the floor, flooded her thinking. She fixated on the gun, couldn't take her eyes off it. She was certain it had not been modified for rubber bullets.

"What I'll enjoy"—Erin raised the gun a fraction—"is watching you hand over Milo Biehle's letters."

"You want Milo's letters?" Hannah knew she sounded stunned, because she was.

"Yes, I do, sweetie. And the sooner the better." She looked around; the gun remained steady. "Jesus, I can see why Vonecker had trouble finding them in this junkyard."

"I don't understand. What's your interest in the letters? Who are you?"

"You're not in a position to ask questions, Hannah, but I'll tell you this. Those letters will make me a rich woman." She paused. "And better than that, they'll give me control. No more sucking up to some aging jerk for handouts."

Hannah still held the full water glass. She toyed with the idea of tossing it in the woman's face, making a run for it. But that would endanger Miranda and Claire.

"Put it down," Erin ordered. Gesturing at the water glass, she flicked the gun barrel. "This is a situation where it pays to be smart, not brave." She took a few steps forward, until the gun was less than three feet from Hannah's face.

Hannah set the glass on the mantel. "You're not Erin Calder." She needed time to think, come up with an idea. If she could get her talking . . .

"Now, aren't you the bright one. Where are the letters?"

"What makes you think the letters are here?" Hannah sank both hands in her sweater pockets. Her right hand closed around the canister of pepper spray, and her heart stammered in her chest. She'd wait her chance and—

"They're here. Morgan told me they were. And while Morgan may be a selfish bastard, he's rat smart and usually right. And if you're going to be difficult—"

"You know Greff!"

Her laugh was unpleasant. "In all ways possible, sweetheart."

Hannah didn't get it all, but it was clear this woman didn't have Greff's welfare at heart—or Miranda's.

Erin looked pointedly toward the open library door. "Where's the old woman?"

It was as if someone had rammed a cattle prod

against her chest, but Hannah kept her voice flat. "I won't let you hurt her."

"Exactly what I was counting on. You'll be happy to know I've got zero interest in hurting the old gal, but what you *need to understand* is I will, if you don't hand over the letters." Her face was grim. "And I'll do it in a heartbeat."

Hannah tightened her grip on the pepper spray, tried to yank it from her pocket. It snagged. She yanked harder, got it out, and sprayed wildly, too low, too wide.

The woman cursed and spun quickly enough to pirouette back into position immediately. Hannah lunged, but she was too late. By the time she got a hand on the woman's shoulder, the gun was pressed into her cheek. "Back off, bitch," the woman growled. "Now!"

Hannah backed off, and as she did, the woman swung the gun hard and flat-edged against her cheek. She stumbled back, and the woman struck again, smashed the gun into her temple. Hannah dropped to her knees on the hearth, put a hand on the side of her head; blood oozed through her fingers. Stars and lights flashed behind her eyelids.

"Get up." The woman, a hand covering one eye— at least some of the spray had found its mark— stood over her and glared, gun pointed. "I said, get up!"

Hannah stayed on her knees, too disoriented to stand, too angry to think—and in too much pain to be agreeable.

She inhaled deeply, made as if to get to her feet and, head down, rammed into Calder's stomach. She heard a whoosh of air when her lungs emptied. She went down backward, her head connecting solidly with the edge of the coffee table.

Calder had to be out cold. Had to be. But the blood was so thick across her eyes, Hannah could barely see. She brushed the blood aside, forced herself to her knees.

The gun was still in Calder's hand. Was the damn thing welded there! Damn, damn, damn.

She had to get it. Had to . . .

She hauled herself to her feet, using the fire screen and then the mantel, but her knees were rubber, and her hand, slippery with blood, didn't hold. She fell backward into the delicate mahogany serving table that sat beside the fireplace, its three tiers displaying an expensive collection of Royal Doulton and Staffordshire figurines. She went down hard in a jumble of splintered wood and broken porcelain.

When she looked up, Calder was on her feet again—and Hannah was out of options.

"You stupid, stupid bitch, I should kill you right now." She was breathing in short sharp gasps, shoving her dark tangled hair off her face. Her lip was cut and bleeding, her face taut with fury.

Hannah, barely able to see through the fresh rush of blood into her eyes, or to think in the solid block of pain that was now her head, got to her knees, and with one hand on what was left of the broken table, looked up.

"Get up, bitch, or I swear to Christ I'll do you on your knees."

Hannah stared into the terrible eyes of Erin Calder and with absolute clarity saw Will and Chris.

"Should be back in a hour, hon. Chris, give your mommy a kiss." Will's quick kiss. Not a last kiss. Never a

*last kiss. The arms of her son around her neck. His damp
kiss on her cheek. "Love Mommy." His bright smile. "Love
you, too, sweetheart. 'Bye. 'Bye. 'Bye . . ."*

This was how they died, falling to the ground,
staring into the face of greed and evil.

Her heart seemed to slow in her breast. A
dream, warm and cloudlike, drifting over it.

She could go now, be with them.

Let the evil win . . .

No!

She staggered to her feet, forced herself not to
lean back and take support from the fireplace.
Where her heart was warm, it chilled.

Blood dripped off her chin, ran like warm syrup
down her throat. She didn't care.

She faced Calder. "You're not going to kill me
or anyone else in this house. You're going to take
your toy"—Hannah nodded at the gun, and pain
bounced wildly in her head, nearly put her back
on her knees—"and get the hell out of my house."

Calder stared at her. She raised the gun, aimed
it square at Hannah's face. Her smile was feral.
"You've got balls, Stuart, I'll hand you that."

"I've got more than balls," Hannah said, her
voice as icy as Calder's heart. "I've got the letters,
and if you kill me there's not a chance in hell
you'll ever find them. And I'll let you pull the trigger and blow my brains out before I hand them
over." Hannah's head wasn't as steady as her heart.
Shadows ebbed and flowed there; she couldn't
seem to clear her vision. Through the encroaching
gray, she stared at Calder. Two Calders. Her vision
blurred.

Confusion briefly showed in the woman's face.

It didn't last, replaced by a grim brutality. "Then I'll have to do the old lady, won't I?"

"I don't think so." The voice came from the open door of the library.

Chapter 27

Calder swung toward the sound of a new threat.

Hannah, nausea welling up, shadows scudding across her mind, blinked to clear the blood from her eyes. She saw Yates—in duplicate—leaning against the wall inside the library. He had a gun in his hand.

Oh God! It was her gun. Her stupid, stupid gun! Fear clotted in her stomach. Yates!

He looked cool, relaxed, and his voice was low—almost pleasant—when he said, "Lena Tenassi. Am I right?"

The woman swung her gun back to Hannah, then to Yates, kept them both in her target arc. Even in her dazed state, Hannah saw the edge of panic in her eyes. She looked cornered, unsure of her next move.

"Put the gun down, Lena," Yates said, his voice board flat. "And no one will get hurt." He lifted the gun in his hand, steadied it.

Hannah swayed, grabbed the mantel for purchase. Terror clawed at her chest. She couldn't breathe, and her knees were giving way. Dear God, she was going to faint.

Lena grinned through her bloodied lips.

"And let you call in the uniforms? I don't think so." She swung to face Yates, leveled the gun.

Hannah curled her fingers around the base of a candlestick.

Can't see. Spots. Doubles. Flashes. Dark light.

Can't. It's too heavy. Going down.

Yates! Throw. Just do it.

The crack of a gun. The crack of her head meeting the stone hearth. A blinding thrust of pain.

Blessed, blessed blackness.

"Hannah! For God's sake, wake up!"

Hannah tried to open her eyelids, only one responded. The other was seized shut. Pain came with awareness, and she closed her one good eye. "Yates?"

"Yes, it's me. I'm here. Wake up now. Please, wake up."

"That woman . . . is she . . ."

"No. She's not dead."

"The police?"

"On their way." He tried to push her hair back from her face, but blood, already drying, held it there. "Take it easy. I've called an ambulance."

She wanted to protest, but darkness threatened. "Yates." His hand rested on her head . . . so gently.

"Uh-huh."

"I'm okay."

She heard him mutter, "I hope so, love. God, I hope so."

"And I . . ." She faded to black, the words "I want to live" a whisper and a wish only she could hear.

The doctor kept Hannah overnight, released her to Libby and Yates only after they gave their assurances they'd monitor her closely for the next few days. Concussion, he'd said, serious enough she'd have to be checked out again in a week or so. Watching Libby listen so soberly to the doctor's instructions, Yates figured Hannah was in for some determined nursing.

When they arrived at the hall, Libby rushed ahead to organize lunch. Yates helped Hannah out of the car, took her arm, and guided her to the front door. He was driving Stella to Sea Tac to catch her plane, so he didn't have much time for the questions Hannah wanted to ask. Questions she'd started to ask the minute she got into the car.

She was steady enough under his hand, but she looked as if she'd fallen off a damn cliff, part of her hair was shaved on the right side of her head—to allow for the twenty-odd stitches, caused by Lena's broadsides with the gun—one eye was barely open, and her face was a smudge of black, yellow, and deep purple.

He wanted to hold her. Kiss her better. But there were words to be said first. Trust to be gained.

"I don't look so hot, do I?" she said, settling herself into the sofa in the library—the room she'd insisted on visiting immediately.

"The bruising will disappear in a few days. What matters is you're alive."

"Thanks to you. If you hadn't come down when you did—"

"Don't." He lifted a hand. Yates knew it could have gone either way. When he'd walked in, saw what was going on, his heart nearly leaped from his chest. He didn't like to think of its condition if something had happened to Hannah. "Are you really okay?"

"I'm okay. I think the stitches hurt more than the bump on my head." She looked around the room with her good eye. No fractured table, no broken glass. "Meara's been busy," she said. "The carpet's gone."

"Bloodstains. She had it taken out this morning." He took off his jacket, sat beside her. He touched her damaged face carefully, tugged her chin so she'd face him when he said, "It's you who did the life saving, Hannah. You sure as hell saved mine."

"I don't remember. I, uh, couldn't see . . ."

"You saw well enough to land a ten-ton candlestick square on Tenassi's back." He pointed to the ceiling. Her gaze followed his hand, until he knew from her intake of breath, she'd spotted the rough splay of broken plaster. "That was meant for me," he added.

She started to shake her head, obviously felt some pain, and stopped on a wince. "I still don't understand. Who exactly is Lena Tenassi? And what possible reason could she have for wanting Milo's letters?"

Yates leaned back in the sofa. "She's my father's partner in the Zanez business—and his mistress. Seems they've had a thing going for a long time."

"I still don't get it."

"You sure you're up for this now? You don't want to rest?"

"I'll rest later." She looked at him expectantly.

"Okay. Why Greff wanted the letters is obvious. They had the power to put him away." He paused. "Which is exactly the reason Lena wanted them. Greff was bent on cashing in his chips and retiring, becoming increasingly paranoid about his luck running out. Lena, apparently, didn't want any part of his, uh, 'effing golden years'—her words not mine. She wanted control of Zanez and its lucrative human trade. Greff was about to sell it out from under her."

"She's obviously capable of killing. Why didn't she—" Hannah stopped as if the words were impossible to say, as if thinking them made her culpable in some way.

"Kill Greff?"

"Yes."

"Because she would have screwed herself. Greff refused to marry her, and he never bothered to make a will. He dies? Zanez comes to Stella and me." What Yates didn't say was this was typical Greff style. The only future he considered was his own. In his view, if he controlled the money, he controlled the game—and everyone in it. "What Tenassi needed was leverage, and Milo's letters would give it to her."

"Greff told her about the letters?" She looked surprised. "Wasn't that risky?"

"Pillow talk." Yates shrugged. "Greff isn't the first man to think he's invincible after sex. Tenassi had known about the letters for a long time, but it wasn't until the Nationeer deal looked like a go that she came up with a plan. Kill Miranda, expose the letters, and watch Greff rot in jail while she played the heartbroken woman faithful to her man. She figured with her on the outside and Greff on the inside, the Nationeer deal would tank and she'd have the control she needed to keep Zanez running its dirty business." He couldn't help himself, he touched her hair, her bandaged face. "When that didn't work, she came after you."

"Then it was Lena who started the fire," Hannah said in stunned amazement.

Yates nodded. "Almost right. She *hired* someone to set the fire. A guy named Wilson Bone. Apparently the cops picked him up last night, south of Portland. A certified wacko according to the arresting officer, half-pyromaniac and mean as a snake—nearly fried the guys who picked him up. It took all of two minutes for him to finger Tenassi. They were already looking for her when I called them in last night."

"How do you know all this?"

"I talked to the cops . . . and Lena before they got here."

"And I suppose none of what she told you was repeated for the benefit of the police."

He shook a negative. "Nope. When they got here, she opened her mouth to demand her lawyer. Period."

"Still no solid link to Greff?"

"Not so far." Yates intended this sorry fact to change, but he wasn't about to tell Hannah until things were nailed down.

She got to her feet, carefully, and he rose with her. "And Miranda? Is she okay?"

"She heard the 'ruckus,' as she called it. I told

her you'd tripped, taken a bad fall, and broken some inventory. What you tell her now is up to you."

"I'll go with that." She faced him. "And your father?"

He hated hearing Greff called that, but didn't correct her. "Still in the Seattle burn unit. So far." Yates paused. "He's already trying to arrange a way out."

Hannah seemed to sag. "I can't believe it."

"About Greff. There's something else you should know."

He saw her wariness, knew he'd started too many lies and evasions with this same opener. He wanted to curse, wondered when—if ever—that particular preface would be a lead-in to good news.

"I forced Greff to turn a ship back to Songkhla in Thailand. The ship was the *Naarmu*. Anne Chapman had received good information it carried another *shipment*. She'd already advised the port authorities and the police of the ship's arrival date. They'd have been all over it and Greff. I didn't want—"

"Greff to be implicated. So you let him go." She looked exhausted, oddly resigned. "God, after all this evil and ugliness . . . nothing's really changed."

"I didn't do it for him." He felt his temper flare.

Hannah ignored him, moved toward the door. "I'm tired, Yates. If you don't mind, I think I'll go lie down for awhile."

"Hannah. Listen." Hell, she still didn't trust him.

She looked back at him, her bruised face puffy and sad-eyed. "It's okay. You did what you thought best. As I did. For Miranda's sake, I made a decision to honor Milo's last wish. A decision that gives

Greff enough time to leave the country. You protected him for Stella's sake and because he's your father. And now, because of us, he'll never pay for anything, not his terrible business, the murder of a family, or Gerry Vonecker." She rubbed at her forehead, winced, and pulled her hand back. "We'll have to live with it, I guess."

"It's not that simple." But Yates knew if his plan didn't work, that's exactly what they'd be doing.

"No. It's anything but simple." At the door, hand on the knob, she looked back at him, so tired and sick his heart ached for her. "Thank you for last night." She walked out.

Yates cursed. How the hell did a man argue with a woman who looked as if she'd been hit by a semi?

The door opened again, and Yates looked up to see Stella. "I saw Hannah heading up the stairs. Did you two get a chance to talk?"

"Some." He looked at his watch. "We'd better get out of here if you want to make that plane."

"I can miss it, Yates. If you need me to." She cocked her head, waited.

Suddenly Yates couldn't wait to get away from Kenninghall. He didn't have any more explaining left in him, nothing that made sense, anyway. He'd played his hand with Greff and with Hannah, and from where he sat right now, neither was a sure thing. The smart thing to do was hold. See how things unfolded. And most important, give Hannah some easing-down time. She'd been on a hell of ride.

He picked up the jacket he'd tossed over the sofa back when he'd sat down. "No, let's go."

Outside, he loaded Stella's bag and walked to the driver's side of his car. He looked up to Hannah's window. She was standing, curtain pulled back, staring down at him. He lifted a hand, more a salute than a wave, and got in the car.

He didn't look back, didn't want to see the curtain fall closed.

Hannah got out of the Saab, locked it, put her head down, and sprinted the short distance to Yates's apartment building through whirling, driving rain and the distant clap of thunder. A smart woman would use an umbrella.

A smart woman wouldn't be here!

She ignored the scary thoughts gathering steam in her brain—all of them saying, "Turn back, you fool"—and told herself to put one foot in front of the other. No matter the task, it was the way things got done.

Through the large double-glass doors, she saw the old man nodding off in his chair, the baseball bat across his knees. The lock on the front door of the dilapidated apartment building was still broken. She walked in and went directly to the elevator.

She tried not to think of why she was here, what she would say, how she would say it—and what Yates would say in response, if he responded at all. She'd been so wrong for so long, she wouldn't know where to start.

The old man stirred but didn't wake when the elevator doors dinged open. Hannah got in, but it took a few seconds and some deep breathing before she worked up the courage to push the button.

The elevator jerked and shuddered its way up. A lot like her heart.

Outside Yates's door, her courage seeped out of her as if she were made of cheap mesh rather than the forged steel she needed to be to see this through.

She raised a hand, made a fist—and the door opened before she laid a knuckle on it.

Yates. He raised a brow, half surprise, half question.

Hannah dropped her hand to her side, and opened her mouth to speak. When nothing popped out, she closed it again.

"You look better," he said, but he didn't stand back or wave her in. He stood there, one hand on the door, the other stuffed in his jeans pocket.

"Yes, well, it's been over a month." She raised a hand to her hair. Libby had cut it an inch or so before she headed back to Portland, and styled it to hide where she'd had the stitches. And most all the bruising was gone, except for a trace of yellow under her right eye.

"Time flies."

She caught the sarcastic tone, sighed. "You're not going to make this easy for me, are you?"

"No."

"Are you going to invite me in?"

He stepped back without a word, and she walked into his large empty space. The hardwood floors gleamed, the kitchen was spotless, and the bed was made with military precision.

Ah, the bed. Memories flooded into her, sensual memories that, if she could, she'd sink into forever.

To ground herself, she glanced around. There was a neat pile of boxes stacked under the windows against the far wall. The rain drummed on the glass like an angry lover.

"You're moving?"

"Getting rid of some junk."

"You don't have any junk."

He ignored her comment and gestured toward the sofa. She sat and he sat beside her. She fidgeted with her bag strap, her mind turning back to the reason she was here, but so tangled, she couldn't line up a coherent sentence.

Yates didn't help, didn't even look interested, for God's sake. She'd made a horrendous mistake in coming here. She started to get to her feet; he touched her knee, his gentle pressure enough to pin her back on the sofa. "Hannah, spit out the apology, will you? So we can get on with things."

She sat back. "I know your dad's in jail." It was all she could think to say.

"He's my father, not my dad. A world of difference."

"How's Stella doing?" Libby had heard from Stella, and told Hannah she'd been questioned by the police about her mom's death. Greff had reached through his pain for vengeance.

"Typical woman, tough as nails when she has to be." He looked away from Hannah to the rain-slicked windows, and for a moment was lost to her. "I underestimated her." His gaze came back to rest on her. "And I underestimated you."

"Anne told me what you did." She hurried on, not wanting to be distracted yet. "How you alerted the Thailand police. She said they were waiting for the *Naarmu* when it docked, and they let all the girls go."

"Go where is still the question. But at least some of them will find home again."

"She said they also picked up the gang members who were waiting for them."

Yates nodded, his expression cynical. "Not sure what that will accomplish either. There seems to be an endless supply of those bastards."

Hannah held her breath. "And they traced the *Naarmu* back to Zanez. Anne says when Greff's able to stand trial, he'll go away for a long time."

"And, because Lena cut a deal to save her skin, they've added Vonecker's murder to the list of charges." His eyes were intense when they looked at her. "One thing Greff won't be doing is leaving the country in this century."

"Because of you."

"I made a statement, gave Anne everything I had; she did the rest. The woman's a bulldog—with serious connections."

"She said Lena would never have talked if you hadn't—"

"Made her see the light?" His smile was grim. "Tenassi was staring into an attempted murder charge; she'd have done anything to mitigate it. She freaked when I told her what I knew about Zanez. I laid it on thick, said maybe I could keep her out of it, if we could have a private chat about Greff's part in things. We had our chat. I got some useful information—and a certain sicko customer list that made the local police happy. It was a no-brainer. Tenassi looks out for Tenassi."

"And you didn't keep the chat private, did you?"

"No." He reached out, touched her hair, ran his knuckles across her cheek. "Now let it go. It's over."

Hannah's neck warmed and tears welled. "I should have trusted you."

He didn't take his eyes from hers, and then a smile, slow and teasing, turned up his lips.

"As apologies go, it'll do. Now come here." He pulled her to him, kissed her hard; his voice was ragged when he said, "Christ, Hannah, I've been going crazy waiting around here for you." He kissed her again, this time slow and deep. She felt her soul lift, her mind fog.

She folded into him, savored the heat of his mouth, then forced herself to push him away. She had one more thing to say. "What's between us, Yates. I plan to be careful about it."

"Careful?"

"When I asked you for . . . sex. That first time? Remember?"

"It's hardly something a man would forget." His lips twitched.

"Yes, well, when I did that? I wasn't thinking about more—if you know what I mean."

"I'm listening."

Hannah got up, paced. "I'm not the same person I was when Milo died. But I'm not . . . new enough, or strong enough, yet, to be sure about my decisions." She walked to the window. "The sex? That was easy. But this"—she touched her heart—"is something entirely different."

"You're afraid."

"Yes. I've been wrong so many times, about Milo, Greff, Libby . . . and you. Especially you." She looked down to where he still sat on the sofa. "How do I know I'm not developing another unhealthy dependency."

"You don't." Yates got up from where he'd been

sitting, watching her, and walked to stand in front of her. "What's happening between us? It's new to me, too. But there's no way in hell I'm not giving it a chance." He gripped her shoulders. "Is it a sure thing? I don't know. All I know is that when I look at you, my heart has a new rhythm." He waved a hand around his cavernous vacant loft. "Without you, for the first time, this place feels empty."

She smiled. "It is empty, Yates."

"Not when you're in it." He took her face in his hands. "So why don't we take it slow? Spend time together—without all the ugliness that came with Greff—and see where it leads." He pulled her to him and rubbed his jaw against her hair. "We'll talk, walk, eat, occasionally sleep, and somewhere in there, you'll make a decision. No pressure." Hannah wrapped her arms around his waist, knowing there was no way to say no to such a carefully thought-out plan.

The room fell to silence, and they held each other, listening to the rain beat on the high, uncovered windows, listened to their own hearts beat in tempo.

There was one other thing . . .

Hannah put her mouth close to Yates's ear. "And when we're not walking, talking, eating, and sleeping, how will we fill our time?"

She felt his smile against her forehead. "I'm a resourceful guy. I'll figure out something."

She smiled back. "I guess I'll have to trust you on that."

His smile faded. He looked down at her, his intelligent eyes hot, intense. "You can trust me, Hannah. Now and forever."

"I believe I can." She caressed his face, her eyes watery again. "And I believe I will."

Epilogue

Six months later

When Hannah reached the front door of Kenninghall, Yates was waiting. He drew her inside and into his arms.

"Done?" he asked.

"Done," she answered, and nestled closer.

"You okay?"

Hannah closed her eyes, pictured the rare and beautiful Chinese ginger jars now side by side, Milo's blue and white, Miranda's a brilliant red.

Ashes to ashes . . .

"I'm good." She took his hand, and they walked toward the kitchen. Hannah sniffed the air, smiled. "Meara's baking again. I notice she's been doing a lot of that since you moved in."

"She's a good woman, Meara, but she's hell on the love handles."

Hannah smiled, and holding both his hands, stepped back to survey his lean frame. "Looks like

you're safe enough on that score." She felt her
smile slip. "Did you take in the letters?"

"I took them to Anne this morning. She said
she'd take care of it."

Hannah nodded. The end, finally the end. Maybe . . .

At the kitchen door, Hannah stopped. "Yates?"

"Uh-huh."

"Do you think they're together? Miranda and
Milo."

"What do you think?" He settled his eyes on her,
curious as always, intense as always.

"I don't know. But I want to believe it." She'd
reached out today, visited Milo . . . touched him,
remembered his endless kindness, and wept for
his ruined, lonely life.

"Then that will have to be enough."

She took Yates's hand again. "Yes, it will."